Caz Finlay lives in Liverpool with her husband, two children, and a grumpy dog named Bert. A qualified probation officer, Caz has always been fascinated by the psychology of human behaviour and the reasons people do the things they do. However, it was the loss of her son in 2016 which prompted her to re-discover her love of writing and write her first novel, *The Boss*.

@cjfinlaywriter
@cazfinlayauthor
cazfinlay.com

Also by Caz Finlay

The Boss
Head of the Firm

Back in the Game

Caz Finlay

OneMoreChapter

One More Chapter
a division of HarperCollins*Publishers*
The News Building
1 London Bridge Street
London SE1 9GF

www.harpercollins.co.uk

This paperback edition 2020

First published in Great Britain in ebook format
by HarperCollins*Publishers* 2020

A catalogue record for this book
is available from the British Library

Ebook ISBN: 978-0-00-834069-8
Paperback ISBN: 978-0-00-834070-4

Set in Birka by Palimpsest Book Production Ltd, Falkirk Stirlingshire

Printed and bound in Great Britain
by CPI Group (UK) Ltd, Croydon CR0 4YY

*For my wonderful Mum, whose love of reading inspired my own.
And my equally wonderful dad, John.*

And as always, for Finlay, Jude and James.

Prologue

The large man's brow furrowed. 'Fucking bastards!' he shouted, spittle flying from his mouth as he ended the call, slamming his smartphone onto the desk in front of him.

Liam McGuinness jumped, spilling his cup of coffee onto his new jeans. 'For fuck's sake, boss,' he snapped as he leaped out of his chair. 'These cost me three hundred quid.'

His boss glared at him in response.

Liam placed his cup onto the desk. 'What's up?' he asked, realising the cost of his designer jeans was inconsequential to the raging man in front of him.

'Our container has gone missing. That's what's fucking up,' he growled.

Liam's mouth dropped open. 'What? That's the second one this month.'

'I know, soft-shite.'

'You know who's behind it, don't you?'

His boss nodded furiously. 'Cheeky little fucker. Who the hell does he think he is?'

Liam snorted. 'He's an arrogant little prick. He'd be no one without Mummy and Daddy's name behind him. It's about time someone taught him what happens to little boys who think they're big men.'

The boss slammed his large fist onto the desk, sending Liam's coffee cup tumbling to the floor. 'He's cost me near on six hundred grand. I don't care what his name is, he's a fucking dead man walking,' he snarled.

Liam smiled. It was about time they stood up to this little prick. If they were going to be the top dogs, then they had to have the balls to take out their main competition, no matter who they were. There was no room in Liverpool for all of them. When that arrogant little shit had walked onto the scene, his name alone had sent shockwaves through the Liverpool underworld. People had automatically fallen in line, as though he was the heir to the fucking throne.

But Liam knew what he really was. A spoiled little boy who was still tied to his mummy's apron strings and who would never be half the gangster his father was. Now that his parents were out of the way, it was the perfect time to make a move.

Liam's boss wasn't from Liverpool, but he knew of the family by reputation. Between them, Grace Sumner and Nathan Conlon had practically ruled Liverpool for years. There was a time when people dared not take a shit without the okay from one of them. And now their son, Jake, had taken up their mantle, although he didn't quite have the same clout as his parents, and in Liam's opinion he never would. Despite Liam's best efforts to persuade him otherwise, his boss had been too cautious to take Jake on. Liam didn't understand why. It wasn't as though he was against getting his hands dirty. The first job he'd taken Liam on had been to get information from a dealer who'd been involved in trying to rip him off. The lad had given up his co-conspirators before they'd laid a finger on him, but his boss had tortured him to death just for the hell of it. It sent a message. That was how he operated.

Liam smiled as he watched his employer taking out the knuckledusters and corkscrew from his desk drawer – it meant their evening was about to get a whole lot more interesting. The boss was pissed off and some poor sod was about to feel his wrath.

'What are we gonna do then?' Liam asked.

The big man stared at him. 'Tonight we're going to pay the McHughs a visit. They're a day late paying me and my patience has worn incredibly thin. As for our other problem, all in good time, lad. But mark my words, Jake Conlon will rue the fucking day he ever tried to mess with me.'

Chapter 1

Grace Sumner smiled at her sleeping daughter as she laid her down in her cot. Belle's dark curls sprawled around her head like a halo. She looked so peaceful. Eight months old and the image of her father. So much so, that sometimes looking at her daughter's face made Grace's stomach contract.

The sound of Grace's mobile phone ringing in the next room snapped her from her quiet reflection. Hurrying out of Belle's bedroom and into her own, she snatched the offending item from her bedside table. In her eagerness to prevent the noise from waking Belle, she'd already swiped right on the screen to answer when she noticed it was a withheld number. *Probably another bloody arsehole asking about the car accident I haven't had!*

'Hello?' she snapped.

'Hello, Grace.'

She recognised the thick Mancunian drawl immediately. Her insides lurched and she contemplated hanging up without speaking another word.

'Sol,' she said instead. 'How the hell did you get this number? And what do you want?'

She heard his throaty laugh before he responded. 'I've always loved your fire, Gracie. It's such a shame we never got together, don't you think?'

No, she thought but didn't say. Solomon Shepherd was a former business associate of hers from Manchester. He dealt in drugs and weapons mostly, which Grace had supplied him with on many occasions. She got on well enough with him, but he had an ego the size of Saturn. 'What do you want, Sol?' she sighed.

'Look, Grace, we've always got on well. We do good business. That's why I'm doing you the courtesy of phoning you about this . . .'

'About what? Just get to the point, will you?' She was not in the mood for his dramatics.

'Okay, don't get your fucking knickers in a twist,' he barked. 'Things have gone tits up since you pissed off. You need to get back home and get your fucking house in order.'

'What?'

'You heard me. I don't know what the fuck is going on over there in la-la-land, but it's causing me no end of aggro. So, fucking sort it.'

'Look, Sol. You know I'm out of that game now. It's Michael you need to be speaking to.'

'I know you're out of it. That's my fucking point. Michael Carter is too fucking stupid to know when he's onto a good thing. He's let everything go to shit. Someone else has taken over. I don't know him, but from what I can gather, he's a fucking weapon who doesn't know his arse from his elbow. He's losing merchandise left, right and centre, and it's disrupting my supply chains.'

Grace frowned. Michael Carter had once been her right-hand man. She had left her considerable empire in his capable hands. He was as hard as they came. So why had he let someone else take over? Shaking her head, she remembered that she was well out of it all now. 'I still don't get what any of this has to do with me, Sol.'

'Oh, yeah, that. Well, that kid of yours is involved somehow as well.'

'Jake?' Grace said as she felt a sudden sickening feeling in the pit of her stomach.

'Yeah. Playing at being a gangster. Stepped right into Daddy's shoes. Trouble is, Daddy's shoes are far too big for him. I've had the filth sniffing round me because of his fucking incompetence. Because he's your son, I've let it go. But I will not do that again, Grace.'

'What are you on about Sol? Jake's not running that kind of business.'

Sol laughed. 'Are you kidding me? You really are out of touch, aren't you? You're living in cloud cuckoo land, Grace, and you need to get your head back in the game before that lad of yours ends up with a bullet in his.'

Grace felt like someone had punched her in the stomach. 'But Jake—' She swallowed, struggling to talk and breathe at the same time.

'But fucking nothing. He's in way over his head. Not a fucking clue what he's doing. There's more to this game than running about sticking guns in people's faces – as you well know. Look, I'm only telling you this because we've got history and I thought you deserved to know. Rein him in, Grace, before someone else does.'

Grace's head spun. What the hell was Sol on about? What the hell was Jake involved in, and why hadn't he mentioned anything when she'd spoken to him that morning? Or any other morning? She needed answers, and fast.

'Thanks for the heads up, Sol.' She hung up the phone.

Grace's legs buckled beneath her. She landed on her bed in a seated position. Dear God! Jake! Her poor, sweet baby boy. What had she left him to?

The murder of Nathan Conlon, her ex-husband and Jake's father, had been a shock to the Liverpool underworld, throwing the cat amongst the proverbial pigeons and causing some unrest while the various factions jockeyed for position in the new world order. For Grace, it had signalled the perfect time to get away. So, that's exactly what she'd done – moving to the sleepy village of Harewood, where the most exciting thing that ever happened was a heated debate at a parish council meeting. She'd been convinced that it would be enough to protect Jake and keep him away from the life she and his father had chosen. She'd been furious with him when he'd declared he was dropping out of university to run his father's seedy little nightclub, The Blue Rooms. But, full of the arrogance and naiveté of a twenty-year-old boy, he'd refused to listen to a word she said. 'Why do a business degree when I can run my own business, Mum?' he'd said with that lovable, lopsided grin on his face.

She'd refused to return to Liverpool with him. She couldn't. There was Belle to think of. But she'd been a fool to believe that Jake wouldn't get sucked into that world. After all, she and Nathan were his parents. She'd stupidly believed him when he'd promised to make The Blue Rooms into a legitimate business to be proud of. God, she'd been so bloody blind.

So, now what?

She had to go back, of course.

Feeling the bile rising in her throat, she swallowed it down. How would she keep her little secret now? She couldn't, could she? It was impossible. And when it all came out, well, all hell would break loose.

Chapter 2

Lifting Belle from her car seat, Grace looked up at the second-floor window of the three-storey house in Canning Street to see Marcus Holden waving at her, a smile plastered across his face. He motioned his hand to indicate he was buzzing her in.

After carrying Belle up the two flights of stairs to Marcus's flat, Grace placed her sleeping charge on Marcus's large sofa, surrounded by pillows.

'I've missed you,' Marcus said, his eyes brimming with tears as he embraced her. 'I'm so glad you're back.'

'I've missed you too,' Grace said as she hugged him. 'Although I'm not so happy to be here,' she said as she untangled herself from his embrace.

'Well, no, I suppose not.' He shook his head. 'Not in the circumstances. You look shattered. How about a brew before you fill me in on everything?'

'That would be great.'

'You take a load off then,' he said indicating his plush sofa. 'And I'll stick the kettle on.'

Sighing, Grace took a seat near Belle. A traffic jam on the M62 meant she'd been driving for over four hours. She'd been hoping to have Belle home and tucked up in bed by eight, but instead it was after nine and she was only just arriving at Marcus's flat to pick up the keys to her house.

Marcus Holden was Grace's oldest and closest friend. He'd been the manager of her pub, The Rose and Crown, before it had been burned to the ground. He was one of the few people who even knew where she lived in Harewood, and he'd visited her and Belle there at least a dozen times. He'd been looking after her house in Formby for her and had been acting as a property manager for the tenants Grace had found. How fortunate it was that they'd moved on a few weeks earlier, or Grace would have had to rent a new place herself.

A few minutes later, Marcus came back into his living room carrying two mugs of tea.

'Thanks,' Grace said as she took the drink from him.

'So, how are you, Grace?' Marcus asked. 'Apart from tired, that is?'

Grace shook her head. 'I don't know, to be honest. Annoyed. Angry. Terrified.'

She hadn't told Marcus the full extent of Jake's troubles, partly because she didn't know yet herself, but also because Marcus had always stayed away from that side of her business and had no place in that world as far as Grace was concerned. It was one of the reasons she'd allowed him to visit her, that and the fact she adored him and missed him like crazy.

Marcus shook his head too. 'So what are you going to do?'

'The first thing I need to do is to find out what's been going on while I've been away. And then I need to speak to that lad of mine and find out what the hell he's playing at.'

'Hmm.' Marcus sipped his tea.

'On that note. Could you do me a favour?'

'Anything.'

'Would you mind staying with me for a while and looking after Belle while I sort some stuff out?'

'Hmm.' Marcus tilted his head as though considering her offer. 'Stay in your gorgeous five-bedroomed house with a home cinema and look after the most incredible little girl in the world? Of course, I will.' He laughed. 'I'll just drink this and then I'll pack a bag.'

'Thanks. You're a legend,' Grace smiled. She didn't know what she'd do without him.

Grace felt Marcus staring at her and knew what he was thinking. Apart from Jake, it was all she'd thought about too.

'So what about your other little problem?' he finally asked.

Grace sighed. 'I have no idea. It's bound to come out, isn't it?'

'Not necessarily,' he said.

Grace raised an eyebrow at him. 'Don't try and make me feel better. How the hell can I keep up the pretence now? It was different while I was in Harewood. But now that I'm back here . . .'

'It will be difficult, but we'll think of something,' he said softly.

Grace shook her head. 'He's going to find out, Marcus. And then the shit will really hit the fan. It's going to be fucking awful.'

Marcus didn't respond. Probably because he knew she was right.

Chapter 3

The tyres of Grace's car crunched on the gravel as she pulled into the driveway of the expensive detached house. She'd settled Belle into her new room and left Marcus babysitting and deciding which bedroom to stake his claim on. It was after midnight and the streets of Mossley Hill were deserted. Only a few amber streetlights buzzed and flickered overhead. Walking up the ornate stone steps, she knocked on the large wooden door and, a few moments later, listened to the sound of the heavy bolts being drawn back. Then the door opened barely an inch and a beady blue eye peered through the crack above the safety chain.

'Jesus Christ, Ivan,' Grace said with a laugh. 'You know it's me. I just bloody phoned you. Is there any need for the Fort Knox level security? Now let me in, it's frigging freezing out here.'

The door opened to reveal Ivan Golding's smiling face. 'You can never be too careful, Grace,' he said. 'You of all people should know that.'

'Who on earth would try and take you on, you daft old sod?' She grinned as she stepped inside his lavish hallway and pulled him into a hug.

Ivan Golding had been Grace's accountant for years and was one of the few people she considered a good friend. She'd kept in limited phone contact with him since she'd left Liverpool, but seeing his round, pleasant face, his grey hair perched jauntily on top, she realised just how much she'd missed him.

'It's so good to see you, Grace,' he said. 'It's been too long.'

'You too, Ivan.' She smiled at him as she took a step back. 'Now how about a cuppa and you can fill me in on all that's been going on since I left?'

'It'll take more than a cuppa, love,' he said with a flash of his eyebrows. 'It'll take a whole bleeding urn!'

Grace followed him down his thickly carpeted hallway into his kitchen. Ivan always did have a flair for drama, but he was a shrewd businessman who had his ear to the ground and knew the ins and outs of almost everyone's business in Liverpool. And if he didn't know, he had the means to find out. As soon as she'd recovered her senses after her phone call from Sol, Grace had phoned him and asked him to start making some enquiries. She was sure, if anyone could fill her in on what had been going on with Jake, then Ivan could.

Sipping her fourth mug of tea since her arrival in Liverpool a few hours earlier, Grace listened as Ivan started to fill her in on some of the comings and goings of the Liverpool underworld over the last eighteen months.

'So Michael's not running my old operations anymore then?' Grace asked.

Ivan shook his head. 'Doesn't have that much to do with the drugs scene now.'

'But why?' Grace didn't understand it. She had left a well-oiled machine in Michael Carter's very capable hands. He'd been onto a great earner. Why would he give it all up?

Ivan took a sip of his tea. 'He's branched out into security instead. Him and his two lads. They seem to be doing well for themselves too. Doing the doors for most of Liverpool now.'

'But still . . .'

'You know Michael, Grace. He's all muscle and aggro.'

'But he's not stupid. I'd never have left him in charge if he was.'

'No.' Ivan shook his head. 'I never said he was stupid, but he's just not cut out for running the show. He prefers being in the thick of it, doesn't he? He can do that with the security.'

'I suppose so. So, who is running my old operations?' she asked.

'Some newcomer called Bobby White has taken over part of it. The rest, well . . .'

'Jake.' Grace sighed. 'So, Michael let Jake take over my old business? My son? The fucking bastard. He knew how I felt about Jake getting caught up in all that.' Grace shook her head. She could happily wring Michael Carter's neck for allowing her son to get sucked into the world she had fought so hard to keep him away from. Despite everything that had happened between them, she had trusted Michael to have her back. More fool her.

Ivan shook his head frantically. 'No, no. That's not how it happened. Michael walked away, and it left a vacuum. You know how it works. And Jake had the means to step into it, at least a part of it anyway.'

'But how? He's a kid, for God's sake!' Grace felt her pulse starting to race. She could hear her heart pounding in her ears. The thought of Jake in trouble – and not just any kind of trouble, but the type that could put him in serious danger – made her want to throw up. She could hardly think straight for the thoughts racing around her head.

'He's also your son, Grace. And Nathan's,' Ivan said, snapping her back to the present. 'His name alone ensured there was a place at the table if he wanted it. And he didn't just inherit Nathan's club, he inherited his workforce too. You know as well as I do that most of those lunatics couldn't wait to get back into the game.'

'Jesus Christ.' Grace put her head in her hands. 'I threw him to the lions, didn't I? He's not even twenty-one yet and I let him come back here on his own.'

Ivan placed his hand on hers. 'Don't say that, Grace. You have your own life to lead. He didn't have to get involved. He *wanted* to.'

'But now he's in some sort of trouble?' Grace asked.

'From what I could gather, someone is sabotaging his shipments and trying to muscle him out of the game altogether. He was supplying to some people in Manchester – I assume some of Sol's men – but that deal went south when the police raided a warehouse he was using. It seems the plod had a tip-off, but thankfully there was nothing to link the drugs to Jake or any of his firm. But instead of keeping his head down, Jake seems to be doing the opposite. He's declared war on anyone who wants to cross him. And he's not shy about sending a message either,' Ivan sucked air through his teeth and shook his head disapprovingly. 'I think he takes after his father in that respect.'

'The stupid little bastard,' Grace snapped. 'After everything I did to keep him away from that life.'

'What will you do now?' Ivan asked.

'I'm not sure yet. But I can't go in there all guns blazing or he'll just shut me out. As much as I love him, he's developed an ego like his father too. He won't admit he's in any trouble, and even if he did, he wouldn't want his mum stepping in to help him out.'

It seems you're in a pickle then,' Ivan said as he sat back in his chair.

'A pickle? I'm in the eye of a fucking shitstorm, Ivan.'

Grace closed her eyes and rested her head on the back of Ivan's leather sofa. She was so bloody tired. Her head was pounding and her limbs ached. She'd been back in Liverpool for less than five hours and already she felt like she was being sucked back into the darkness she'd tried so hard to escape. And if that wasn't enough to contend with, she had to walk around wondering when her cover would be blown and her dirty laundry would be out in the open for all the world to see.

She knew it was only a matter of time.

Chapter 4

Liam McGuinness crossed the tarmac and ducked behind a shipping container, sticking to the shadows in case one of the security cameras picked him up. If they did, they'd see a man of average build wearing a dark hoodie, which could fit the description of half the people in Liverpool. He waited in the darkness until he saw the unmistakeable form of Nudge Richards walking out of the security office towards him.

'You been waiting long?' Nudge asked as he approached.

Liam shook his head. 'Only a few minutes.'

'Had to square things with my buddies in there first,' Nudge said. 'They'll leave us in peace.'

'Great,' Liam said.

'So what have you got for me?' Nudge asked, indicating the container Liam was standing in front of.

'Fifty kilos of coke. Six Baikals and two machine guns.'

Nudge gave a low whistle. 'Heavy-duty stuff. That's not so easy to shift, lad. If you give me some time, I can get you top whack for them, otherwise you'll have to take what I can find. And my cut will be the same, regardless of how much you get.'

'I understand that. But like I said, I need them gone fast.'

'Which nutter did you nick 'em off then?' Nudge said with a grin.

'None of your fucking business,' Liam growled. 'Not backing out, are you?'

Nudge shook his head and laughed. 'Nope. Let's get this moved before your boss finds out, eh?'

Liam frowned. Did Nudge know more than he was letting on? 'I can count on you keeping your mouth shut, can't I, Nudge?'

Nudge, whose demeanour up until that point had been friendly, squared up to Liam. Having almost a foot on him, Nudge had to bend his head to bring his face close to the younger man's. 'Don't you fucking question my integrity, you little shit,' Nudge spat. 'I've been doing this job longer than you've been alive, and if I was a betting man, which I am, I'd put my life's earnings on the fact I'll still be doing it when you're six feet under.'

Liam nodded and took a step back. 'Just making sure we're on the same page.'

Satisfied with his response, Nudge backed off. 'Let's get this loaded into my van then,' he said.

'Anything you say,' Liam replied, now desperate to get out of the dockyard and away from the stolen merchandise. He was going to end up selling it for a fraction of its worth, he knew that, but it wasn't about the money; it was about his boss finally doing something about Jake fucking Conlon. Liam just wanted the stuff gone as quickly as possible, before his boss got even the slightest sniff of what had really happened to his lost shipment. Nudge Richards was the best fence in Liverpool. He could get anything for anyone, and get rid of anything too. Because of that, he was untouchable. There were few people who hadn't had cause to use Nudge's services at one time or another. Not that Nudge would admit that. He was the embodiment of discretion, and that was why he was so bloody good at his job.

* * *

Nudge Richards drove his old transit van through the quiet streets of Liverpool with his newly acquired stash safely tucked away in the false bottom in the back, should he be stopped for any reason. He had to get rid of it as soon as. That shit was so hot it might burn a hole through the floor if he didn't move it soon. He knew Liam had nicked it off his own boss, but he had no idea why. It wasn't like he was going to make a life-changing sum of money from it. Nudge had made it clear that moving merchandise like that in a matter of days limited his buying pool and he'd have to sell it at rock-bottom prices. But Nudge didn't care. He didn't ask questions. What was it to him if these gangsters insisted on ripping each other off? What he did know was that Liam's boss was a vicious fucker, and if he ever found out, the lad would wish he'd never been born.

Nudge shook his head. He sometimes wondered why he still did this shit. He was getting on for sixty. He should be thinking about retiring. If only he could stop gambling his money away at the bookies, or paying for women, he might have built himself a little nest egg. Instead he was facing a few more years being the go-between of every gangster in Merseyside, and sometimes beyond. He had no affiliation or loyalty to any of them. It was his number one rule and one which had kept him alive and in business for this long. Well, all except for Grace Sumner – but she was different. She wasn't like those narcissistic egomaniacs, running around waving their dicks at each other to see whose was the biggest. She was a businesswoman, pure and simple. She was a stunner too. Besides, he owed Grace. Years earlier she had saved him from losing absolutely everything and he had never forgotten it.

As he turned the corner into his scrapyard, Nudge was already lining up potential buyers in his head. He had some contacts in Cheshire who would bite his hand off for some cheap, clean guns, and there was a bloke in Fazakerley trying to make a name for himself who'd take the coke and wouldn't care where it came from. He'd have it all moved within two days and earn a decent wedge in the process.

Chapter 5

Pushing open the double glass doors of The Blue Rooms, Grace suppressed a shudder. The last time she'd been in this place had been to see her ex-husband, Nathan. It had changed a lot since then. Jake had spruced the place up, with new tiled floors and a professional paint job. Taking advantage of the regeneration of the Dock Road area, The Blue Rooms was no longer a seedy lap-dancing club but an up-and-coming nightclub which booked some of the best DJs in the country. Despite all that, the place still felt the same in so many ways. The smell. The neon lighting. The way Grace's skin prickled as soon as she walked through the doors.

Grace's heels clicked along the tiled floor as she made her way through to the manager's office – now Jake's office. She wondered if he had any idea of the things that had happened in there. The great Tommy McNulty had been murdered in that very room. She shivered at the thought of her last few visits there, when Nathan had pawed at her clothes and she'd had to allow him to touch her, to kiss her. She shook her head in annoyance. Nathan was gone. He'd been dead for eighteen months. Six feet under with a hole in his chest. When would she stop allowing him to have a hold over her?

The office door was open and Grace could see Jake as she

approached, talking to someone on the phone. No doubt one of his employees, judging by the tone of his voice.

'Just fucking sort it, Vinnie,' he snapped before ending the call.

God, he looked so much like his father it made her stomach churn.

'Mum,' he said as he looked up, unable to hide the shock on his face. Then, remembering his manners, he stood up and walked towards her, pulling her into a warm hug. 'What are you doing here?'

'I missed you. Thought I'd pay you a visit. I'm getting bored in that big old house in the middle of nowhere.'

'Really? I thought you loved that place?' He raised an eyebrow at her.

'I do. But it can get a bit boring when the only company you have is an eight-month-old baby whose solitary word is bloody Dada.' She laughed.

Stepping back, Jake eyed her suspiciously. 'Why the sudden visit though? I only spoke to you yesterday and you never mentioned you were coming.'

'It was a last-minute decision. I wanted to surprise you. Now, aren't you going to offer your old mum a drink?'

Jake laughed. 'Sorry, Mum. Remy do you?' he asked as he took the bottle from the cabinet near his desk.

Grace watched him pour them both a generous measure of brandy. At least he didn't drink whisky like his father. Just the smell of that still made her nauseous.

'So are you down for a few days, Mum? And where's Belle? I can't wait to see her. Do you need me to get Siobhan to sort out the spare room for you both?'

Grace sat in the chair opposite Jake's desk, thankful that he'd changed the furniture in here too, and sipped her drink. Her boy was a bit wet behind the ears but he wasn't stupid; she had to think of a convincing reason for being there. 'I'll be staying at the house. I'm planning on sticking around for a few months,' she said casually. 'I'm thinking of getting back into the restaurant business so I'm looking for the right premises. Ivan's going to help me. You remember him, don't you?'

'Yeah, but I thought you were done with the restaurants too?' he said as he sat down, unbuttoning his jacket as he did so, another habit he'd inherited from his father.

'I thought I was, but like I said, I was getting bored,' she lied. 'I need something to keep me busy, Jake. I always enjoyed the planning and the bustle of setting up a business. So, I'm hoping to get one up and running, and then I'll go back to my quiet little life in Harewood. Until I get restless again, anyway.'

'What about the horses and chickens?'

'Those two girls from the village, Lol and Beth, are going to look after them for me.'

Jake rolled his eyes. Lol and Beth were two sixteen-year-old girls who loved horses and were always happy to help Grace mucking out her stables in exchange for some riding time. However, whenever Jake visited, they found as many excuses as possible to call at the house. Then they spent most of their time following him around, giggling and bombarding him with questions. Jake's girlfriend, Siobhan, found it all amusing, but it annoyed Jake no end.

'Oh, right,' he said as he continued to eye her suspiciously.

She wondered if he believed her. It was a plausible lie. At least she thought so. Why wouldn't someone like Grace, who had always been in the thick of it, not get fed up living in the arse end of nowhere? But now came the more difficult part. Convincing him that he needed her in his club. 'But that won't keep me too busy, so I was hoping you might have a use here for me?' She smiled at him.

'Me? Why?' Jake snapped, and then, remembering who he was talking to, said more softly, 'Why would you want to work here, Mum? You hate the place.'

She shook her head. 'I used to hate the place, when it was your father's. But now that it's yours, well, I'd love to help you make a success of it. I did run a pub for twenty years, in case you've forgotten about that?'

'I know. It's just . . . I'm not sure what you'd do, to be honest.'

'Well, how about the books? Knowing you, they're probably your least favourite job, and I bet they're nowhere near up to date,' she said.

The way Jake averted her gaze and fiddled with his collar confirmed her suspicions. 'I know you're busy with *other* stuff,' she said pointedly. 'Let me sort out the books and some of the admin in this place for you. Leave you more time to focus on your other, more pressing, business?'

'I don't know, Mum.'

'Look, Jake. Have I taught you nothing? I know you've taken on more of your dad's businesses than just this club. If you're involved in anything like he was, like I was, then one of the most important things you need to do is to keep your legitimate front appearing legitimate. Even your dad knew that. He kept dodgy books, but he kept books.'

Jake blinked at her. He acted the big tough guy, but in a lot of ways he was still a little boy learning the ropes, and there was no doubt in her mind that he knew it too.

'Okay, Mum,' he sighed. 'But just the books.'

'Just the books,' she agreed.

'And maybe the staff rotas?' he added. 'The bar manager,

Martin, has been doing them, but he's causing murder by giving his mates the best shifts.'

'Anything I can do to help, son.' She smiled.

Before long, she'd know exactly what he was up to.

Chapter 6

Grace walked into The Blue Rooms for her first day of work. After almost eighteen months of wearing maternity clothes or her go-to mum uniform of jeans and a T-shirt, it had felt strange putting on smart clothes again. Smoothing her skirt over her hips she walked through the club and into the manager's office at the back, leaving her handbag and coat on Jake's chair when she saw he wasn't in.

It didn't take long for Grace to get back into the swing of things. She'd run her own pub for over twenty years and it was second nature to her. She was going through the previous week's stock order when Jake came bursting through the door.

'Mum?' he said. 'What are you doing here?'

Grace frowned at him. 'I'm working here. We discussed it yesterday.'

'Oh yeah, right. I just didn't realise you'd be here today – and in my office.'

Grace looked at him. She hadn't even considered that this was his office and she really had no right being in there without him. 'I assumed it would be okay. There isn't really anywhere else for me to work.'

He shook his head and stared at her. 'But you can't be in here. This is my office.'

Grace stared at him in surprise as she waited for the sting of his response to lessen. Suddenly she realised that she was working for her son. It hadn't crossed her mind until now that he was technically her boss, and she wasn't used to having to answer to anyone – not anymore. Now here was her son, the person she had taught to read, how to use a bloody spoon, telling her that she wasn't welcome in his space. He was treating her like a spare part – or, worse, a nuisance. It saddened and infuriated her at the same time. If only he knew the real reason she was there. With that in mind she closed her eyes and took a deep breath. 'Don't worry, I'll find myself somewhere else.' She forced a smile as she picked up her handbag. She supposed she couldn't blame him. This was his place, not hers. It couldn't be easy for him allowing her into his domain, not given who she was – who she had been.

Grace hadn't considered that it wouldn't be easy for her either. Coming back to Liverpool and not knowing where she fitted in the new order of things. She had been on top for so long, it felt like the place she most belonged.

'I'll catch up with you later, Mum,' Jake said as she walked out of his office.

'Yeah, okay,' she said, as she wondered where on earth in this club she could find somewhere she could call her own.

Grace felt the tension building in her shoulders and creeping up her neck as she walked down the tiled hallway. No doubt Jake was sitting in his office feeling as annoyed as she was. He was probably contemplating his empire, with no idea of the trouble he was actually in. With no clue that she had been drafted back in to save his skin. It irritated her that he thought he was helping her out by giving her something to keep her busy. If she wasn't so worried about him, it would be bloody infuriating.

But, as she rubbed her neck with her free hand, she reminded herself that he was her son, and just like she always had, she would do anything for him – even if it meant stepping back into a world she'd tried so hard to leave behind.

Chapter 7

Grace placed the ledger back in the safe. With Jake's agreement, she'd turned one of the old unused rooms into an office for herself. It had been used for a similar purpose in an old life and although it had no windows, she'd brightened it up with a good clean and some antique furniture from an old acquaintance of hers.

With Ivan's help, it had taken her almost a week to put Jake's accounts in order. They'd been in such a state she'd hardly been able to make sense of them and it seemed he'd barely touched them since he'd taken over the running of the place a year earlier. Last year's tax return had been filed, but that was about the extent of the accounts upkeep.

Of course, she'd been preoccupied with her real reason for being there – to find out just how much trouble her son was in, who was trying to take over his business, and, more importantly, how she could fix it – all without Jake's knowledge, if she could help it. Getting information about her son's extra-curricular activities was proving a much simpler task.

It was quite clear that Bobby White was the man trying to take over Jake's business. He was the obvious candidate seeing as he was the one who was in direct competition with him. Grace didn't know Bobby; in fact, nobody seemed to know very much about him at all. Ivan had mentioned he was a newcomer and Grace was sure she'd find out who he was before the week was out. She'd spoken to all of Jake's employees at The Blue Rooms, all under the pretence that she was interviewing them about their shift patterns and preferences, in preparation for taking over the staff rotas. She was good at getting information from people without them even realising. It was laughable how much people trusted her simply because she was a woman. Despite being brunette, she knew how to act like the proverbial dumb blonde when required, and when she did, most men were happy to give her the benefit of their wisdom and expertise.

Although she was Grace Sumner, who'd once run one of the biggest drug operations this side of the Mersey, one of them had even explained the various drugs terminology to her. She'd sat, nodding at him and pretending to be enthralled by his dazzling insight, while desperately trying to keep a straight face.

In a few days, Grace had learned that few people employed at The Blue Rooms were loyal to Jake, and very soon she'd be giving most of them their marching orders. A few choice words in their ears about Jake not knowing what he was doing had most of them willing to throw their boss under the bus for the promise of more or better shifts.

What was clear was that Jake had no idea how to run a business – at least not a legitimate business. It seemed he was faring better, if only slightly, in his criminal activities – but due to sheer brute force, stubbornness, and stupidity rather than anything else. He had the brass neck to front anyone, and he wasn't shy of using extreme violence when the occasion called for it. All of which was earning him a reputation to rival his father's back in the day. No doubt the ghost of Nathan had played a part too, as well as the fact that many of Nathan's former minions were now happy to serve Jake instead.

If the stories Grace had heard were to be believed, Nathan Conlon's son was turning out to be as ruthless as he was. It made her feel sick to think that everything she'd done to keep her son away from this life had been for nothing. He was like his father in so many ways, it was alarming.

Grace sighed as she sat down in the chair in her office. As much as Jake was like Nathan, he was like her too. She had to hold onto that. Now, if only he could learn to use his brain along with his muscle, she had no doubt that he'd be running Liverpool before long. It was her worst fear, but now she knew it was a path she'd never be able to deter him from. It was in his blood.

So, until then, while he was still learning the ropes, she would have to lend a helping hand – and try to make sure he didn't get himself killed.

Chapter 8

John Brennan's large frame almost filled the doorway of Grace's office. She hadn't seen him since before Nathan's murder but he hadn't changed a bit. Unsure of the reception she'd get from him, she had been anxious about inviting him in. But as soon as she saw his face, she knew she'd made the right decision. John had one of those smiles that was infectious. Nathan had always called him the Smiling Assassin and Grace had to admit it suited him. John might look like a gentle giant, but he was a vicious bastard when he needed to be. He was one of the few people who'd worked for Nathan who hadn't continued working for Jake too. Grace had heard he was doing well on his own. Nothing too major, dodgy fags and booze mostly, along with a bit of weed, but he was still a man with a fearsome reputation and few would be stupid enough to try and cross him.

'Hiya, Grace,' he said, beaming, as he walked into the room. 'Long time no see.'

'Hi, John.' She returned his smile as she stood up to be hugged. But a hug from John felt like a hug from a grizzly and she was eager to escape. 'Can I get you a drink?' she asked him.

'I wouldn't say no,' he replied as he released her.

Grace poured him a glass of her best brandy and sat on the desk beside him.

'So what brings you back to these parts?' John asked as he sipped his drink.

'Jake.'

'Of course.' He'd known Jake and Grace for years through his connection with Nathan. Grace often wondered if, in another life, she and John could have been friends. Whatever they were, they had a healthy respect for each other.

'I thought you wouldn't be too pleased about his new career choice,' he said, shaking his head. 'Stupid kid. After everything you did for him. He should have stayed in uni and made something of himself.'

'I couldn't agree more, John. But it is what it is. He's made his choice and nothing I, or anyone else, can say will persuade him otherwise.'

John nodded in agreement.

They both sat in silence for a moment until John spoke again. 'Although it's nice to see you, Grace, I'm sure you didn't just invite me here for small talk . . .?'

'Of course. I know you must be busy, so I'll get straight to it. I want you to come and work for me.'

John laughed. 'Are you serious?'

'Deadly.'

'Are you *back* then? To be honest, I'd hoped you were when I heard you were home. There are a lot of people out there who would be very happy about your return, Grace.'

Grace laughed. 'And some not so much.'

John took a sip of his brandy. 'Not many. It was definitely much calmer when you were in charge.'

'Well, that may be. But, no, I'm not *back*. Not in the way you'd hoped anyway.'

'So why do you need me to work for you?' He frowned.

'Well, you'd be working for Jake really, I suppose.'

John laughed again. 'So what you really want me to do is to spy on your son?'

'No,' Grace snapped, before realising that John had a point. 'It's just that you'd be so good for him, John. I wish you'd stayed on with him. I know you've got your own thing going on, but . . .'

'But?'

'It's not exactly playing to your strengths, is it? Smuggling booze and ciggies?'

'It's good money. I'm my own boss. It's less hassle.'

'You're wasted, John. I think you should consider working for Jake. If we say you're working for me he won't be able to question it. Then when I move back to Leeds, it would make sense for you to stay on. I'll speak to Jake.'

John sighed. 'You make it all sound so easy, Grace.'

'Isn't it?'

John shook his head. 'I don't work for Jake because he didn't want me to.'

'What? He told me you left of your own accord to go it on your own.'

'I did. But only because he made it impossible for me to stay.'

Grace shook her head. What the hell was Jake playing at, letting one of his biggest assets go?

'Look, Grace. He's a young kid. He's got big boots to fill. He wants to do things his own way, make his own mark. Not have his dad's old buddies telling him what he's doing wrong.'

'I'm sorry, John. I didn't know. It looks like I've wasted your time.'

John downed the last of his brandy and shook his head. 'Not at all. It was good to see you.' He stood up to leave. 'And if you

ever do decide to get your head back in the game, let me know.
I'll come and work for you any time.'

Grace stood up to show him out. 'Thanks, John,' she said as
she gave him a parting hug. 'That means a lot.'

'It's true.' He smiled. 'And I'm not the only one.'

Chapter 9

Picking up the invoice from the brewery, Grace walked into the bar area of The Blue Rooms.

'Hi, Grace,' Jake's girlfriend, Siobhan Davies, said, her large smile lighting up her pale, freckled face.

'Hiya, Siobhan,' Grace replied, pulling the younger woman into a hug as she reached her. Jake adored Siobhan, and Grace liked her too. She'd been over the moon when she and Jake had finally got together. He'd pined over the girl throughout the last few years of school and then through college too. Siobhan was smart, funny, and kind and she always had a smile on her face and rarely a bad word to say about anybody. Because of that, people trusted her, and sometimes took her for a fool. But she was far from it. Grace knew Siobhan was as savvy as the best of them. She was an asset, but Jake didn't seem to be able to see her true value and had her pottering about behind the bar instead. Grace intended to utilise her considerable talent and business acumen as soon as possible, so that when she returned to Harewood, the management of The Blue Rooms could be left in Siobhan's capable hands.

'It's so nice to have you back. Jake has really missed you, and Belle.'

'I know, I miss him too. I'm glad he has you to keep him

company though. I hear the two of you have bought a flat on the waterfront?'

'It's absolutely gorgeous, Grace. You and Belle should come visit us. How about Sunday? I do a mean roast dinner.'

'Sounds good to me. It's not very often someone cooks for me these days. I seem to live on cereal and toast,' she said, laughing.

'It's a date then. I'll pick up a leg of lamb from that butcher's on the high street.'

Grace pulled Siobhan to one side. 'Who orders the stock around here?'

Siobhan pulled a face. 'Martin is supposed to do it, when he remembers. But most of the time it's Olly.'

'Well, neither of them appears to be any good at it. I can see we've run out of bottles of Bud already, and it's only Saturday.'

Siobhan shook her head. 'They're a pair of idiots if you ask me.'

'I couldn't agree more.' Grace had only met the pair of them on a handful of occasions. They were supposed to be the bar managers, but they seemed more interested in pulling women and shagging on their break.

'What about you? Why hasn't Jake got you doing this stuff?'

Siobhan sighed. 'Don't ask me. He says he doesn't want me having to work all hours in this place. He only lets me do shifts when he knows he'll be here too. I think he has some old-fashioned ideas about looking after me and needing to be the breadwinner.' She raised her eyebrows in amusement.

Grace shook her head in despair. It didn't surprise her. His father had been a misogynistic prick who'd treated women like dirt. She had hoped she'd raised Jake to be the opposite of that, and he probably believed that he was. She had no doubt that her son thought it was enough that he treated Siobhan like a princess. But what he obviously didn't realise was that his own thinking was simply oppression in a different guise. A gilded cage was still a cage.

'I'll have a word with him. Between you and me, I'll be letting those pair of lazy bastards go in the next few weeks. I think you should take over the stock ordering from this week. I can walk you through it, but I think you'll pick it up no problem.'

'I couldn't be any worse than that pair, could I?'

Grace laughed. She liked Siobhan's confidence. She'd make a club manager out of her in no time.

Chapter 10

Liam McGuinness sat at the bar nursing his pint and watching the redhead walking around the place with a clipboard and pen. She was pretty, but she had that annoying holier-than-thou thing going on. He'd bet she thought she was too good to talk to the likes of him. The other bar staff were friendly enough and he'd spent the past few Monday nights enjoying a drink at The Blue Rooms.

It soon became clear why the redhead had such a stick up her arse when Jake Conlon walked up behind her and put his arms around her waist and she spun around and kissed him.

Liam frowned as he watched Jake Conlon talking and laughing with her. It was Jake he was there to see, or at least to observe. He wanted to find out as much as he could about his competition. He hated that pretentious, privileged little shit so much it made his head hurt.

Liam had been twenty-one when he'd first met Jake's dad, Nathan Conlon in Frankland prison. He'd been serving six years for wounding and couldn't believe he'd been lucky enough to share a wing with the great man himself. Liam already had a growing reputation of his own and he'd made it his business to ingratiate himself with the man who could help him make it to the top. It had taken months of careful preparation and planning. Always being there at the right time. Taking the rap for an assault on a screw that Nathan would have got a few extra months for. Being there when he was jumped by a group of Manchester lads. Both situations planned and carefully executed by Liam to ensure he became an asset to the man who had become his hero.

Before long, he and Nathan were padded up in the same cell together and they remained that way for another two years. Nathan had promised him a long and illustrious career in his firm. He'd said he'd make him one of the most feared and respected enforcers in Merseyside. Nathan had told Liam he was like a son to him, which to Liam, whose own father was a useless waste of oxygen who'd overdosed when Liam was just a toddler, had been powerful stuff. When Liam got out, he'd done various jobs for Nathan while he was still inside, and was quietly and methodically cementing his place in Nathan's firm. It had all been going well – until this snot-nosed little wank-stain had turned up.

Liam clenched his jaw as he remembered the day it happened. Nathan had just got out and Liam was supposed to meet him for a drink. Liam had just done a big job for him and he knew it was the day Nathan was going to bring him into the fold – into his inner circle. They'd spoken on the phone and Nathan had been happy with the way Liam had handled himself. He said he'd made him proud and that had made Liam happier than he'd ever felt in his life. Then, ten minutes before they were supposed to meet, Nathan had called to say he was going to meet up with his son instead. But to add insult to injury, he'd sounded so fucking excited about it. As though Liam was his second choice, to be discarded whenever someone better came along. As if it was Jake who had been the one seeing to his every fucking need for the past few years. Liam had voiced his displeasure about the whole thing and that was it. Nathan had told him to grow up and stop being such a ponce, and Liam never heard from him again. All because of Jake fucking Conlon.

'Can I get you anything else, love?' The blonde barmaid smiled at him.

'Another pint, gorgeous.' He winked at her.

'Coming right up,' she said with a giggle.

Liam put a note on the bar and continued watching Jake Conlon out of the corner of his eye. The blonde placed his pint in front of him and took the money. 'Keep the change, babe.' He grinned at her and she smiled back at him while fluttering her eyelashes. He'd take her home later and give her a good seeing to. That always made him feel a bit better. She looked a bit like his Leanne too so that was a bonus. He wondered briefly what she was doing tonight. Probably being fucked up the arse by Bobby White, he thought bitterly, which only served to further his bad mood.

Chapter 11

Grace looked up from her paperwork as she heard her office door open. Although her heart started thumping in her ears at the sight of them, she couldn't help but smile at her two visitors. She'd been back in Liverpool for over a week and had wondered how long it would be before they'd make an appearance.

'Hello, stranger,' they chorused.

'Hello, you two,' she replied. Smiling, she stood up as Patrick and Sean Carter walked towards her.

Patrick looked so much older than she remembered. Her eyes were instantly drawn to the two missing digits on his left hand and she felt a pang of guilt. He walked with a stick now too. Both lasting reminders of a beating from Nathan which had landed him in intensive care and almost killed him. Patrick had been the man responsible for her rise to the top of the Liverpool underworld. He'd seen something in her that no one else had before. He'd worked for her for a long time and, along with his youngest son, Michael, had been her most trusted confidante.

Patrick's eldest son, Sean, hadn't aged a day, still cutting a handsome figure in his suit and tie. He and Grace had opened a string of successful Italian restaurants in Liverpool which he still owned and ran, although Grace had left them behind too and sold her shares to the rest of the Carter family.

Grace embraced each of them in turn.

'So this is where you're hiding yourself away then?' Sean asked.

'Between this place and Belle, I'm kept pretty busy.'

'We heard you'd had a baby girl,' Patrick said. 'Congratulations. How old is she now?'

'Nine and a half months,' Grace lied. 'How are you both?' she asked, trying to change the subject.

'Not bad, considering,' Patrick said as he indicated his stick.

'Enough of the small talk, eh?' Sean said. 'We could ask you why you never bothered your arse to speak to any of us since you buggered off to live in the country. We could complain that it fucking hurt when you dropped us all like a tonne of bricks. But what we really came to say is it's good to have you back, Grace. We all missed you.'

Grace smiled. She knew she'd hurt them all, but it had been the only way for her to move on. 'I've missed you all too,' she said and she meant it.

'Look, it's Nicola's birthday party on Sunday. You do remember my daughter, don't you? I assume you'll be coming now you're home. Bring Belle too. Everyone is dying to meet her.'

'I don't know, Sean—' she started.

'Look, Grace,' he said. 'We heard nothing from you for almost eighteen months. Complete radio silence. We had to rely on Marcus to hear how you were doing, and even then it was like pulling teeth. We understand why you wanted to move on and put everything behind you, but you're back now. It's all water under the bridge, isn't it? We're family. You're my daughter's godmother, for fuck's sake. We'll see you at our place at one,' he said.

'Come on, love,' Patrick said. 'Everyone would love to see you.'

Grace had to admit she would love to see all of them too.

She had forgotten how much she enjoyed being in their company. Although taking Belle was out of the question.

'Okay,' she said. 'I'll be there.'

'Good,' Sean and Patrick chorused. 'See you Sunday.'

'Shall I bring anything?'

'Just yourself and that daughter of yours,' Sean said. 'We'd better let you get on. Come on, Dad. I'll treat you to a pint.'

As the two men got up to leave, Grace felt a lump in her throat. She'd missed them more than she'd care to admit.

It felt good to be home.

Chapter 12

Grace shifted from one foot to the other as she knocked on the familiar door of Sean Carter's house on Sunday. She could hear the laughter and conversation from the partygoers outside.

'Grace!' Sean's wife, Sophia, shrieked as she answered the door before pulling her into a warm hug.

'Aunty Grace,' Nicola and Beth chimed behind their mother.

'Hey, you two,' she said, crouching down to hug them both. 'I've missed you guys.' The girls, aged eight and six now, had shot up in height since Grace had last seen them. They looked just like their mother, unlike their older sister, Steph, who was the double of her father, Sean.

Grace gave Nicola her birthday present and both girls skipped off to open it. Sean placed a glass of champagne in Grace's hand and led her into the dining room where most of the guests were.

'Where's Belle?' Sophia asked. 'I've been dying to meet her.'

'Oh, she's not feeling well,' Grace said. 'Jake and Siobhan are looking after her.'

'Oh no, poor thing,' Sophia said as she made a sad face.

'It's just a cold and a bit of a temperature. She'll be fine in a few days.'

Grace made her way through the room, passing a stream of familiar faces, all of whom seemed happy to see her, hugging and kissing her as she passed. Finally, she reached her intended target: Patrick Carter. Her old friend and confidante. God, she'd missed him. She hadn't realised just how much until he'd come strolling into her office the other day.

'Hello, love. I'm so glad you came,' Patrick said as she approached, giving her a kiss on the cheek. 'Have you met Sue?' He introduced the elegant-looking lady with the grey hair standing next to him.

'No, I don't believe I've had the pleasure,' Grace said as Sue held out her hand, showing off the giant rock on her ring finger. Grace had barely managed to congratulate them on their recent engagement, when she was accosted by Sean's daughter Steph, who hugged her as though she'd just returned from a decade-long expedition to Everest, enveloping her in a cloud of Chanel Mademoiselle perfume.

'Grace,' Steph squealed. 'It's so good to see you.'

'You too,' Grace said with a smile.

'I've been dying to come visit, but Jake and Marcus are so bloody secretive with your new address.'

'I know. I'm sorry about that, they're so protective,' she lied. She had made them swear that they wouldn't reveal her new address to anyone, not even Steph, whom she loved like a little sister. 'Anyway, tell me how the love life is going. Is Steve still in the picture?'

Steph shook her head. 'Oh God, no. He was another one who turned out to be a complete bell-end.'

Grace laughed. Steph's dating history was more colourful than Joseph's infamous coat. 'But I thought he was the one?'

Steph rolled her eyes. 'So did I. Anyway, I'm seeing Chris now.' She smiled. 'He's lovely. He's a barrister.'

'Really?' Grace raised her eyebrows in surprise. Any barrister in his right mind would be crazy to get involved with one of the Carter family, but she kept that thought to herself.

'Steph, can you give me a hand?' her mother, Sophia, shouted from across the room.

Steph waved to signal she was coming, then turned to Grace. 'We need a proper catch-up. I've got so much to tell you about. How about I cook you lunch tomorrow? At Antonelli's?'

Antonelli's had been her and Sean's flagship restaurant. It would be good to see the place again, and Steph was an incredible chef. 'I have a meeting at one. But I could get there about two?'

'It's a date.' Steph smiled and then headed over to her mother.

Grace was standing near the kitchen sink talking to an old friend when she saw Michael Carter and his wife, Hannah, walk into the room. Her mouth suddenly felt dry and her pulse began to race as she remembered the last time she and Michael had spoken. It was a painful memory and she had to take a second to compose herself. Michael had been her right-hand man back in the day, and one of her closest friends – but not anymore. Grace held her head high. She wouldn't let him know his presence had any effect on her.

It was Hannah who made her way over first. 'Hello, Grace,' she said brusquely. 'What brings you back here?'

'Hello, Hannah. I'm just here to help my son out for a while. I'll be going back to Leeds in a few months, I expect.'

'Oh, that's nice,' she said dismissively.

'Grace.' Michael nodded at her before following his wife out of the kitchen.

Patrick sidled over to her. 'He can't half pick 'em,' he chuckled in Grace's ear. 'Another stuck-up cow who hates us all.'

Grace laughed. 'She's all right really. You should be nicer to her, Pat.'

'Ha. If she gave me the time of day, maybe I would.'

After three hours at the party, Grace made her excuses to leave. She didn't like to leave Belle for too long and Siobhan was making a lamb roast for dinner. It took her almost half an hour to get out of the place, with the need to say goodbye and exchange hugs with everyone, and promise that she would see them all again soon.

She was just about to open her car when she saw Michael walking back towards the house. She'd hardly seen him all afternoon and wasn't aware he'd left the party.

'Hey.' He smiled.

'Hey,' she replied. 'Where's Hannah?'

'She had to go to work. I've just dropped her off.'

'Oh. Well, enjoy the rest of the party,' she said as she opened her car door.

'Grace,' he said, taking hold of her arm.

'What, Michael?'

He swallowed. 'It's good to see you.'

'Yeah, you too,' she said before climbing into her car.

Glancing in her rear-view mirror she saw him standing in the driveway, hands in his pockets, watching as she drove away.

Chapter 13

Michael Carter watched as Grace's car drove down Calderstones Avenue, and sighed. Their first meeting had been as awkward as he'd expected. It wasn't so long ago that he and Grace had been the best of mates. Always comfortable in each other's company. She could, and often did, make him laugh in even the most inappropriate of situations. He smiled as he remembered the time she'd had him in stitches in a funeral parlour. They'd been there to pay their respects to an old friend of his dad's. He couldn't even remember what the joke was now, but he could recall the pair of them holding on to each other with tears rolling down their cheeks and Grace proclaiming loudly that she was going to pee herself.

They had thought there was no one else in there at the time, but unbeknownst to them, his dad had turned up too. He'd given him a right bollocking afterwards. He hadn't said a word to Grace about it though. She could walk on water as far as his dad was concerned.

Michael was about to rejoin the party when his mobile phone rang. He saw the name of one of his bouncers, John King, flashing on the screen.

'Yeah, John?' he answered.

'There's been some trouble in town today, boss.'

'What?'

'Cody, that new kid you took on, he's been stabbed in the neck.'

Michael sucked air through his teeth. 'Fucking hell. Is he okay?'

'He's on his way to the Royal. They blue-lighted him.'

'Shit. What happened?'

'The usual. Bunch of wannabes turned up and started kicking off and one of them had a knife. He came straight at Cody. None of us saw it coming.'

'And what happened to the wannabes?' he snapped.

'Don't worry. They're all dealt with, boss.'

'Good. I'll get down to the hospital and see how he is.'

'Maybe wait until tomorrow. The plods were crawling all over the place.'

Michael sighed. 'Does his mum know?'

'Police will be telling her, I imagine.'

'Okay, well, make sure she's looked after, John. Anything she needs, okay?'

'Will do.'

Michael hung up the phone. 'Fucking cunts,' he muttered under his breath. He'd started up his security firm six months ago when there'd been a gap in the market. He'd wanted out of the drugs business and security seemed a much better fit for him. He'd been hoping it would be a bit less hassle too, but he'd been wrong on that score. He'd needed something of his own though. The business Grace had walked away from and left him in charge of just wasn't the same without her. She'd left a gaping hole in his life in more ways than one, and now she was back, he wondered if things could ever be the same between them. He hoped so at least.

Chapter 14

Grace looked up as the young man walked through the door of her office.

'Hello, Grace,' he said with a smile.

'Eddie Redman,' she replied. The last time she'd seen Eddie he'd been a pimply-faced teenager. He'd shot up about two feet since then. Eddie was Nathan's other biological son, not that he knew that, of course. She and Eddie's mother, Sandra, had agreed that they would keep that secret a long time ago. When he was a chubby-faced child, his resemblance to Nathan had been clear, but now he bore no likeness at all to the man who'd fathered him.

Grace had been surprised to receive a phone call from Eddie the previous day, asking if he could meet with her. He'd told her it was urgent, claiming that she'd want to hear what he had to say. Assuming it had something to do with his mother, Grace agreed. She and Sandra had been close friends at one time, but, as with everyone else in Grace's life, they had drifted apart since Grace had moved to Harewood.

'Take a seat,' Grace said, indicating the chair on the opposite side of her desk.

Eddie took the proffered seat and, to Grace's annoyance, helped himself to one of the boiled sweets from the open bag on her desk. Not that she begrudged him a sweet – they were Siobhan's anyway – but it was good manners to ask first.

'What can I do for you, Eddie? What do you have to tell me that's so urgent?' she asked.

Leaning back in his chair, Eddie grinned at her, revealing a row of perfectly straight, if slightly yellowed, teeth. 'I know what really happened the night of the fire,' he said.

'What?' she snapped, at first having no idea what he was on about.

'I know what really happened to the Rose and Crown. You pretended to be the innocent victim, but you did it. You torched the place yourself, and you tried to burn Nathan Conlon with it.'

Grace felt like she'd been kicked in the stomach. The Rose and Crown had been her father's pub, and then hers. She'd lived at the place almost her whole life and it had nearly killed her to see the place razed to the ground. But at the time she'd seen it as the only way to finally be rid of her psychopathic ex-husband. She'd worked hard to store the memory of that night away in the darkest recesses of her mind, and here was Eddie talking about it like he'd been there. How could he possibly know? She studied his face. The cocky grin now seemed permanently etched onto his face. Suddenly, he looked just like his father after all, and that only made Grace dislike him even more.

It was then that it hit her. There could only be one reason for him knowing the truth. He had been there. On that awful night when she had burned down her own pub in an attempt to kill her ex-husband once and for all. Except it had gone spectacularly wrong. Nathan had survived and Ben McKinley had died instead. Grace had always wondered who had saved Nathan and hit Ben over the head, leaving him for dead. Well, now she knew. It was Eddie. It must have been. It was the only way he could have known. She had to stop herself from jumping up and throttling the life out of him. She had loved Ben, and Eddie had left him to die like an animal. She fought to steady her breathing and remain calm. 'And what?' she shrugged.

'And what? I want some compensation for my silence. It's ate me up inside, it has.' He feigned a sad face. 'It's been so hard to keep it all to myself.'

'You're a no one, Eddie. Who would believe you anyway?'

'I could go to the police. I'm sure they'd be very interested to know what really happened.'

She laughed. 'I'm sure they would. And will you tell them you murdered the poor bastard they found dead in there instead? Do you even know who that was?'

'Nathan's mate, Ben McKinley.' He shrugged, as though Ben's life meant nothing. 'So, I can't go to the police. I'm not a grass anyway. But I could tell everyone else. What would people think if they knew the truth, Grace? I'm sure your precious Jakey wouldn't be happy that you tried to burn his dad to a crisp while he was still alive, would he?'

He glared at her, no doubt expecting her to break down and beg him to keep quiet, asking him how much money would buy his silence.

Instead Grace started to laugh. 'You really haven't thought this through, have you?'

Eddie frowned at her, deep furrows lining his young forehead. 'Don't fucking laugh at me,' he snarled. 'I'm not messing about.'

Grace stopped laughing and glared at him. 'You know who I am, Eddie. You know who my friends are. You also know that I killed Nathan Conlon, one of the biggest gangsters Liverpool has ever seen, not to mention my husband. And I tried to burn him alive, and when that didn't work, I shot him. Yet you think that you, some little no-mark who couldn't drop his own pants, can come into my son's club and threaten me! You really are as thick as you look, sunshine. Now fuck off out of my office, and if I see you in here again, I'll kick your arse myself.'

Eddie glared at Grace as he stood, his fists clenched by his side. Grace had always kept tabs on Eddie – just in case he ever found out who his father really was and started to cause a problem for Jake. It was obvious he wasn't used to being spoken to with so little respect. In his local neighbourhood, he was a small-time pot dealer and a massive bully, and no doubt enjoyed a bit of kudos because of it. But in Grace's world, he was nothing more than shark-bait.

Without another word, Eddie stormed out of her office, slamming the door behind him as he went. Grace leaned back in her chair and closed her eyes. Memories of Ben came flooding back to her. The way he smelled. His smile. How his arms felt when he held her. She missed him so much. Fighting back tears, she thought about Eddie. His threatening her was laughable, and she wasn't overly concerned about that, but she couldn't let him get away with murdering Ben. He obviously didn't realise who Ben had been to her, or he never would have revealed, even inadvertently, that he was responsible for his death.

Pouring herself a glass of the good brandy she kept in her office drawer for visitors, Grace wondered what to do about him. He deserved to die as painful a death as Ben had. But what about Sandra? Eddie was her son and she loved him just as much as Grace loved Jake. The thought of anything happening to Jake made Grace's heart fall through her stomach. How could she do that to Sandra, a woman who had always been there when she needed her? Besides, Grace was trying to be a better person now. A better role model for Belle. There would be no more deaths on her hands.

No. Eddie would live. But one day soon he'd know terror like he'd never imagined. Grace would make sure of that.

Chapter 15

Setting down her fork, Grace pushed the half-eaten plate of pasta away from her.

'That was incredible, Steph,' she said. 'But I'm fit to burst.'

'You'd never make an Italian.' Steph laughed good-naturedly. 'You barely eat.'

'What? I've tasted half of your menu,' Grace replied. 'All of it delicious, by the way.'

'I do try,' Steph said as she picked at a stray olive from Grace's plate.

Steph had invited Grace to Antonelli's for lunch and she'd jumped at the chance to see the place where she'd once been co-owner. It was one of three restaurants Grace had opened with Steph's father, Sean, but Antonelli's had always been her favourite. Sean had called it their flagship. They'd planned on opening half a dozen more across the country, but after Grace had left Liverpool, that dream seemed to have stalled. Steph was now co-owner and she was doing her best to keep the place as current and trendy as it had been the day it had opened.

'Speaking of trying'—Steph bent her head towards the door as her cousins, Connor and Paul Carter, sauntered through the restaurant, full of swagger and confidence—'I'd better get back to the kitchen and make a start on dessert anyway.' She gave them a brief wave before disappearing through the crowded room.

Dressed smartly in suits, the Carter twins looked the part, and drew the attention of most of the females in the busy restaurant. Paul and Connor Carter had once worked for Grace and now worked for their father, Michael, as well as having a lucrative sideline cleaning up other people's messes, if the rumours Grace had heard were true.

'Hey, Grace.' Paul smiled as he approached her table.

'Long time, no see, boss,' Connor piped up from behind him.

'Hey, boys,' Grace said. 'What brings you two here?'

'Steph mentioned she was trying out some new recipes on you. We missed you at the party yesterday. You'd left by the time we got there, so we thought we'd drop by and see if the rumours were true or whether everyone was having us on,' Connor said as he and his brother took a seat each at Grace's table.

'What rumours?' Grace asked.

'The ones about the boss lady being back in the Pool.' Connor laughed. 'We had to see you for ourselves.'

'Well, as you can see, I'm here,' Grace said. 'But I'm not the boss lady. Not anymore.'

'You'll always be the boss lady, Grace,' the twins chorused before signalling the waitress for two beers.

Grace laughed. She had a soft spot for the twins, always had. They'd caused her no end of grief when they'd worked for her, but they seemed to have matured in the eighteen months she'd been away. Now they were a couple of men to be reckoned with. From what she'd heard, it seemed their brains had finally caught up to their brawn.

'Anything you need doing, Grace, just ask. Isn't that right, Paul?' Connor said as his brother nodded.

'Actually boys, there is something you could help me with,' Grace said, as she was struck by an idea. 'Can I count on your discretion?'

They nodded in response.

'Great. I could use your help sorting out a little problem. Can you come to my office tomorrow afternoon? About twelve, before anyone else gets in, would be ideal.'

The twins grinned at her and she was reminded of their youth. 'Is it the kind of problem we enjoy sorting?' Paul asked.

'Yes. Your favourite kind.'

'Nice one.' They laughed just as the waitress arrived with their drinks.

Connor raised his bottle in a toast. 'To the Boss Lady. It's good to have you back.'

'I'll drink to that,' Paul said as he lifted his bottle to Connor's.

Grace raised her wine glass to join their toast and smiled.

It was good to be back.

Chapter 16

The twins arrived at midday the following afternoon as requested. Grace let them in through the side door and they followed her through to her office.

'What's this job you've got for us then?' Connor asked once they were all seated, his eyes twinkling. Grace remembered how the pair of them were always up for getting their hands dirty. Always eager to get stuck in and bang some heads together. In their youth and stupidity, they'd once tried to take out her ex-husband and had failed miserably, causing a shitstorm for Grace to clean up after them. She'd wanted to murder them herself at the time, but in hindsight, it had probably been the best thing that could have happened to them, teaching them a salutary lesson. The twins were no longer as eager to go off half-cocked as they used to be. Grace was willing to give them another shot to see whether they could be trusted.

'Yeah, we're dying to know,' Paul piped up, reminding Grace they were waiting for her to speak.

'There's a little no-mark I need dealing with. His name's Eddie Redman. Have you heard of him?'

The twins shook their heads. 'Nah, doesn't ring a bell,' Connor said as he sat forward in his chair.

'That doesn't surprise me. As I said, he's a no-mark. But he needs to be taught a lesson, boys. Namely that he cannot walk in here and threaten me.'

The twins nodded enthusiastically. 'Want him to disappear?' Paul asked.

Grace sighed. She'd gone over and over this question herself and still wasn't confident she'd made the right decision. 'No, not disappear. At least, not yet. Don't do too much damage. But let's make sure he has enough reasons to regret his decision to try and cross me, and that I don't live to regret mine.'

'Consider it done, boss,' Connor said and Paul nodded in agreement.

'Thanks, boys. You'll find him hanging around The King's Arms in Bootle. It's a shit-hole pub off the Dock Road. He deals out of there. Can I ask you to keep this to yourselves? I'd rather no one knows I've had anything to do with the little prick.'

'Of course,' they said. They didn't ask any questions, as Grace knew they wouldn't. They trusted that she'd tell them if they needed to know.

'Great. Now that we've got that out of the way, how about a drink?' she said as she took the bottle of Remy Martin XO out of her office drawer.

'Sounds good to me,' Paul said, grinning as Connor took three crystal tumblers from the tray on Grace's desk.

Pouring them a generous measure each before handing the twins their glasses, Grace thanked them again.

'No problem at all,' Connor said.

'Anything for you, boss,' Paul said before downing his drink in one.

Grace smiled as Connor did the same, the pair of them wincing as the expensive cognac burned their throats. She should have given them the cheap stuff she kept on her desk instead.

They would never have tasted the difference. They might dress in expensive Armani suits, but the twins had a lot to learn about appreciating the finer things in life.

Chapter 17

Connor Carter pushed open the doors of The King's Arms and walked inside, with his brother Paul close behind him. Together they walked over to the corner of the room and approached the man who fitted Eddie's description.

'Eddie Redman?' Connor asked him

He looked up and scowled at the pair of them. 'Who's asking?'

Connor couldn't blame him for his reaction. Eddie couldn't afford to lose face in his local boozer, where he no doubt thrived on the regulars being scared of him.

'I'd say this is him, wouldn't you, Paul?' Connor asked.

'Fits the description. But we'd better check. Just in case.'

Paul lifted Eddie from his seat by the neck of his T-shirt. Despite Eddie struggling and attempting to free himself from Paul's grasp, Paul dragged him towards the exit.

'Fuck off. Get off me,' Eddie snarled, but his protests fell on deaf ears.

'Next round's on me if anyone can give me the name of this dickhead,' Connor shouted as he walked behind his brother.

'Eddie Redman,' a couple of voices from the other side of the pub shouted.

'Much obliged, gents,' Connor said as he held up five £20 notes and then placed them on a nearby table.

Paul laughed as he dragged Eddie out of the doors. 'See how easily they gave you up, lad.'

Two minutes later, Eddie was bundled into the back of the twins' old van, with Paul for company while Connor drove.

Eddie was already bleeding and pleading for his life by the time Connor pulled up at their destination.

'Get out,' Paul shouted as Connor dragged Eddie out of the back of the van.

'Fucking hell, what were you two doing back there?' Connor laughed as he saw that Eddie's nose, eye and lip were already bleeding.

'Eddie here decided to get a little bit mouthy during our trip,' Paul grinned.

Connor shook his head and grabbed Eddie by the arm. 'I really wouldn't wind my brother up, Edward,' he whispered in his ear. 'He's a bit of an animal.'

Eddie looked up at him, his eyes wide with fear, and Connor laughed. No doubt, during their twenty-minute journey, Paul had convinced Eddie he was a sadistic psychopath.

Paul held open the doors of the old garage and Connor dragged Eddie inside. He sat him on the single chair that was positioned in the centre of the room. Eddie sat with his head hanging low.

'Look up, Eddie,' Connor taunted him. 'We have something we'd like you to see.'

Paul stood behind him and lifted Eddie's head. 'Look,' he snapped.

Eddie opened his eyes, blinking a few times to acclimatise to the dim light. Connor smiled as Eddie's eyes widened in fear. The sight of two giant meat hooks hanging from the ceiling would be enough to make any man tremble with the fear of what might happen next. Eddie started to shake his head violently and tried to scramble from the chair but Paul held him firm with his powerful arms.

Paul started to laugh. 'Calm down, lad,' he said. 'You haven't seen the best stuff yet.'

Connor walked over to him and placed a large parcel at his feet. Unfurling it, he revealed a wide array of medical instruments and tools. Scalpels, hammers and pliers of various sizes were laid out before Eddie's feet.

'No. No,' Eddie screamed.

Connor knelt down so he could look Eddie directly in the eyes. 'You have seen a rare glimpse into my brother's little playroom here today, Eddie,' he said quietly. 'Should you ever threaten Grace Sumner again, we will bring you back here and you will never see the light of another day. Do you understand me?'

Eddie nodded furiously.

'Good,' Connor smiled. Then he hit Eddie on the temple, knocking him unconscious.

'Did you see his face?' Paul laughed as Connor drove the three of them back towards Bootle, an unconscious Eddie now alone in the back of the van.

Connor laughed too. 'I thought he was going to have a heart attack for a minute.'

'You went over and above with your little toolkit there, bro,' Paul snorted. 'Where did you get it all from?'

'An old friend of ours. Anyway, never mind me. What the hell did you say to him when you were back there with him? He was as white as a sheet when I pulled him out of there.'

Paul shrugged. 'I hardly touched him. But I told him what I

liked to do to people who threatened my friends, and I embellished a little.'

Connor smiled at him. 'Mission accomplished then?'

'I think our little show will make him think twice before he even thinks of Grace's name again.'

'Good. Now where are we dropping him off? I need a drink.'

'There's a pub up the road. We can drop him off outside there. It's quiet, but someone will find him soon enough. Or he'll come round and he can get himself a pint.' Paul grinned.

Chapter 18

Jake watched Siobhan from behind the bar as she tied her long red hair up into a ponytail. She saw him watching and grinned at him. He winked in response, remembering the incredible blowjob she'd just given him in his office. It was one of the many perks of being the boss, he thought, smiling to himself as she disappeared into the back room to help Libby with the stocktaking.

He was still smiling when his mobile phone rang. Fishing it from his pocket, he looked at the screen to see it was Vinnie Black calling. Jake had inherited him along with the club. He was loyal, but he was also as thick as rhino shite.

'All right, mate?' Jake said as he answered the phone.

'Jake,' Vinnie started, and Jake already knew by the tone of Vinnie's voice that his good mood was about to disappear faster than a rat up a drainpipe.

'What?' Jake sighed.

'Someone has tampered with the container again,' Vinnie said.

'What?' Jake shouted, barely able to believe what he was hearing. He started to walk to his office where he could have a private conversation.

'We opened the container, and it's not in there. It's all gone,' Vinnie stuttered.

'But it came into the docks, didn't it?' Jake snapped.

'Yeah.'

'So, somewhere between Liverpool and Glasgow, you've managed to lose fifty kilos of coke and four handguns? Are you fucking shitting me, Vinnie?'

'I know, boss. Maybe someone switched them? Or they put the wrong container on the lorry,' he mumbled.

'What?' Jake shouted. 'Didn't you watch them putting it on? Are you fucking stupid or something? What were you doing while my money was being nicked? Who was watching the lorry?'

'I was chatting to Blind Macca, boss.'

'Chatting! Fucking chatting! Are you fucking kidding me? I've fucking warned you about Blind Macca. He's a scumbag who would sell his own granny down the river if he thought he'd get a bung out of it.'

'I'll talk to him . . .'

'You'd better do more than talk to him, lad.'

'I will, boss. And I'll get the stuff back, I swear.'

'You better fucking had, Vinnie. Don't come back here until you have,' Jake snapped before throwing his mobile phone at the wall and watching it break into pieces.

Jake shook his head. This was the fourth shipment in two months that had either been nicked or almost nicked. No doubt he would never see his missing drugs again. They'd be cut up and sold off before Vinnie remembered what day it was. He had a good idea who'd taken them, and he would wring Bobby White's neck once he got his hands on him, but that bastard was as slippery as a stripper covered in baby oil.

Vinnie was a fucking liability who couldn't find his own arse with both hands, let alone Jake's drugs. Instead, he'd turn up with his tail between his legs, begging for forgiveness. But he had fucked up one too many times and Jake had run out of patience with him. Vinnie would repay the debt he now owed, one way or another.

Jake needed someone working with him who had brains as well as balls. He almost regretted letting John Brennan go. Almost. He'd always had the distinct feeling that John was looking over his shoulder, waiting for him to fuck up, or to remind him that his dear old dad would never do things that way. Jake sometimes hated being Nathan Conlon's son. There was always someone willing to tell him either what a legend or what a massive cunt his dad was. Either way, they were big shoes to fill.

There was a lot about his father that Jake admired – his head for business and his ability to get anything he wanted from anyone he wanted. People said he was a lot like him and Jake supposed he was. They certainly looked alike. Jake had seen enough photographs of his dad in his twenties to know that they were dead ringers. He sometimes wondered if that was hard on his mum – having to look at the same face as the man who'd caused her so much pain and misery. If it did, she never showed it. She thought the sun shone out of Jake's arse and would do anything for him. And though he was a grown man, and he would never admit it to anyone, somehow that knowledge made him feel invincible. His mum was a Liverpool legend. The queen of the underworld – until she'd given it all up to move to the sticks and have his baby sister. But he'd never felt the need to fill her shoes in the same way he did his dad's.

The one thing he knew for sure was that he wanted to do things better than his dad had. Nathan Conlon had been known as a ruthless fucker and when he'd been at the top of his game, no one had dared to challenge him. But he had too many weaknesses – women, drugs and booze. Jake was never going to go down that road. He'd never had any interest in drugs – not in taking them at least – and although he liked the odd drink, he could count on one hand the number of times he'd been completely wasted. But most importantly, he loved Siobhan. She was his soulmate. Women threw themselves at him all the time. Barely a day went by when he wasn't propositioned by someone offering it to him on a plate. He knew it was all about the power. Some people were just drawn to it like a smackhead to their next fix. But he would never do anything to hurt Siobhan. She was the only woman he'd ever loved.

Chapter 19

Grace looked up from her desk and was surprised to see Michael Carter strolling through the door of her office.

'Hello, stranger,' she said. 'What are you doing here?' Last time they'd met, he hadn't exactly given her a warm welcome.

'Thought I owed you a visit.'

'You don't owe me anything, Michael,' she said as she closed her laptop with a snap and rested her hands on top of it.

'I think maybe I do,' he said before closing the door and sitting on the chair opposite her.

She looked at him. He looked good, dressed in a suit as usual, his shirt open at the collar. They had once been so close but now it felt like they were strangers. There was an awkwardness between them that made Grace feel almost vulnerable around him. Although perhaps it was all in her imagination?

'Drink?' she asked him.

He shook his head. 'I'm driving.'

'Well, why is it you think you owe me a visit then?'

He sighed. 'I wanted to explain about Jake. I had no idea he was in so deep until it was too late. I would have warned you but I had no way of contacting you. I should have looked out for him, Grace. Made sure he stayed away from Nathan's old followers. When I found out what he was into, I came to see him.'

'Did you?'

'Of course I did. I know you didn't want this life for him. I tried to help him out a bit. You know, give him some advice.'

'Ha.' Grace laughed. 'I bet that went down like a lead balloon.'

Michael smiled. 'You know lads his age. They think they know everything.'

'So he told you to sod off then?'

'Well, he wasn't quite so blunt. He gave me some bollocks about wanting to stand on his own two feet.'

'Well, I appreciate you trying anyway.'

'I know you'd do the same for me,' he replied.

'So what happened with you then? I hear you've left our old business behind and branched into security instead?'

'It wasn't the same after you left. You know I can't stand all that arse-kissing and ego stroking that goes on when you're negotiating with the Sol Shepherds of the world. And I was fed up looking over my shoulder all the time, to be honest. I felt like a quiet life for a while. As you can see, I ain't no young man anymore.'

'Behave yourself,' she said, laughing. 'You're only forty-four.'

He laughed too. 'Yeah, but sometimes I feel seventy-four. I've been in this game for almost thirty years, Grace.'

'So the security business is nice and relaxing, is it? A quiet life?' she asked sarcastically.

'Nope. But it's a hell of a lot more straightforward.'

Michael's phone started to ring and Grace watched him as he took it from his inside pocket and looked at the name on the screen before returning it, unanswered.

'Wasn't that important?' Grace asked, suspecting it had been his wife, Hannah.

'It can wait.'

'Can I ask you something?'

'Of course. Always.' He sat forward in his chair.

'I'm going to fire the bouncers here as soon as I've got a new security firm in place.'

'Really?'

'Yep. I was going to ask the twins to speak to you about taking over. But now you're here, I can ask you myself.'

'You weren't going to ask me yourself anyway?' he asked, his brow furrowed in annoyance.

'Well, we didn't part on the best terms, did we?'

'Grace.' He swallowed. 'About that.'

Grace waved her hand in dismissal, pretending she no longer cared. 'Never mind. It doesn't matter now. Will you take over the doors here then, or what?'

'Of course. But what about Jake? Does he need to approve this?'

'Leave Jake to me. He's left me in charge of the staffing, and bouncers are staff, so it's my decision.'

'You've only been back a couple of weeks and now I'm working for you again?' He laughed. 'How did that just happen?'

She shook her head. 'You're not working for me. I won't be sticking around for long anyway. I'll feel better knowing that you're around, to be honest. Jake could use your expertise. Even if he would never admit it.'

'How long are you staying then?'

'A couple of months, and then I'm off back to Leeds.'

'Oh, right.' He stood up. 'I'd better get going. Let me know when you want my boys to start.'

'Why not tomorrow? I'm meeting with Karl Morgan in a few hours. I'll let him know that he and his shower of piss-takers are no longer needed back here after tonight.'

'Fucking hell, Grace. You don't hang around, do you? That'll cause murder, you know that?'

'Your boys can handle it, can't they?'

'Of course they can. I'll tell them to start tonight instead. Once you tell the other lot to sling their hook, there's no way they'll be hanging around here protecting your club. They're more likely to come back armed to the teeth and try and do the place over.'

'Tonight it is then.'

'Stay away for the night then, eh?' he said as he was walking out of the door.

'Don't be daft.' She laughed at him. 'I'm a big girl, Michael.'

'Yeah, I know you are. But can you just stay away for one night. Please? I'd rather not have to worry about you getting caught in the crossfire.'

She sighed. 'Okay then.' The truth was she preferred staying home with Belle in the evenings anyway.

'Thanks.' He disappeared through the door.

Grace leaned back in her chair. Michael Carter working in the club was a good thing for Jake. A good thing for The Blue Rooms. But it was a potential minefield for her. One she would have to navigate very carefully.

Chapter 20

Grace laughed as Libby Baxter told her about the drunken antics of some of the customers on a hen do the night before. Grace had recently promoted Libby to be the new assistant bar manager after realising she was bright, loyal and knew when to keep her mouth shut. She'd let the previous occupier of the position go for being a complete balloon who didn't have a clue what he was doing, or have an ounce of loyalty in his body. Libby was someone Grace already considered a friend. They had a similar sense of humour too and Grace enjoyed spending time in her company. When the time came for Grace to move back to Harewood, Libby would be the perfect assistant for Siobhan. The pair of them would be a force to be reckoned with and would make sure The Blue Rooms thrived.

Grace and Libby were going over the rotas when Grace saw Karl Morgan stroll into The Blue Rooms like he owned the place, half an hour early for the meeting she'd arranged with him. Karl was the owner of Trident Securities, who managed the doors of the club, but he was such an arrogant prick Grace wondered how Jake had ever agreed to do business with him. He grinned as he sauntered over to where Grace and Libby were standing at the bar.

'All right, girls?' he said with a wink.

'We're no girls, son,' Libby snapped. 'I'll finish up, Grace,' she said before walking away.

Karl shrugged as he watched Libby's retreating rear. She was probably just his type, Grace thought – blonde, tanned skin, long legs and a tiny waist. Unfortunately for Karl, Libby was happily engaged to her fiancée, Maria, and Karl's charm was entirely wasted on her.

'You wanted to see me, Grace?' he said, turning his full attention to her instead.

'Yes. You're early. Come through to my office.'

'Anything you say, darling.'

Closing the door to her office, Grace was hit by the pungent smell of Karl's aftershave, which he'd obviously applied with a bucket. She contemplated opening the door again, but thought the privacy was worth the price of having to breathe through her mouth for the next five minutes. She didn't need the rest of the staff hearing her business.

Karl sat on Grace's desk rather than the chair she offered. She sat down herself and for a few seconds she just watched him as he looked her up and down, his eyes lingering on her breasts for much longer than could be considered polite. Karl considered himself a hit with the ladies. Stocky, with a shaved head and piercing blue eyes, he had a certain appeal, she supposed, but she found him creepy. He'd been flirting with her for weeks, making vulgar comments and crude innuendoes. He thought all he had to do was smile at a woman and she'd drop her knickers. Well, not Grace. She hadn't invited him to her office for a social visit.

'So, what can I do for you, darling?' he said, grinning at her suggestively.

'I asked you here out of courtesy to you, Karl. I wanted to

tell you to your face that I'm letting you go,' she said matter-of-factly. She watched him shake his head as though he couldn't possibly have heard her correctly.

'What?'

'You heard me. I'm letting you go. As of today, The Blue Rooms will no longer require the services of Trident Security. You can tell your boys not to bother turning up for their shifts tonight. They'll be paid for the rest of the week.'

Grace watched as the whole of Karl's face changed in an instant. Gone was the seemingly permanent grin and the twinkling blue eyes. His face twisted in anger as his cheeks flushed and his eyes narrowed. He rose from the desk and stood over her.

'Who the fuck do you think you are?' he shouted, so close to Grace's face she could feel the spittle flying from his mouth. 'You're letting me go? You cheeky fucking bitch. Who do you think would look after this place as well as me?' he snarled.

Grace stood, and although he was almost twice the size of her, she brought her face close to his. 'A fucking monkey could protect this place better than you, you useless piece of shit. Where were your boys when Martin Mitchell put a bar stool though the mirror behind the bar and threatened Libby with a knife?'

Karl glared at her, his whole body shaking with anger. She knew he wanted to lamp her one. But she also knew he wouldn't dare. She was Grace Sumner, after all.

'You had that coming,' he snapped. 'You sacked half the fucking bar staff. If you go around giving people the boot for no good reason, you're bound to get some comeback. Martin Mitchell is connected, or didn't you know that? And now you've fired your security too? You're a fucking nutcase.'

Grace smiled at him. 'We'll see,' she said. 'Now get your shit and go.'

'You'll fucking regret this,' he growled as he stormed out of her office.

Sitting in her chair, Grace leaned back against the headrest. That hadn't gone as badly as she'd expected. She could act as cool as an ice cube in a snow storm in those situations, but her insides were shaking. She hoped Karl and his boys didn't cause too much trouble when they inevitably came back to show their displeasure at her decision. In time, Karl would realise that it was just business. Hotheads like him always calmed down eventually.

Grace thought about Martin Mitchell. He'd been the bar manager until she'd fired him the week before. He was useless. But connected? That was a laugh. He was the nephew of Kevin Mitchell. Kevin had been a well-known face a few years earlier, until he'd been left eating through a straw for the rest of his days. Kevin had been a pain in Grace's arse, and if he hadn't become too greedy and started to have ideas above his station, then he'd still have full use of all of his faculties.

Chapter 21

'So you're okay with Michael's firm taking over the security then, Jake?' Grace asked him.

'Yeah, Mum. Whatever,' he said distractedly.

She shook her head as she walked out of his office. Sometimes that boy was a complete mystery. If she did something as simple as adding to the list of lagers they sold, he accused her of meddling in his business, but firing the security team and replacing them with Carter's firm was no big deal? Something was obviously on his mind, but whatever it was, she was getting an easy life for the time being and she could roll with that.

'Hey, boss,' Grace heard from behind her.

Turning around she saw Connor and Paul Carter. 'Hello, boys, what are you two doing here?'

'Come to make sure everything's set up for tonight.' Paul said.

'Shouldn't you be going?' Connor asked.

'I'm leaving in ten minutes,' she sighed. 'Is that why you're really here? To make sure I've gone?'

'No,' Connor protested. 'But we were *instructed* to make sure you were off the premises by six o'clock at the latest.'

'Your father is a control freak,' she said.

'He controls because he cares.' Connor grinned at her. 'Is there somewhere we could use as a base? We've got some paperwork and stuff we could do with leaving here.'

'Bring them to my office,' she said. 'It's too big for just me anyway. It would be nice to have some occasional company. There's a spare desk in there too.'

'Brilliant,' said Paul. 'Dad will be made up he's finally got a proper desk.'

Of course, Grace thought to herself. The twins didn't do paperwork, Michael did. And now she'd just given him his own desk in her office. Hopefully he would hardly be there during the day anyway, and she rarely worked nights, preferring to be at home with Belle. She would just have to avoid him as much as she could.

'Hey, Jake,' Paul called as he noticed him in his office.

'All right lads. Fancy a drink?' Jake called back.

The twins looked at each other, then at Grace, then at the briefcase Connor was holding.

'I'll take that for you,' Grace said. 'Go and have a drink with Jake. He can show you where my office is later.'

'Because you'll be gone in ten minutes, won't you?' Connor asked looking at his watch.

'Yes,' she sighed.

Connor handed her the briefcase and she watched the pair of them stroll into Jake's office and close the door.

Jake smiled as the Carter twins closed the door to his office.

'How's it going, Jake? What's it like being the head man?' Paul laughed.

Jake shook his head. 'Don't fucking ask, lads. That cunt Bobby White is crawling up my arse every time I turn around.'

'He's a cocksucker if ever I met one,' Connor said as he sat down. 'Greasy little fucker. Wouldn't trust him as far as I could throw him.'

'To be fair, I bet you could throw him pretty far though, mate,' Jake said and the three of them started to laugh.

'How's things with you then, lads?' Jake asked as he poured them all a drink. 'I see your firm's taking over the security at the club. Will that mean you two are around here more often?'

'We're here tonight because we're expecting a bit of a kick-off. But we won't be involved much after that,' Connor answered.

'We prefer to keep busy in other ways,' Paul said with a smile. Jake nodded. He knew the twins did freelance work for some of the most powerful gangsters across the whole of England and Scotland. They were colloquially known as 'the cleaners' because they were brought in to clear up other people's messes, and they were good at it too.

'The security business is a bit too tame for us, isn't it, Con?' Paul said.

Connor nodded.

'I hear you get to travel a lot though?' Jake said, grinning.

'Yeah, but we're looking to set up something a bit closer to home though, aren't we, Paul?' Connor replied.

'Well, if I hear of anything, I'll let you know,' Jake said.

'Sound,' Paul said as the three of them finished their drinks.

'Will you be about tonight, Jake?' Paul asked. 'It should be a good kick-off.'

'Wouldn't miss it, lads.'

Jake watched as the twins left his office. He wondered what exactly they'd meant by setting up closer to home. He liked the twins; they were a pair of vicious bastards, but they also had a code that they stuck to. They never hurt women or children. They had a solid reputation because they kept their mouths shut about what they did and who they did it for. And they kept their word, which was rare in their game. Apart from his mum and Siobhan, Jake could count on one finger the people who worked for him that he trusted.

He sighed and ran his hands through his hair. She probably didn't know it, but his mum had done him a massive favour getting Michael to take over the security at the club.

Chapter 22

Grace walked up the rickety wooden steps leading to Nudge Richards's portakabin. She and Nudge had been friends for a long time and since Grace had once helped him out of a tricky situation, he was always happy to return the favour in any way he could.

'Grace, love,' he smiled as he opened the door to her. His large frame almost filling the doorway, he had to step aside to let her in.

'Hiya, Nudge. How are things?' she asked.

'Not bad, girl. You know how it is. I get by.'

Nudge owned a successful scrapyard, but was also well known for being able to get his hands on absolutely anything. He could probably get you the Hope Diamond for the right price.

'Fancy a brew?' Nudge asked as he indicated for her to take a seat.

'Only if you wash the mugs first, Nudge. I don't fancy getting dysentery.' She laughed as she took off her coat and sat down.

'For you, girl, I'll even use the Fairy liquid.'

When they were both settled with a hot mug of tea, Nudge started to talk. 'So, I used the information you gave me to do a little digging. I even visited my old mate, Annie, down the knocking shop.' He grinned.

Grace shook her head. No doubt information wasn't the only thing he got in there. 'And?' she asked.

'You were right. Bobby White is the one trying to take over Jake's business.'

'I knew it. It makes sense. But what I can't figure out is who he is and where the hell he's come from.'

'Seems to be from all over the place. Some people say Manchester, some Newcastle, Scotland. One fella told me he was from fucking Cornwall!'

'I've never even heard of him, and I haven't been away *that* long.'

'No. I hadn't heard of him until recently either. He came to me looking for some crossbows. Not the sort of stuff you can get hold of easily either. The really nasty ones he was after.'

'Did you get them for him?"

'Of course,' Nudge said with a look of pride on his face.

'So what's he like?'

'Same as most of them. Arrogant prick. Thinks he's God's gift. Fat fucker. Face like the arse end of a bus.' He laughed at his own joke. 'Anyway, if you want to get hold of him, he's got a bar near the Baltic Triangle.'

'Oh?'

'Yep. Some fancy gin place. His wife, Leanne, runs it. She's from round here like.'

Grace sipped her tea. Nudge had given her plenty to think about. So now she knew who Bobby was, she just needed to find a way to get one over on him. She needed an edge and she would find one. She always did. Maybe she'd give her old friend Sandra Redman a call? Grace didn't particularly relish the thought of meeting up with Sandra again, especially given her son Eddie's antics and the fact that the twins had recently beaten him up. But Sandra worked as a doctor's receptionist and had always been happy to search the NHS records for information. She was someone else whom Grace had helped out in a time of need and she was always happy to repay the favour. And people like Bobby always had a skeleton or two in their closets.

Little did Grace know, Bobby had a whole graveyard.

Chapter 23

Grace sat in one of the comfortable chairs sipping her gin and tonic and wishing it was a brandy, while she waited for Sandra in Bobby White's bar, Gin Blossom. She looked around and decided it was a nice enough place, if a little pretentious. Full of hipsters and stockbroker and banker types, Grace thought, rather than the men in suits she was used to. She wondered if Bobby would even show his face in the place, but she'd heard he liked to mix with the cool people and enjoyed being lord of the manor. Besides, she was meeting Sandra anyway and it was a worth a try.

Twenty minutes late, as usual, Sandra came rushing through the doors, shaking the rain from her coat and long blonde hair as she did. Grace waved to her and she made her way over.

'Hi, stranger,' Sandra said as she embraced Grace in an awkward fashion, no doubt to try and prevent soaking Grace's thin dress with rainwater. 'It's just started chucking it down out there.'

'I can tell.' Grace replied. 'I got you a gin. Elderflower and rosehip,' she said with a flash of her eyebrows.

'Ooh fancy.' Sandra took a seat opposite her friend.

'I'm sorry I've hardly been in touch,' Grace said. 'I just—'

'Don't worry about it.' Sandra waved her hand dismissively.

'I know you had to get away. After everything that happened, who could blame you? I'm just glad to see you now. You're looking so well. And tell me all about this baby girl of yours.'

Grace told Sandra about Belle and how besotted with her she was.

'She must be one soon then?' Sandra asked.

Grace nodded. 'So how is Eddie?' she asked. She'd been apprehensive about contacting Sandra after what happened with Eddie. But she'd thought it was worth the risk. Eddie would never tell his mother the truth about why he'd ended up taking a beating that landed him in hospital.

'To be honest, Grace, I rarely see him these days,' she sighed. 'I haven't seen him for weeks. He phones me now and then, but he only turns up when he wants something, usually money. I have no idea where he's even living. I don't know what I did wrong with that lad, I really don't.' She shook her head.

'You did nothing wrong, Sandra. Maybe it's his father's genes coming out in him?' Grace said, relieved that Sandra didn't even appear to know that Eddie had been beaten up.

Sandra bristled and Grace regretted her statement immediately. It was one thing to criticise your own child, but having someone else do it was an entirely different matter.

'I'm sorry, Sandra. I didn't mean . . . I'm sure Eddie will get himself sorted soon,' she said, hoping that it was true. Because the way he was going, he'd end up in an unmarked grave, or floating facedown in the Mersey.

'I know.' Sandra sniffed. 'I just worry about him so much. But enough of my troubles. How is Jake doing? It must be hard on him not having you around?'

'Oh, he's okay,' Grace lied. 'He's taken over Nathan's club, The Blue Rooms, so he's trying to make a go of that. I've come back to help him out for a few months, just while he learns the ropes.' Grace would never tell her friend about Jake's troubles. It was a world Sandra wasn't a part of and knew little about. No doubt she'd be horrified to learn what Jake really did, and what her own son considered his day job too.

Grace ordered another round of drinks from the waitress and handed over the cash.

'I'll pay for these,' Sandra said but Grace would have none of it. 'It's my treat for being such a poor friend lately.' She was about to ask Sandra a favour and plying her with a few gin and tonics beforehand would probably grease the wheels a little.

Grace marvelled at how quickly she had been sucked back into her old life – her old ways. Here she was, about to take advantage of a friend, someone she hadn't seen for ages. It made her feel awkward, but nevertheless, it had to be done. It was for Jake, after all.

The waitress placed their drinks on the table and Grace was about to ask Sandra to dig up some information on Bobby White when she heard a multitude of voices raised in greeting.

'All right.'

'Nice to see you.'

'Hello, big fella.'

She craned her neck to see as the recipient walked towards the bar. It had to be Bobby White. Tall. Wide. Slicked-back hair. He certainly walked through the place like he owned it. He had his back to Grace, but then someone tapped his shoulder and he turned around giving Grace a good view of his face.

She almost shouted his name with delight. She knew him. He was older, and much wider, but she would never have forgotten that face. She smiled.

'What are you looking so pleased about?' Sandra said.

'What?' Grace said, for a moment forgetting Sandra was there. 'Oh, nothing.' She picked up her glass and raised it towards Sandra. 'To old friends.' She smiled.

Chapter 24

Sandra returned the magazine to her handbag as the train trundled slowly along the track. Pressing her head against the window, she watched the rivulets of rain running down the glass and thought about her evening with Grace.

She loved Grace. She'd missed her when she'd moved away and apart from the odd text message and occasional phone call, they'd barely had any contact. And even though Sandra had understood Grace's decision, it didn't make it hurt any less. She wasn't great at making friends, and Grace was one of the few people she counted as one. Now that Eddie barely had time for her either, she was always lonely. Her husband, Richie, was busy at work or with his hobbies – Airfix and cycling, two things she had absolutely no interest in.

Poor Eddie. He was so messed up. Whenever she saw him, he was drunk, or on something. She knew he took drugs; she could tell by the way his eyes were always glazed over. She'd tried so hard to help him but he threw it all back in her face.

Of course, he hadn't had it easy growing up; with no father around and little money, it had been hard for him. Not like Grace's son, Jake. Nathan had seemed to dote on that kid and he always had the best of everything. Why was he any different to Eddie? Just because he had a different mother. Eddie was as much Nathan's son as Jake was. And now Eddie was struggling to make ends meet, while Jake was living the high life as a club owner. A club that Eddie should rightfully have half of.

Sandra shook her head in despair. Her jealousy of Grace Sumner was how Eddie came to be born in the first place. She'd tried to let it go, but the alcohol was making her feel melancholy. By the time the train pulled into Seaforth station, she felt like the whole world was against her.

When she let herself into her house, and realised Richie was still out, Sandra could have cried with loneliness. Instead, she opened herself a bottle of wine and poured a large glass. Turning on the television, she curled up on the sofa to watch her favourite soaps on catch-up. That always made her feel better. Sometimes she felt like soap characters were the only ones with lives more messed up than hers.

Sandra was nodding off when she heard the knock at the door. She had finished half a bottle of wine and was feeling decidedly drunk. Her head spun as she stood up from the sofa. She cursed under her breath. Richie must have forgotten his key.

Instead, she was greeted by Eddie's face when she opened the door.

'Hiya, Mum,' he slurred.

'Eddie,' she sighed. 'What do you want at this hour?'

'Is that any way to speak to your only son?' he snapped as he pushed his way past her.

Sandra followed him into the kitchen where he was inspecting the half bottle of wine on the worktop. He poured the remaining contents into a coffee mug and began to drink it.

'Where have you been anyway?' Sandra asked. 'I haven't seen you for weeks. Is that a black eye?'

'Fucking hell, Ma. Stop with the twenty questions, will you?' he snapped. 'And you wonder why I never come round here. You're always on my case.'

'I'm just worried about you.'

'Well, in that case, have you got fifty quid to lend me until next week?'

Sandra shook her head. 'You still haven't paid me back from the last three times I've lent you money.'

'So you're keeping count then?' he snarled. 'I'm your fucking son! Would you rather I starved?'

Sandra felt the colour flushing her cheeks. She was so angry she felt like slapping him. The alcohol. Eddie. Her conversation with Grace. It was all making her head spin.

'Well, you're not just my son,' she snapped. 'Perhaps you should go after some of your bloody father's fortune.'

Eddie lowered the mug from his lips and stared at her, his mouth open in surprise. 'You told me you never knew who my dad was,' he growled.

Sandra regretted the words the instant they'd left her mouth. What had she done? But then, fuelled by the alcohol, she convinced herself that no harm could come from revealing the truth now. Nathan was dead. He couldn't hurt her any more. He couldn't hurt Eddie. And Eddie deserved half of that club.

'Well, I do. It was Nathan Conlon,' she said, her arms across her chest and her jaw set defiantly.

'What?' Eddie screamed and threw the coffee mug he was holding across the kitchen. Sandra ducked out of the way and it smashed against the wall.

'Why didn't you tell me?' he yelled in her face, the anger radiating from him in waves.

'Eddie?' she pleaded.

'You fucking bitch!' he snarled as he started to stomp around the kitchen, smashing everything in sight.

'Eddie, please, stop!' Sandra wailed, but it was as though he couldn't hear her.

Finally, he stopped ranting and turned to her. 'I'll never forgive you for this,' he spat. Then he was gone, slamming the door behind him so hard it almost came off its hinges. Sandra sank to the floor and began to sob.

What had she done?

Chapter 25

Grace sat in the rocking chair in Belle's bedroom, watching her daughter sleep. Listening to her baby's soft snores was one of her favourite things to do, especially when she couldn't sleep herself. Tonight she was full of adrenaline. She couldn't believe her luck. Who would have thought Bobby White would actually turn out to be Robert Whitehead? She wondered how she hadn't made the connection before – but then neither had anyone else.

Robert had changed a lot, but then it had been almost twelve years since she'd last seen him. Grace had first met Robert when he'd worked for Solomon Shepherd. Robert had been twenty years old at the time and one of Sol's many minions. But even then he'd had his sights set on bigger things. The trouble for Robert was that he went entirely the wrong way about it.

Sol had one child, a daughter, Chantelle. Fourteen years old and the apple of her daddy's eye. His little princess. When she'd told him she was five months pregnant he had been intent on murdering every red-blooded male in Manchester in an attempt to find out who had taken such a liberty with his baby girl.

But Chantelle would never tell him. And no one else knew. That was until Chantelle confided in Grace one rainy afternoon when she had found the young girl in tears. The poor girl had been terrified. Of her father, who had sworn she was going to give the child up for adoption, and also of the thought of having to give birth. Grace had comforted her and talked about her own experience of having a baby, assuring her she'd be fine and that her father would come round once he met his grandchild.

Grace had always had a way of getting information from people – even when she didn't want to. She didn't want to be the one to know who the father was, and either send him to a painful and drawn-out death or have to keep it from Sol. But Chantelle had told her anyway. It was Robert Whitehead. Chantelle had told Robert she was sixteen when they'd first met and he'd believed her. She loved him, he loved her, and Chantelle believed that once the baby was born they were going to run off into the sunset together. Grace, on the other hand, knew that such fairy tales rarely came true.

Two weeks later Chantelle went into labour, but in her youth and naiveté, as well as the fear of her father's wrath whenever the baby was mentioned, she hadn't mentioned that she hadn't felt the baby move for weeks and Chantelle's beautiful little girl was stillborn. Consumed with guilt, and anger at her father and Robert, Chantelle started popping pills like Smarties. A few months later she was dead too.

Grace had had nothing against Robert at the time. She'd thought he was a creep for sleeping with a fourteen-year-old girl, and a coward for abandoning her and their baby, but Sol would have flayed him alive and fed his testicles to his dogs before he let Robert and Chantelle be together. Grace knew that for a fact. So, she never told a soul. What would have been the point? It wouldn't have saved poor Chantelle or her baby.

Sol, on the other hand, had never got over the death of his daughter and granddaughter and would give his granny and his mother to find out who the father was. Because as far as Sol was concerned, that man was directly responsible for their deaths.

Robert had left Sol's employ shortly after and had never been heard from again. And now Grace knew why. He'd reinvented himself as Bobby White. And now Grace had her edge. As tragic as the whole situation was, Grace was not above using it to her advantage.

Chapter 26

Grace walked into the small office at the back of Gin Blossom and knocked on the open door to get Bobby's attention.

He looked up, a mixture of shock and confusion on his face. 'What are you doing here?' he snapped.

'Oh, so you do remember me then, Bobby? Or should I say Robert?'

Bobby flinched at the mention of his name but he quickly regained his composure. 'I know who you are. Who doesn't? But how do you know me?'

Grace walked into his office and sat down. 'I worked with Solomon Shepherd a long time ago. When you worked for him too. Don't you remember me?'

He shook his head. 'Those were crazy times. It was a lifetime ago, that.'

Grace nodded sympathetically. 'Yeah, and you were more interested in fourteen-year-old girls back then, weren't you?'

Bobby stood up and closed his office door. The colour had drained from his face. 'I don't know what you're on about,' he snapped.

'Oh, I think you do, Robert. Unless there was more than one fourteen-year-old girl? Are you that much of a perv? I assumed it was only the one and you'd thought she was older?'

'Of course there was only one,' he snapped. 'She told me she was sixteen. How do you even know that?'

'Chantelle told me. She told me everything.'

'You've got no proof,' he growled.

Grace laughed. 'Do you think Sol is interested in proof? You had means and motive, Bobby boy. He'll skin you alive when he finds out, and that would just be for starters. Do you remember how livid he was when he found out she was pregnant?'

Bobby didn't answer so Grace went on. 'He was apoplectic, wasn't he? Remember that poor kid from her school he almost turned into a eunuch?' Grace continued to laugh. 'And then when she died, he went to a whole other level. He went nuclear. He's still out for blood after all these years, you know. He told me it's his biggest regret in life not knowing who was responsible for the deaths of his little girl and her baby.'

'I wasn't responsible,' Bobby spat. 'If anyone was, it was him. Scared her to fucking death, he did.'

'Well, by all means, you can explain that to him yourself when you see him, Robert. I'm sure he'll be wanting to pay you a visit once I tell him your little secret.'

'So what the fuck do you want then? Money?'

Grace shook her head. 'I don't need money.'

'What then?'

Grace leaned on the desk. 'I want you to stay the hell away from my son. You've got a big enough slice of the pie, so leave his alone.'

Bobby laughed. 'Does he always need his mummy's protection?'

Grace glared at him. 'Are you fucking kidding me, Robert? Did I just hear you insult my son?'

He shook his head, sufficiently chastised. 'How do I know you'll keep your end of the bargain?'

'I've known for twelve years and I've never told Sol. But I will be up the M62 quicker than a rat up a drainpipe if you go near Jake or his business again. And should anything happen to me, my solicitor has a letter to Sol which he'll personally deliver. Okay?'

'Okay.' He pouted, like a petulant child.

Grace stood up to leave, but couldn't resist asking him. 'Don't you feel any guilt for what happened to that poor girl? To your daughter? Do you have any remorse?'

He shook his head. 'It was another lifetime. I told you that.'

'You're a real piece of shit, Bobby White,' Grace spat before walking out.

Chapter 27

Bobby White frowned at his wife, Leanne, as she busied herself clearing his desk.

'Leave it,' he snapped. 'The lads will be here in a minute, and I don't need you fucking hanging around distracting them.'

'All right, Bobby,' she whined. 'I'm only trying to help.'

He scoffed. 'Help! Don't think I haven't noticed you giving Liam the eye. Now get your arse back out there and put them tits I paid for to good use.'

Leanne shot him a venomous look and turned on her heel, flouncing out of his office and back into the bar.

A few moments later, Bobby's two most trusted employees, Liam McGuinness and Harry Bolger, sauntered through his office door with a bottle of Becks each. No doubt, Leanne had made sure she'd greeted them personally. She was a flirt of the highest order, but the punters fucking loved her. Bobby was sure she'd never actually act on any of her banter, if only because she knew he'd break every bone in her body if she did.

'All right, boss,' Harry said as the two of them sat down opposite him.

'All right, lads,' Bobby sighed.

'What's up?' Liam asked as he placed his untouched bottle of lager on Bobby's desk.

'Sunday is off,' Bobby said.

'What?' Harry had been taking a swig of his beer and almost choked on it.

'But we're all set. Everything is in place.' Liam frowned at him.

'It's off. That's all you need to know,' Bobby snarled.

Harry sat back in his chair and continued to drink his lager. He was happy to do whatever Bobby told him to, but Liam was young and eager, and he'd been looking forward to Sunday night for weeks.

'But this is our chance to take Jake Conlon out for good. It will be quick and clean. The arrogant prick won't see it coming. And we can pin it all on Reuben and walk away scot-free. I told you, boss, we're all set. Reuben doesn't have a fucking clue. He thinks he's going to be your next big protégé.'

Bobby shook his head. 'We're leaving Jake Conlon alone. I don't need the aggro. I certainly don't need his business. I've got enough of my own to be getting on with.'

Liam shook his head, his face screwed up in anger – or disgust. 'I don't fucking believe this. You hate Jake Conlon as much as I do. He stole your gear. He's an arrogant little twat who only got where he is today because of his name. This is ours for the taking, boss.'

Bobby glared at Liam. He knew why Liam wouldn't let it go. He wouldn't either if he were in Liam's shoes. Their plan was bloody brilliant. Jake Conlon was going to end up buried in a field in the middle of nowhere, and Reuben McBride was the perfect fall guy. Reuben would be the one in the frame and Bobby and his lads would be in the clear. Not that Bobby was scared to take anyone on – ordinarily he would have been happy to let it be known he'd taken out his biggest rival – but for once he'd used his head and decided he didn't need a war with Grace

Sumner, or her friends the Carters. But now she'd brought a potential war to him and his hands were bloody tied. There was a reason no one ever dared to cross her. She was a fucking shrewd businesswoman. He'd admire her if he didn't hate her so much. It didn't matter that she'd been away; now she was back and it seemed the whole of Liverpool was falling back into line.

Bobby had liked working for Sol. He'd ruled Manchester for years, and you didn't get to do that without being a vicious bastard, but he was fair too. However, Sol's reach was far and wide, and if he ever found out the truth about who'd got Chantelle pregnant, he would torture him in ways Bobby couldn't even begin to imagine.

Grace Sumner had him over a barrel and for the time being, at least, there was not a single bloody thing he could do about it.

'Has someone got to you?' Liam asked, snapping Bobby from his thoughts.

'No. Just fucking let it go, will you? I said it's off and that's my final word. You just focus on my next shipment and getting our Scottish friends to pay up on time.'

Sufficiently chastised, Liam sat back in his seat and took his bottle of lager from the table. Bobby smiled. He didn't like to be challenged. He was the boss and his word was law.

Chapter 28

'Do you really need to leave your stuff everywhere, Michael?' Grace snapped as she moved his coffee mug from the papers on her desk for what felt like the hundredth time that afternoon. She'd assumed he wouldn't be around the club much during the day, but he seemed to be there as much as she was and it was driving her crazy.

'Sorry,' he said as he took the mug from her.

'It's like sharing an office with a bloody teenager,' she sighed. 'Can you just tidy up after yourself like a grown-up?'

'All right, Grace,' he snapped. 'What the fuck's crawled up your arse today?'

'I'm sorry,' she said. It wasn't his fault she found it so hard to be in the same room as him. He had no idea. And she had offered him the use of the spare desk – she just hadn't thought he'd get quite so much use out of it. 'I'm just feeling a bit on edge today, that's all.'

'Anything I can help with?'

'Not unless you're a qualified masseuse,' she said.

'Pardon?'

She smiled. 'I have a knot in my shoulders the size of a football, and my head is pounding.'

'Oh, I see.'

Grace sat at her desk and was continuing with the staff rotas when Michael piped up. 'So, if I was a qualified masseuse, do you think it would be a good idea for me to give you a massage in the office?'

'What?' she said.

He grinned. 'I'm just saying, it wouldn't look very professional of us if you were sitting at your desk with your top off and I was giving you a back rub, would it? What if someone walked in?'

'Who said I'd have my top off?' she said, laughing.

'Have you ever actually had a massage, Grace?' he asked incredulously. 'You have to take your top off. They have to use special oils and shit to get rid of those knots.' He grinned.

'The pain is only in my shoulders and my head, Michael. I don't think it would require removing any of my clothes.'

'Shame,' he mumbled so quietly she almost didn't hear him.

'What did you just say?'

'Nothing.' He shook his head, feigning innocence. 'Why don't you have an early dart and go home. I'm sure a nice hot bath would do the trick.'

'You think so, do you?'

'I imagine so, yes.'

'So now you're imagining me in the bath? A minute ago you were trying to get me to take my clothes off so you could rub my shoulders. There are laws against this sort of thing, you know. If you're not careful, people will start to think you're some kind of sex pest.'

He stuck his middle finger up at her in response.

'Anyway, I can't have an early dart. My car is in having a service. Libby's going to drop me off when her shift finishes at six.'

'I could drive you home,' he offered.

'No,' she said a little too quickly and felt bad when he looked offended. 'I need to finish these anyway.'

'Okay.' He quietly went back to his laptop.

Grace felt a pang of guilt. They had once had such an easy relationship but now it would never be the same, and she only had herself to blame. She wanted nothing more than to sit and talk to him for hours, to tell him everything. But she couldn't. She had done something unforgiveable, and it was only a matter of time before he found out.

Chapter 29

Martin Mitchell shuffled through the door of Bobby's office at the back of his bar, Gin Blossom, and stood in front of his desk. Bobby didn't look up from the newspaper he was reading. Martin cleared his throat as if to announce his arrival.

Bobby looked up with a sigh. 'Martin Mitchell. What the fuck do you want?'

'I've got some information about Jake Conlon,' he said, his chin tilted defiantly.

'Oh?' Bobby sat a little straighter. 'What kind of information?'

'He stole your gear,' Martin said.

'I fucking know that,' Bobby snapped. 'So, if there's nothing else, fuck off!'

'I know who he's working with,' Martin offered.

Bobby frowned at him. He'd never quite figured Martin out. When Bobby had first moved to Liverpool, he'd used Martin to move some dodgy spirits through the pub he'd been working at. Martin came from a family of criminals. His uncle, Kevin Mitchell, had once been someone to be reckoned with, before he'd had the shit beaten out of him and ended up a cabbage – a hazard of the job. Martin had seemed like he wanted to follow in his uncle's footsteps, but when Bobby had offered him a bigger slice of the pie, he'd backed off and gone and got himself a job working for Jake Conlon.

'What's in this for you?' Bobby asked.

'He fucking fired me,' Martin moaned. 'Well, his bitch of a ma did, anyway. She fucking swans around the place, doing fuck all, and she has the balls to fire me. Had the bouncers throw me out too, in front of my fucking girlfriend. I've had enough of them fucking Conlons, Bobby. Someone needs to teach them a lesson.'

'And you think that someone is you, do you?' Bobby laughed.

'No. But I could help you do it.'

'Who is he working with then?' Bobby asked, indicating the seat in front of his desk.

Martin sat down. 'Michael Carter,' he said, triumphantly.

Bobby glared at him, his eyes narrowed. 'Are you sure?'

'Yep. I've seen them together. Michael's taken over security at the club. Him and Jake are in business together. I'd bet my life on it.'

'If you're lying to me . . .'

'I'm not, Bobby. I swear,' Martin stuttered.

Bobby had heard Michael Carter was out of the drugs game after he'd set up his own security business. If Michael was back in the game, then his boys were too, and possibly his brother. The Carter family were well known in Liverpool, and were treated like royalty – they would not be an easy family to take down. A Conlon–Carter alliance was Bobby's worst nightmare. And if things couldn't get any worse for him, Grace Sumner was back too. The Carters, for all their reputation and power, were basically her personal protection detail.

Bobby admired Grace. She had come from a powerful family herself and had worked her way up to the very top. There was a time when she had practically run Liverpool, with the Carters as her lapdogs, and then she'd just walked away from it all. It was her departure, and Nathan Conlon's death, that had heralded Bobby's move to the city. Before that he'd been floating around Glasgow and Newcastle, but there wasn't the same money to be made there. There was no way he could go back to Manchester, London was all sewn up, so Liverpool was the next best place to be as far as he was concerned. But now Grace was back, and she knew about his involvement with Sol Shepherd's daughter. He had no doubt she would use that information if she needed to. So he had to plan his next move carefully.

'So?' Martin said, interrupting Bobby's thoughts. 'What are you going to do?'

Bobby considered the man sitting before him. He seemed eager to witness the downfall of the Conlon–Sumner dynasty. But if he thought Bobby would do all of the work and let him sit back and watch, he had another think coming. If Bobby played his cards right, he could get rid of Jake and Michael and pin it all on someone else. He already had one scapegoat lined up in the form of Reuben McBride, and here was another one offering himself on a plate.

'You mean, what are *we* going to do, Martin?' he asked.

Martin's face paled, but then he sat up straighter in his chair and nodded.

'I appreciate the information. Let me think about our next move and I'll be in touch. Have a few drinks in the bar before you go. Leanne will look after you.' Bobby smiled at him.

Martin smiled back. 'Thanks, Bobby,' he said as he stood up and backed out of the room, almost genuflecting as he did so.

Bobby laughed to himself. That's right, lad, bow to your king.

Chapter 30

Eddie squinted as sunlight streamed through the windows of his mate Ando's flat. Groaning, he straightened his legs out along the old sofa. His whole body ached. He'd slept in an awkward position, and he still hadn't fully recovered from the vicious beating he'd taken a couple of weeks earlier. He knew Grace Sumner was behind it. He hated that woman. One day someone would give that vile bitch exactly what was coming to her, and it couldn't come soon enough as far as he was concerned.

Eddie shook his head. His brain felt like it was made of candyfloss and his mouth was so dry he couldn't even swallow. Reaching his hand out, he fished around for anything that might quench his thirst, and settled on a half-empty can of Strongbow. Swigging the contents back, he almost gagged at the stale, sweet taste of the now flat cider. Wiping his mouth with the back of his hand, he let out a large belch and sat up. Ando's living room looked and smelled like the inside of an old boozer. Bottles, cans and cigarette stumps littered the small room. Ando himself was comatose on the floor in front of the gas fire, wearing what looked like at least three layers of clothing.

Eddie rubbed his eyes and his stomach growled in hunger. It had been a few days since he'd eaten anything substantial. He'd been on a bender to end all benders – ever since the night his lying whore of a mother had told him that Nathan Conlon was his father – and food wasn't top on his list of priorities. That had been two weeks ago now, and he'd come straight to Ando's place, and together the pair of them had been drunk and stoned ever since – funding their extended party by nicking whatever they could get their hands on.

The trick to dealing with difficult news, in Eddie's experience, was to blot it out for as long as possible, until it didn't make his head hurt quite as much. If he stayed just the right amount of wasted, then the hurt and anger remained around the edges, like a dull ache, rather than an all-consuming agony that occupied his every waking moment.

Looking at the bag of skunk on the coffee table, he wondered whether it was time to start sobering up and deciding just what he would do with his new-found knowledge about his father, or whether he should roll a big, fat spliff and sink back into oblivion. He was Nathan Conlon's son. Fuck! It was mind-blowing. Why hadn't his mum told him? Why on earth would she choose to keep such important information from him? As the rage started to prickle underneath his skin, he decided that the skunk was his best option. He had plenty of time to figure out his next move.

Chapter 31

Grace was lying on the floor of her sitting room playing trains with Belle when she heard her mobile phone ringing. Glancing at the screen she saw it was her accountant, Ivan, calling.

'Hi, Ivan. What can I do for you?' she asked.

'Grace, love. There's a client of mine here who could really use your help.'

'Oh, who?'

'Steven Porter. Do you remember him?'

Grace paused while she tried to recall how she might know him.

'He sold you the building for yours and Sean's first restaurant,' he reminded her.

'Oh yeah,' Grace said. 'Grazia's. What help does he need from me?'

'It's a little delicate. Would you mind meeting him at my office?'

Grace sighed. She had a rare day off, but she knew Ivan wouldn't ask a favour of her unless he needed to. 'I'll wait for Belle to take her nap and ask Marcus to watch her for me. Is two o'clock okay?'

'Perfect,' he said. 'Thanks, my love. I'll see you at two.'

Grace hung up the phone and returned to her game with Belle, feeling somewhat distracted. She hadn't seen Steven Porter for years; what the hell could he want from her?

Grace walked up the steps to Ivan's office and knocked on his door. He opened it and greeted her with a smile and a warm hug. She noticed Steven sitting on a chair as she walked in, looking pale and clammy, which Grace assumed wasn't a good sign. God, what had he done?

Ivan re-introduced them both and Steven shook Grace's hand with a sweaty palm.

'So, what am I doing here, gentlemen?' Grace asked as she sat down.

'It's my daughter,' Steven began. 'She's in trouble.'

He went on to explain that his sixteen-year-old daughter, Megan, had got herself involved with an older man, Leo Baines, who Steven later discovered was basically a pimp. Wouldn't you know, Steven's sweet little daughter was now Leo's number one commodity. Megan had left home, got hooked on drugs and was living in a filthy flat in Kirkdale. Steven had tried to bring her home but Leo had given him a hiding and threatened to do the same to his wife and their two younger daughters if he ever went near Megan again. Megan managed to escape and make it home herself one day, only for Leo to turn up and forcibly remove her from the house, swearing that if anyone phoned the police he would murder them all in their beds. He was a nasty piece of work with fewer morals than brains and he had them all terrified of him.

Grace knew what was coming. It was a headache she could do without, but being a parent herself, it was hard to watch Steven as he sobbed in front of her.

'So, what is it you want from me, Steven?' Grace asked.

He stared at her. 'Ivan said you might be able to get her back?' he said as he choked back the tears.

'I know of Leo Baines. He is a nasty, horrible bastard. He holds a grudge too. Fortunately for you, I happen to know some people who can be much nastier than him, and who don't look fondly upon men who use women and girls for their own disgusting ends.'

Steven looked up at her gratefully.

'*If* I help you with this, nobody knows about it. Not your mates down the pub. Not your neighbour or your business partner. Not Megan. Not even your wife. I don't need any aggravation from the likes of Leo Baines right now. Understood?'

Steven nodded furiously. 'Yes. I won't tell a soul. I promise.'

'Do you have a photograph of her?'

Steven passed Grace a well-thumbed photograph. She looked at the face of a bright-eyed teenager smiling into the camera and her heart almost broke.

'Right. Well, go home. Don't tell anyone about this meeting and Megan will be back within the next couple of days.'

He stared at her as though she'd just revealed she was the Virgin Mary. At any moment, she thought he was going to throw himself at her feet. 'Thank you, Grace,' he sobbed. 'Thank you so much. What can I do to repay you? I have money.'

'I don't need money, Steven. Just remember your promise to keep this to yourself. And who knows, one day you might be able to help me out. I may open another restaurant again in the future.'

He took hold of her hands. 'Of course, Grace. And thank you.'

Grace smiled at him. 'No problem. Now I have to get back to my own daughter.' She smiled. 'She'll be back soon, Steven. I promise you.'

* * *

Grace climbed into her Mercedes and phoned Connor Carter. His voice filled the car when he answered.

'Hiya Boss,' he said.

'Connor. I need a favour. Another one.'

'Anything.'

'It's the type of job that's just up your street.'

'Great,' he laughed.

'Can you and Paul meet me at my place in an hour?'

'Consider it done.'

Grace watched Paul and Connor as they drank their tea and casually digested the information she'd just given them.

'I don't want any of this to come back on me or the club,' she said. 'I could really do without the aggro right now.'

'Of course it won't,' Connor said.

'No one will even know we were there, Grace,' Paul added.

'Make sure the girl gets home safe. This is her,' she said as she handed them the photograph of Megan.

'Nice-looking kid,' Paul said. 'How did she get mixed up with that piece of shit?'

Grace shook her head. 'Who knows?'

Less than twenty-four hours later, a very grateful Megan Porter was returned home to her loving parents Steven and Anne. Leo Baines, on the other hand, had the shit and the teeth kicked out of him and the word 'paedo' carved into his forehead by two masked intruders.

Chapter 32

Grace was putting some money in the safe when she heard the fracas in the hallway outside. It was a Wednesday night and they were usually quiet. As she stepped outside her office, she had to duck behind one of the bouncers as a body came hurtling down the corridor.

'I'll fucking cut your nuts off if you come back in here, you little cunt,' Michael bellowed from the distance.

'You're a shower of bullies, you lot,' a woman screeched as she was forcibly marched past Grace's office.

'And you can fuck off and all. I don't want to see either of you in here again. Do you hear me?' Michael shouted as he walked towards Grace.

'What the hell was that about?' Grace asked him.

'That daft old cow was demanding to be served after the barmaid cut her off because she can barely fucking stand. And Romeo there'—Michael nodded towards the door—'decided to leap to her defence and came at Libby with a broken bottle.' He shook his head as he held up his bleeding hand. 'Pair of fucking loons.'

'She's been in here a few times. She gets a bit lairy when she's had one too many,' Grace said. 'She's seemed pretty harmless before though.'

'She's as mad as a box of frogs,' Michael said. 'Her and her fucking drinking buddy. Look at my hand.'

'Come on. I've got a first aid box in my office,' Grace said. He followed her inside and sat on her desk as she cleaned his wound with alcohol before starting to wrap it with a bandage.

'Ow, that fucking hurts,' he said, wincing.

'Don't be such a baby,' she told him, trying, and failing, to suppress a smile.

'I think you're enjoying this.' He smiled at her, his brown eyes twinkling.

'Well, it's bringing back memories, me cleaning up your war wounds,' she said as she finished wrapping the bandage. 'There, all done.' Then she unconsciously lifted his hand to her face and kissed the palm, as though it was the most normal thing in the world. She felt momentarily embarrassed by the overt show of affection for him but it soon disappeared when he placed the same hand on her face, rubbing the pad of his thumb across the flushed skin of her cheek.

It was as though she had only just become aware of how close they were, only just realised that she was standing between his legs and their thighs were lightly touching. She could feel the heat from his body, hear his fast, steady breathing. Looking up at him, she saw him staring at her intently, his pupils dilated, making his brown eyes look almost black. In one swift move, he was up off the desk, spinning her around so she was on it, sitting as he had been only seconds before. Then before she could even think about what was going to happen next, his mouth was on hers.

Pushing her back onto the desk, Michael slid her skirt up her thighs until it was bunched around her waist. All of Grace's senses were heightened. She was hyper aware of everything. The heat of his fingertips as they brushed her skin. The smell of his Tom Ford aftershave – the one she loved. The one that always reminded her of him. The taste of the coffee he had been drinking earlier and the peppermint sweets he loved. Then she heard the unmistakeable sound of him undoing his belt buckle and she thought it was quite possibly the sexiest thing she had ever heard in her life.

'Stop,' she said, pushing his hands away. *What the hell was she doing? He was a married man, for Christ's sake.* 'What about Hannah?'

He shook his head. 'There is no Hannah. Not anymore. We're getting divorced.'

'I'm sorry,' she whispered.

'I'm not,' he breathed.

Then he was kissing her again and this time she didn't stop him. His lips only left hers for a moment when he used his teeth to tear open the foil packet on the condom he'd pulled out of his pocket. For a second, Grace wondered why he had one, until she was too busy being grateful that he did.

'Well, that was an unexpected turn of events,' Michael said breathlessly as he zipped up his trousers.

'Was it?'

'Hmm.' He put his arms around her waist and nuzzled her neck. 'I was beginning to think you'd never succumb to my charms.'

Before she could respond they were interrupted by a knock at the door.

'Shit,' he snapped, and then he straightened her skirt and fastened his belt in two fluid movements, before Grace could even think of a response for their unwelcome intruder.

'Come in,' he said before Grace had fully regained her composure. The door opened and Ali, one of the new barmaids, walked into Grace's office. Grace could see from the look on Ali's face that she knew something had been going on. Grace was so embarrassed that she could barely look the girl in the eye. Michael, on the other hand, didn't miss a beat.

'What can we do for you, Ali?' he asked nonchalantly.

'There's someone here to see you, Michael.' She smiled sweetly at him.

'Oh shit, I forgot.' Looking slightly flustered, he started to head off out of the door. Ali waited for him in the doorway, preventing Grace from talking to him about what had just happened. Just as she thought he was going to walk out of there without saying a word, without any acknowledgement of what has just happened between them, he turned to her.

'Thank you for sorting me out, Grace,' he said, while holding up his bandaged hand. His tone was serious but she could see the wicked glint in his eye and hoped Ali didn't notice her blushing in the dimly lit office.

Eddie Redman watched as the bouncers manhandled the man and woman out of The Blue Rooms and wondered what mortal sin the pair of them had committed to warrant their punishment. Probably told that stuck-up cow Grace that her arse was getting fat. He laughed to himself.

'Why the fuck are we sitting out here still, Ed?' Ando Williams groaned in the passenger seat beside him. 'Let's go and get some more scran. I'm fucking starving.'

Eddie rolled his eyes and resisted the urge to punch Ando in the face and tell him to get out of the car – it was Ando's motor, after all. 'Here, have these and shut the fuck up.' He tossed a paper bag containing three cold chicken nuggets into Ando's lap.

Ando grumbled as he opened the bag before stuffing one of the nuggets into his mouth.

'I wonder what they've done.' Eddie nodded his head towards the two clubgoers who'd just been ejected by the bouncers as they staggered towards the direction of the car.

Ando shrugged. 'Who gives a fuck?'

'I bet that bitch had them thrown out for nothing.'

'You're fucking obsessed with her,' Ando chuckled through a mouthful of cold processed chicken.

Eddie turned in his seat to give Ando a slap when there was a loud bang on the bonnet. The drunk woman had stumbled and fallen onto the front of the car. She was clearly unhurt as she cackled and squealed while her companion helped her up.

'Sorry, lads,' she shouted loudly as she gave a half-hearted wave at them through the windscreen.

'Oh, fucking hell, I know her,' Ando groaned as he ducked low in his seat. 'Let's get out of here before she recognises me.'

Eddie started the engine. He was starting to sober up, his skin prickled with nervous energy and repressed anger and he knew he needed something to take the edge off – and fast. He would resume his monitoring of Grace Sumner another night. She wasn't going anywhere.

'Who is she?' Eddie asked as he pulled the car away from the kerb, startling the drunken woman and causing her to give him the finger as he drove past.

'Some old crank who used to live by us in Birkenhead when I was a kid. Her and me ma used to be mates but even she realised what a nutter that one was, and as you know me ma will talk to anyone.' Ando laughed. 'She disappeared for a few years then turned up at me ma's house a few months ago on the sniff for a few quid. Me ma told her to fuck off.'

Eddie liked Ando's mum, Angie. She could talk the skin off a cat and was always in the know about who everyone was and what they were up to. Although Eddie wasn't that bothered about the neighbourhood gossip, he liked that she'd always treated him like he was a grown-up. She'd even given him his first spliff when he was thirteen. She was nothing like his own mother, who tried to constantly baby him and make him do stuff he had no interest in, like going to school or fucking cycling with Richie, her useless cunt of a husband. No, Angie just let him be who he wanted to be. She cooked the best cheese toasties he'd ever tasted as well. Eddie's stomach rumbled as he realised he'd given Ando the last of his McDonalds.

'Reckon your ma will be up?' he asked Ando. 'I could fucking murder a cheese toastie.'

'She's always up,' said Ando. 'She'll have some good weed an' all. Her new fella, Dave, just started selling it.'

'Sound.' Eddie smiled as he made his way towards the Birkenhead tunnel.

The rest of the night passed in an uneventful blur for Grace, who'd been so busy, she'd barely had time to think, which was probably a good thing given what had happened earlier with Michael. Realising she hadn't seen him since he left her office, she wondered whether things would be awkward between them. Aside from the obvious, he was going through a divorce. She was a single mother. After everything they'd been through, she wasn't sure she wanted anything more right now. But did he? It would certainly complicate things if he did.

As she was locking up and letting out the last of her staff,

Grace saw a car parked outside with its lights on and the engine running. She recognised it as Michael's Audi. He stuck his head out of the driver's window as she approached.

'Can I give you a lift home?' He grinned and she couldn't help but smile at him. Walking over, she leaned inside the window.

'I have a perfectly good car there.' She indicated her silver Mercedes.

'I know you have.' He smiled. 'But I can promise you it will be much more fun driving home with me. And don't worry, your car will be safe in here. I know the head of security. I'll bring you back for it in the morning.'

'You're very sure of yourself, aren't you?'

'Well, I have reason to believe you fancy the pants off me.'

She laughed. She'd forgotten how funny he was.

'But don't worry, the feeling is mutual.' He winked. 'Now come on. Get in.'

'I can't let you take me home. Belle is there.'

'She's a baby. She'll be asleep, and I'll leave before she wakes up. Promise. I'll get your car dropped off instead. Come on. What have you got to lose?'

'Er, everything.' She laughed. If only he knew! Going home with him was opening herself up to a whole host of trouble. He was going to find out about the secret she'd been keeping from him – from everyone. And when he did, none of their worlds would ever be the same.

'Come on,' he pleaded.

She looked at him. He was just her type really. She'd never let herself think about that when Ben was alive. Dark hair. A neat beard. Eyes that crinkled when he smiled. One muscular arm resting on the car door, his rolled-up shirt sleeve offering a glimpse of one of his many tattoos.

'Okay,' she said. 'But we'll have to go to your place and I'll need to be home before Belle wakes up. I'll ask Marcus to stay the night at mine. He won't mind.'

'My place it is then.' He grinned. 'Jump in.'

So Grace did as she was told and climbed into his warm car.

'So how long since you and Hannah . . .?' she asked as he drove.

'About six weeks now.'

'I didn't realise. You came to Nicola's birthday party together?'

'That was just for appearances. I wanted to tell the boys first and Hannah wanted to find herself a house by her mum's before we made it official.'

'I'm sorry it didn't work out for you both.'

He shook his head. 'We should never have got married in the first place. We've always wanted different things. We should have split up ages ago,' he sighed. 'I feel like I've wasted years of her life. She deserves someone who can give her everything she wants.'

'I'm sure she'll find someone when she's ready.'

'I hope so.'

'So have you been seeing anyone else?'

He looked at her like she'd just asked him if he'd shot his granny. 'Of course not. I told you it's only been a few weeks.'

'Oh, right. It's none of my business anyway. It's just . . .'

'Just what?'

'You had a condom?' It had been playing on her mind. She was glad he'd had one, obviously. But Michael had never been into one-night stands or casual sex – at least he never used to be.

He started to laugh. 'Billy's daughter works in the STD clinic. He always brings a bagful in for the lads. I always take a few or I never hear the end of them taking the piss out of me.'

'Oh, I see.' She smiled to herself. Jealousy was an unfamiliar emotion for her, and one she didn't relish experiencing again any time soon.

'I've never had cause to use one before, if that's what you're getting at,' he assured her. 'How about you? Is there anyone else I should know about?'

'Nope,' she shook her head. 'There's been no one since . . .' She didn't finish her sentence. He knew.

Grace smiled as she leaned her head against the passenger window, despite knowing that she was making a huge mistake. She would pay dearly for this, she knew, but at that exact moment, she didn't care.

Chapter 33

Jake watched as Connor and Paul Carter strolled into Eric's boxing gym and placed their sports bags near the ring.

'Ready for a good scrap, lads?' Eric asked.

'Always,' they said, grinning.

Jake Conlon watched as the twins proceeded to knock seven shades of shite out of each other for twelve rounds. Neither one of them would concede and Eric was forced to declare their match a draw.

Taking off their head-guards, they patted each other on the back and it was hard to believe they'd just been trying their best to knock each other out.

'Is this how you two usually work out?' Jake asked as he handed them a towel each.

'Only when we've had a bad day,' Connor said with a laugh.

'Fancy a go, Jake?' Paul asked him.

'No thanks.' He liked a good scrap as much as the next man, but he didn't fancy being beaten to a pulp by one of the Carter twins, not even one who'd already done twelve rounds.

'So what did you want to talk to us about, Jake?' Connor asked and Eric sensibly made himself scarce. He was used to opening his gym after hours for the boys and he knew to keep his nose out of their business. They rewarded him by making sure that no one ever took the piss.

'I have a business proposition for you both.'

'Oh?' Connor said as he raised an eyebrow. 'Sounds promising.'

'It is. I want to take over Bobby White's firm.'

'Why?' Paul asked.

'Why not? Bobby is a prick. Nobody likes him. He's not even from round here. With our contacts we could take it all. We could be as big as my old man, and yours was, back in the day.'

Connor laughed. 'I think you'll find it was your mum who really ran the show.'

Jake shrugged. 'Whoever it was, we could be bigger.'

'What exactly do you have in mind?' Connor asked as he wiped some of the sweat from his hair with a towel. 'We just go in there and take it from him?'

'Why not? Between us, we've got the manpower.'

'Sounds like a plan to me,' said Paul.

Connor shook his head. 'I'm not against it, Jake. We've been thinking about making a move ourselves, haven't we, Paul? But we have to think it through. If we're going to go to war, then we need to have a plan. Bobby mightn't be from round here, but he's no mug.'

'Bobby has already been sniffing around my business. He's gone quiet again now, but it's only a matter of time before he makes a move himself. If I don't act, then he will.'

'Well, if he does, we'll be ready for him, won't we?' Connor replied.

'This means you're in then?' Jake asked.

Connor and Paul looked at each other and smiled. 'We're in.'

'Then welcome aboard.' Jake smiled back.

'Equal partners?' Connor said.

'Of course,' Jake replied.

'The Carters and the Conlons. A truly unholy alliance,' Eric said as he shuffled past with a smirk on his face.

'All the more protection for you then, Eric,' Paul called after him. 'You nosy sod.'

Chapter 34

Bobby White handed his two most loyal employees, Liam and Harry, a glass of scotch each and indicated that they should take a seat in his office.

'Are we celebrating, boss?' Harry asked, pointing to the bottle of expensive whisky on Bobby's desk.

A grin spread across Bobby's face. 'We certainly are, H. We are about to pull off a job that will make Jake Conlon and his motley crew look like a bunch of amateurs.'

Liam smiled at him. He was still smarting from Bobby backing out of their plan to get rid of Jake permanently, and it was about time they did something to put the smarmy little shit in his place. 'Nice. So, what is it?'

'I told you about that guy I knew from Newcastle whose brother is over in Colombia. Well, he has just sorted me with a cracking deal on some of the best quality shit money can buy. This shipment is gonna make us rich, lads. Everyone from Scotland to Crewe will want in on this shit. It will blow Jake Conlon's gear out of the water, and we've got a whole fucking truckload of it coming in on Sunday night.'

Harry nodded in anticipation and Liam started to laugh. 'Nice one, boss,' he said. 'What do you need us to do?'

'After all the bother we've had with our containers, I want

you two nowhere near this one until the gear is safely in our hands. Your faces are too well known. No one can get a sniff of this, lads. I cannot afford to lose this shipment. I'll have Reuben drive it to Sammy's warehouse and you can unload it there.'

Liam nodded. Sammy was his cousin on his mother's side. He had an electronics warehouse on Brasenose Road and he was more than happy for Liam to use it when he needed, providing the price was right. 'Have you spoken to Reuben?'

Bobby shook his head. 'No. I'll leave that to you. You know I can hardly stand the little gobshite. Make sure he knows no more than he needs to.'

'Will do.'

'Make sure he doesn't fuck this up,' Bobby warned.

'He won't. I know he's a bit of a dickhead, but he knows what he's doing.'

Bobby stared at him. 'He'd better.'

Chapter 35

'I told you I haven't seen him, Mum,' Connor snapped at the blonde woman standing before him. Grace was about to walk into her office when she'd overheard the exchange. Not wanting to intrude, she'd lingered outside until Connor looked up and waved his hand for her to come in.

'Sorry, Grace. This is my mum, Cheryl. Mum, this is Grace.'

Grace watched as Michael's first wife looked her up and down, a smug grin on her face. Cheryl had been one of Nathan's many conquests in the past. Michael, who had still been married to Cheryl at the time, didn't know that – at least Grace didn't think he did – and Grace hadn't thought it was information worth telling him. Nathan probably didn't even remember screwing her; she was simply another one in a long list of women. But she was just his type – blonde hair and giant knockers. She'd obviously been a looker back in the day, but she'd struggled to maintain her expensive beauty regime once the twins had turned eighteen and Michael had stopped paying her a hefty monthly allowance. Grace knew that the twins kept their mum in the lifestyle to which they thought she should be accustomed, but they never seemed that close to her. Ever since they were young, she was always swanning off to Turkey to meet one of her many toyboys. A different one every year.

Grace smiled at her. 'Hello, Cheryl. Nice to finally meet you.'

'Hmm.' She sniffed. 'Tell your dad I'm around if he needs anyone to talk to, Connor,' she said and then she sashayed out of the room in a cloud of cheap perfume.

Connor shook his head as his mother left the room. 'As if my dad would be talking to her of all people. He can't stand her.'

'Why would he need someone to talk to?' Grace asked.

'He doesn't. But she's only just heard he's getting a divorce and the deluded mare thinks she's got a chance of getting him back. I almost feel sorry for her.'

'You shouldn't talk about your mum like that,' Grace admonished him while suppressing a smile. Connor was only confirming what she already knew. Michael despised his ex-wife. He'd been devastated when he'd come out of prison to find she'd been sleeping with any Tom, Dick or Harry who'd looked twice at her.

'What?' Connor protested. 'It's true. I love the woman, but she made her own bed, Grace.'

Grace couldn't argue with that. 'Where's your other half anyway?' she asked, referring to Paul.

'He's out with Jake.'

'Oh?'

'Just business.' Connor grinned and, despite her stomach churning, Grace sensed not to pry any further. She loved the twins but she knew exactly what business they were in and the thought of Jake getting involved with them made her feel sick with worry. The twins were going to go far, but would Jake go along with them? She'd find out soon enough, no doubt.

* * *

Paul watched Jake and his associate talking animatedly outside the bookies, their hot breaths creating clouds of fog around their faces. Despite the cold weather, the car was warm. Smiling to himself, he rested his head against the warm leather seat and thought about the events of earlier that afternoon. It seemed Jake loved a good scrap just as much as he did.

He'd convinced Jake to go to his mum's house with him to pay her boyfriend a visit and put a stop to him spreading unsavoury rumours about Paul's character. Jake didn't ask any questions, he just agreed to go along. And when things got a bit out of hand, Jake helped him clean up the mess he'd made, and deposited his mum's hopefully now ex-boyfriend at the nearest A&E. Thankfully, his mum hadn't been in, or she'd have gone ballistic and he'd have ended up having to pay for a decorator to come and redo the whole place. As it was, they'd had to bin the cream rug, but apart from that, you'd never know they'd been there.

'What are you smiling about?' Jake asked as he climbed into the car.

Paul's eyes snapped open. 'Nothing,' he said.

'Liar.' Jake grinned at him.

'Did your mate know anything?' Paul asked as he put the car into gear.

'Hmm. Seems our mate Bobby has a massive shipment coming in on Sunday night.'

Paul smiled. 'Nice one.' He knew Jake was still smarting at Vinnie losing him a fortune a few weeks earlier. Jake was sure Bobby had been behind it, and now it was time for payback. 'So we're taking it from him then?' Paul asked.

'Course we are, lad,' Jake laughed. 'Get us back to the club so we can fill Connor in. He'll be wondering where we are.

We said we'd only be an hour and that was three fucking hours ago.'

'Well, you shouldn't be such a fucking bad influence then.' Paul winked at him.

Chapter 36

Michael walked up behind Grace as she was putting some paperwork on the shelf. Wrapping his arms around her waist, he whispered in her ear, 'Fancy getting out of here and coming home with me tonight? I'll make it worth your while.'

'Behave yourself. I'm busy,' she said, although she made no attempt to move from his embrace and instead leaned into his body. He buried his face in her hair, inhaling the smell of her perfume, and began to wonder whether he'd even be able to make it home before he buried himself inside her.

'How exactly will you make it worth my while?' she purred and he felt a familiar stirring in his groin area.

'You already know how,' he growled in her ear.

'Yes, but I want feeding too. I've been stuck in here all day and I'm starving.'

'Fine. I'll pick us up a Chinese on the way home, and I'll make you a breakfast fit for a queen in the morning. Will that do you?'

'Hmm, I suppose,' she said and then she turned in his arms and took his face in her hands.

He was about to kiss her when the door to their office was opened. They both turned in surprise to see who had rudely interrupted them without even knocking. Michael was about to give whoever it was a mouthful of abuse and tell them they were fired, but when he saw who it was, he groaned instead.

'Oh, don't tell me you're fucking *her*?' his ex-wife Cheryl spat angrily

'What the fuck are you doing here?' he snarled as he and Grace stepped away from each other. 'Don't you know how to fucking knock?'

'I need to talk to you,' she snapped. 'Alone!'

'Anything you have to say, you can say in front of Grace,' he replied.

'It's okay. I'll leave you two to it,' Grace said as she started to put on her coat. Michael was about to protest about her leaving when she leaned over and kissed him so hard he almost forgot his annoying ex-wife was in the room. 'I'll wait for you in the bar.' She smiled as she glided out of the room. 'Bye, Cheryl. Don't keep him too long, will you?'

Michael watched Cheryl staring after her, her face red with anger.

'Are you really screwing her?' she spat when Grace left.

'Oh, fuck off, Cheryl. It's none of your business who I am or am not screwing.'

'I thought you had better taste.'

'Well, it's certainly improved since I married you.'

She glared at him and he could hardly believe he'd once thought she was the love of his life. His family had never taken to her. They said she was so far up her own arse she could lick her ribs clean, but he used to think she was full of class.

'What do you want, Cheryl?' His patience was growing thinner by the second. All he could think of was Grace waiting for him.

She sighed dramatically. 'One of your lunatic children has put my Terry in hospital.'

Terry the Turk was Cheryl's latest boyfriend. He seemed to have lasted longer than most of the others and had been hanging around for a few years by this point. But Michael had heard whispers of the rumours Terry was spreading about Paul and had planned on giving the cheeky little fucker a good slap himself. When he heard Terry was in hospital with a broken jaw, a concussion and three broken ribs, he assumed one of his boys had heard the rumours too and saved him a job.

'It's funny how they're always *my* children when you're pissed off with them, isn't it?'

'Well, it's your fault they've turned out the way they have. Pair of animals.' She shook her head.

'You're not saying that when they're giving you money though, are you?'

She blushed and he hoped she at least felt some shame for being such a horrible fucking mother.

'It's none of your business what them boys give me. Anyway, are you going to have a word? My Terry will be in hospital for weeks.'

Michael laughed. 'It serves him fucking right. He's lucky he's still breathing.'

'You just can't stand to see me happy, can you?' she spat. 'You and your bloody thug mates have turned our sons into vicious little bastards too, just like you.'

Michael stepped closer to her and leaned in so his face was close to hers. She blinked rapidly at him and then started to smile. She leaned towards him, as though she thought he was going to kiss her. 'You never complained about my mates when you were fucking them behind my back, did you?' he snarled and then watched as the smile slipped from her face. She took a step back from him and lifted her hand to slap his face. He'd taken the odd slap from her back in the day – she was a woman with a temper – and he'd never hit a woman in his life, but this time he caught her by the wrist and stopped her, realising he was squeezing her arm when she winced in pain. When he let go, she looked up at him, her face full of venom.

'Tell that little whore of yours I screwed her husband too,' she cackled.

'Get out before I have someone throw you out,' he growled at her.

'Tell them boys to leave my Terry alone,' she said over her shoulder as she headed out the door.

Michael put his jacket on and closed the office door behind him before going to find Grace. He'd suspected that Nathan had been one of Cheryl's many suitors but he'd never told Grace that. He wondered if she knew. He wasn't planning on telling her anyway. Nathan was dead and all it would do was remind Grace what a vile scumbag she'd once been married to. He made a mental note to speak to the twins in the morning and warn them Cheryl was on the rampage. Not for her benefit but for theirs.

Michael walked out into the bar area and scanned the room for Grace. She was standing by the bar talking to a guy who was clearly three sheets to the wind and who kept trying to grab her arse. Michael's instinct was to go over there and break the drunken fucker's fingers, but he watched her instead, knowing that she wouldn't appreciate his intervention. She was perfectly capable of handling herself, as she repeatedly liked to remind him. After moving his hand three times, she'd obviously had enough and she kneed him in the groin so hard that he doubled over and dropped to the floor. Michael laughed to himself as one of his bouncers stepped in and escorted the man from the premises.

'Ready?' she said breezily as she walked over to him.

'Still fancy a Chinese?'

'Yeah. I'm famished. What did Cruella De Vil want?'

Michael laughed. 'Nothing important. Come on, let's go,' he said as he put his arm around her shoulder. They walked out of The Blue Rooms like any other couple in love and Michael felt a pang of sadness, wondering how long it would be before it all came crashing down around him. Grace Sumner was like lightning in a bottle. He could never manage to hold onto her for too long.

Chapter 37

Grace smiled at Michael as he slipped beneath the sheets of his king-size bed.

'Here you go. Breakfast in bed.' He laughed as he handed her a protein bar.

'Are you kidding me, Michael Carter?' she said as she threw it back at him. He caught it as it bounced off his chest. 'After last night, I want a full fry-up. At the very least, I expect some toast.'

'What? That's full of goodness, that. Plenty of protein to keep your strength up.' He winked.

'I'll go out and get my own breakfast then,' she said, pouting, pretending to be offended, as she pulled back the covers to get out of bed.

'Hang on. Not so fast.' He pulled her towards him. 'I've got some bacon and eggs in the fridge.' He silenced her with a kiss.

Grace wandered into the kitchen to see Michael standing beside the oven over a sizzling frying pan. The radio played a nineties scouse-house song in the background and she laughed quietly to herself as she watched him nodding his head to the music and humming along. The smell of bacon made her stomach growl and she realised they'd barely eaten the night before, having discarded their Chinese takeaway as they'd headed straight up to bed. She smiled at the memory.

What was wrong with her? She was behaving like a horny teenager. Perhaps it was because they both knew their time together would be brief. Grace would be going back to Harewood in a few months, and Michael would be staying in Liverpool. She couldn't stay and he couldn't leave.

'You're finally dressed then?' Michael said and Grace realised he'd turned around and was smiling at her.

'This better be good, Carter.' She indicated the food he was preparing. 'You promised me a queen's breakfast last night if I came home with you again.' She laughed as she took a seat at his kitchen table.

'And it will be.' He walked over to her, tea towel slung over his bare shoulder, half covering the large Celtic symbol tattooed on his chest – a nod to his mother's Irish roots – and planted a kiss on the top of her head.

Five minutes later, the two of them were sitting at the table, eating a large plate of bacon, egg, toast and beans, which, Grace had to admit, tasted as good as any she'd ever eaten before. Despite having her head down, concentrating on buttering her toast, she felt Michael's gaze, hot on her neck.

'What?' she snapped as she looked up.

'I'm just watching you.'

'Well, stop it, will you? I'm trying to eat my breakfast.'

'What is this, Grace?' he asked then, catching her off-guard.

'Well, you cooked it. But I think it's a fry-up. Well, it's supposed to be at least. No sausage or black pudding though, is there?' She laughed, trying to keep the mood light.

Michael sighed. 'Stop taking the piss. You know what I mean.'

Grace stared at him. 'You mean us?'

He nodded as he bit a chunk off his toast.

'You know what it is. We're just having some fun, aren't we? That's what you said that first night you persuaded me to get into your car anyway. Fun!'

'I know that. But—'

'But nothing, Michael. You're in the middle of a divorce and I'm moving back home in a few months.'

'This is your home.'

'Not any more. I can't stay here.'

'But you belong here.'

Grace shook her head and focused on the plate of food in front of her so Michael wouldn't see the tears pricking her eyes. He was right and she knew it. But she couldn't stay. She couldn't stay with him, as much as she desperately wanted to. She should never have agreed to start anything with him. She was going to break his heart.

Stay or go – he would hate her eventually.

Chapter 38

Reuben McBride grinned at his own reflection in the lorry's large wing mirror. He had finally hit the big time and was feeling incredibly pleased with himself. Liam had introduced him to Bobby White and Reuben had liked Bobby straight away. He was a no-nonsense, old-school hard man. He took no shit and he crushed anyone who tried to cross him. Reuben knew exactly how to play people like Bobby – it was all about stroking their considerable ego. Reuben had done his best to impress him, and realised it had worked when Bobby offered him an in on a big job he had planned. He needed someone who could drive an HGV from Liverpool to Glasgow and Reuben had offered his services. He'd been driving HGVs since Michael Carter had put an end to his previous career as an armed robber. He'd fucked up a massive job because of the hiding Michael had given him. He'd been deaf in his right ear ever since, and all because that little faggot mate of Grace Sumner's, Marcus Holden, took offence at the way he spoke to him. Reuben liked to conveniently forget about the fact that he'd barged into Grace's office and threatened her too.

It still pissed Reuben off when he thought about it, but he didn't want to make an enemy of Grace Sumner or the Carters so he'd had to bite his lip and let it go. Anyway, Bobby White was his meal ticket now. He was on his way to the top, and Reuben was happy to ride his coat tails.

Reuben was still smiling when he pulled up at the temporary traffic lights just before his turning. It didn't even register in his head that the regular traffic lights at the junction of Derby Road and Millers Bridge fifty yards ahead were in perfect working order. It was one in the morning and there were no workmen around. If he had been a smarter man, or one who was more concerned with his surroundings rather than how pleased he was with himself, he might have thought it odd and driven straight through them.

But he wasn't. Reuben didn't stand a chance when a masked man wrenched open the door of the cab and pulled him out of it, tossing him onto the tarmac as though he was a used johnny. Reuben bounced like an overdone Brussels sprout and landed in a seated position. What the hell had just happened? How had he gone from Cloud Nine to Shit Street in less than ten seconds? He heard laughter in the cab and realised his attacker had been joined by someone else. Looking up, he saw another figure running down the street towards them. This idiot wasn't wearing a mask though and Reuben recognised him as he disappeared behind the passenger side of the cab. Before Reuben could stand up the cab doors slammed shut and he watched as the lorry, along with Bobby White's drugs, and Reuben's future, drove away down Derby Road and into the night.

'Jake, where's your fucking mask?' Connor snapped at him.

Jake shrugged. 'In my pocket. It's pitch fucking black, Con. No one saw me. And so what if they did? Bobby will know it was us. Just like I know it was him who had me off.'

'We agreed masks. We had a fucking plan.'

'Oh, calm down, lad.' Paul sighed. 'No one fucking saw him. The poor fella you just face-planted onto the tarmac couldn't have anyway,' he sniggered.

'Did you see who he was?' Jake asked.

Connor shook his head as he drove. 'No. Didn't recognise him. I didn't get much time to look at him anyway as he flew past me onto the road.' He grinned. 'He didn't see me anyway. Because I was wearing my fucking *mask*.'

'All right, Con. I'll stick to the plan in future,' Jake said.

'Good. Let's get this dropped off and we can celebrate.'

'Sounds like a plan,' said Paul.

'Good to me,' Jake agreed.

The three of them chattered away, full of adrenaline, as Connor drove them to Charnock Richard service station on the M6, where some of their Scottish counterparts were waiting to take delivery of the shipment of cocaine and weapons that they'd just stolen. A shipment they were paying handsomely for. Connor had to admit, Jake had come up with a good plan. He'd found out all the details of Bobby's shipment, even the route it was taking from the docks. It was Jake who'd had the temporary traffic lights nicked and set up at exactly the right place so the driver would stop. He'd been waiting ahead in the car they'd stolen, just in case Plan A hadn't worked. Then their plan B was to simply follow the lorry and hijack it at the most convenient opportunity.

Connor smiled as he watched Jake and his brother laughing in the cab beside him. He had the feeling this was going to be the beginning of a lucrative partnership.

'Here he is – where the fuck have you been? We've been waiting for you,' Connor shouted good-naturedly as Jake walked into his office at The Blue Rooms.

'I had to see to the girlfriend before she went home,' he said with a grin.

'Come here, lad,' Paul said as he pulled Jake into a bear hug and tousled his hair. The three of them had just pulled off a massive job and were a whole lot richer for it. But more than that, they had earned their place as the new top firm in Liverpool, a firm who were not to be fucked with.

'I think tonight went even better than we'd planned,' Jake said as he poured the three of them a shot of his most expensive vodka.

'Too fucking right,' Connor said. 'I wish I could see Bobby White's face when he realises someone has driven off with his lorry-load of coke.'

The three of them started to laugh, so full of adrenaline that the vodka had no effect at all and Jake poured them another.

'Let's go somewhere for a proper celebration, eh?' Connor suggested as they downed their next shot.

'Sounds like a plan,' Paul agreed.

'Where?' Jake asked. 'It's nearly three in the morning. And I don't fancy one of them all-night dives in town.'

'We know a place,' said Paul, and winked at him.

Bobby White hung up the phone and sat on the bed beside his sleeping wife, Leanne. His heart thumped violently in his chest as he thought about the container of finest quality Colombian marching powder he'd just lost. He'd gambled almost all of his spare cash on that job and had made promises to some very dangerous people in the process. This could ruin him. He resisted the urge to throw his phone at the wall and punch his way through every piece of furniture in the bedroom, knowing it would wake Leanne and she'd start asking questions that he didn't want to answer. Instead he sat there, silently seething as he contemplated his next move. He no longer cared about the dirt Grace Sumner had on him. He could not let this go. Jake Conlon was a dead man walking.

Half an hour after leaving The Blue Rooms, Jake, Paul and Connor were in a private members' club in Liverpool city centre, knee deep in beautiful women, expensive cigars and the finest Russian vodka money could buy. Jake's head buzzed with the thrill of it all. He loved working with the Carter twins. They were professional, cold and calculating when they were working – and a good laugh when they weren't. The private club wasn't usually Jake's kind of scene, but the twins were obviously good customers and were treated like kings. Sitting back in the expensive leather chair, Jake surveyed the scene unfolding around him. One of the waiters was placing a bottle of Bollinger in the ice bucket beside them – a bottle that neither he nor the twins had ordered, but that some well-wisher had sent over in a bid to ingratiate themselves.

Jake smiled. Life was good. He had made it. People thought he couldn't live up to his old man – but here he was being treated like fucking royalty. All of the staff practically fell over themselves to serve them. The other customers were in awe of them, and the women flocked around them like seagulls to a chip butty van.

One in particular obviously had her eye on Jake and kept rubbing her tits, which were very expensive by the looks of them, up against him every chance she got. Eventually he told her to piss off. She was wasting her time. He would never cheat on Siobhan.

Chapter 39

Jake's head was pounding. Reaching out his arm to feel Siobhan's familiar warmth, his fingertips brushed against skin, but it wasn't hers. Opening his eyes, he remembered where he was. And then he remembered last night, or more precisely, earlier that morning. Feeling the bile rising in his throat, he swallowed it down, trying to swallow the feelings of guilt and shame along with it.

Paul Carter stirred beside him, disturbing the sheet as he moved and revealing a glimpse of his toned, hard torso. Jake closed his eyes and remembered Connor leaving the club with two women. He and Paul had stayed behind and carried on celebrating. The women who had previously swarmed around them seemed to drift away until there was only Paul and Jake left. When Paul had invited him to sleep at his place, Jake had convinced himself he'd only agreed because it was close to the club. He'd phoned Siobhan and left a voicemail telling her he was shitfaced and wouldn't be home until later.

Jake lay still and willed himself to get out of the bed but he already felt the familiar twitching in his dick that only someone like Paul could give him. He was still lying there with his eyes closed when he felt a calloused hand running down his chest towards his groin.

'Morning, handsome,' Paul said. His deep, hoarse voice seemed at odds with his words.

Jake didn't move. He didn't speak, afraid that if he did, he'd say something he would regret. In his head, it could go one of two ways. He would either declare his undying love for his new business partner and make a complete tit of himself. Or he'd confess his disgust at what they had done the night before. At what they quite obviously were. Men like them weren't supposed to be queer. They had women falling at their feet. They were idolised. Like gods. If people found out they were actually a pair of fags, they'd be a laughing stock. They would never live it down. Jake had been at school with a few lads who'd been branded gay, whether they were or not, and the grief they'd been given was both relentless and merciless. Their schooldays had been made a living hell.

Jake had known back then that he liked boys far more than girls, but he decided that was a route he would never go down. Aside from the bullying at school, there was his dad too. King shagger himself, he would have balked at the idea of his son being a queer. No, Jake wouldn't leave himself open to ridicule for the sake of a few sexual encounters. He'd buried his urges so deep, he'd almost convinced himself he no longer had them. And now one night with Paul Carter threatened to undo it all.

When Jake had met Siobhan, he'd been surprised that he'd even fancied her, at least more than any other girl he'd ever met. But it was her laugh and her personality that attracted him to her. He did love her though. She was the only woman he'd ever had any interest in. She was his best mate. But she had never made him feel the way Paul had. He could only describe it as pure lust. The tearing of clothes and the marking of skin in that frantic need to be as much as part of the other person as possible. His and Siobhan's lovemaking had always been pleasant enough and she gave amazing head. But as much as he hated to admit it, he usually closed his eyes and fantasised that it wasn't her going down on him but some muscular Adonis with a six-pack and more tattoos than a sailor. Until last night, he'd never acted on any of those fantasies, convincing himself he could live with that. But now he felt like he'd crossed a line and it made him feel like he was going to throw up.

Opening his eyes, Jake decided he was going to smile politely and leave. He would pretend that last night was due to one too many vodkas and over-excitement at their latest business venture succeeding. But he looked up to see Paul's dark head disappearing under the covers and he groaned in pleasure instead, cursing his treacherous body for betraying him and refusing to allow him to move.

Jake stared at the ceiling while Paul stared at him, his head resting on one elbow, his firm body pressed against Jake's side.

'First time?' Paul asked.

'And only time,' Jake snapped.

Paul shrugged. 'That's the guilt talking, mate. You'll soon get over it. How long have you known?'

Jake stared at him. He contemplated arguing and claiming that he wasn't gay, that he'd made a mistake and had been curious, that was all. But something about Paul and the way he looked at him made him want to spill his guts. 'Since I was about fourteen. You?'

'I've always known.'

'Have you done this before?' Jake asked.

Paul laughed. 'After what I just did to you, what do you think?'

Jake felt like he was going to vomit again and jumped out of bed. He scrabbled around the floor for his clothes.

Paul stopped laughing. 'There's nothing to be embarrassed about, you know,' he said as softly as his voice allowed.

Jake glared at him as he put on his jeans. He'd had no inkling at all that Paul was gay. 'How do you manage to keep it a secret?'

'I'm discreet. It's not that hard to do. I'm discreet about the women I fuck too.'

'You're bi?'

'I'm greedy.' Paul winked.

'Does Connor know?'

'Of course. It's not a big deal,' Paul replied.

'And your dad?'

'Probably. He doesn't ask questions about my love life.'

Jake dressed quietly, contemplating the fact that Paul Carter was bisexual. That some of his family knew, probably all of them, as the Carters were a close lot. Yet he'd never heard even the faintest rumour about him.

'So, I'll see you later then.' Paul smiled at him.

Jake's body tensed and he glared at Paul while he wondered how to answer. He thought he'd made himself clear that this wasn't going to happen again.

'At the club, I mean.' Paul laughed. 'Look, Jake, don't start worrying I'm going to fall in love with you or anything. We can pretend this never happened if you like.'

'Yeah. That's probably for the best, isn't it? With us working together and that.'

'Whatever you say, mate.'

'Brilliant. See you later then.' Jake said as he bolted for the door. As soon as he was outside in the fresh air he stopped and took a deep breath. The cool air flooding his lungs felt almost cleansing. Yes, he would forget last night ever happened.

If only he could.

Lying in bed, Paul Carter stretched his arms above his head and smiled. He'd fancied Jake Conlon for years. It was hard not to. He looked like he'd stepped out of the pages of *Esquire* – all designer stubble and swagger. Paul had always wondered at Jake's ability to turn a blind eye to the constant stream of women who threw themselves at him, but he'd never dared to imagine that it was because Jake was in the closet. Paul's gaydar was finely tuned and he could usually spot them a mile off, but he'd had no idea about Jake. Not until they'd been sat together in Xcalibur the night before, laughing and reminiscing. Then Jake had stared into his eyes and Paul knew. He'd got a semi on just sitting there with him then, knowing that in a few hours he'd have Jake exactly where he wanted him.

Paul knew Jake was feeling guilty now. The first time was hard for men like him when they'd convinced themselves they were straight all their lives. Plus, he'd cheated on Siobhan, and Paul knew that he did love the girl. But the guilt would soon pass. Paul knew that from experience, and he was very experienced. He'd given Jake his first taste of incredible sex and he knew it. It was only a matter of time before he came back for more.

Chapter 40

Jake went behind the bar of The Blue Rooms and helped himself to a large whisky. He didn't usually drink the stuff but he'd already had five glasses of brandy and it had barely touched the sides.

The place was quiet. They opened in the early afternoon Thursday to Sunday to accommodate the hen and stag party crowds and after-work drinkers. Jake took a seat on one of the barstools and placed his forehead on the cool wooden bar. His head was pounding. He'd had an argument with everyone he'd met today. His mum, Siobhan, Michael, Vinnie. Everyone was pushing his buttons.

Swallowing a mouthful of whisky, he grunted at one of the barmaids to top up his glass. What the hell was wrong with him? He'd tried to forget about what happened two nights ago with Paul. It was a drunken mistake and the pair of them hadn't spoken of it since. But Jake couldn't get it out of his head. He'd fought those urges for so fucking long, and just like that he'd given in. And with Paul Carter of all people. God, if people found out he'd be a fucking laughing stock. A pariah. There was no room in their world for queers. And he was no queer. He was Nathan Conlon's son, for fuck's sake.

He took another swig of his whisky as the barmaid walked

over with the bottle for a refill. 'Just leave it there,' he snapped.

As he poured himself another whisky, he noticed the old blonde who'd been sitting at the bar sidling over to him. He'd seen her in the place a lot, although he never paid much attention to her. The only reason she'd caught his eye was because she'd looked so out of place. She must have been well into her sixties, and she usually drank alone.

'You look like you've lost a pound and found a penny there, lad,' she cackled.

Jake looked sideways at her. 'Hmm,' he said, in no mood for a chat with her.

'I suppose people don't really understand how hard it is being you, do they?' she asked.

'What?' He looked at her now. What the hell was she on about? Who was this woman?

'I'm Eve,' she said, raising her glass in greeting, as though she'd read his mind. 'You do own this place, don't you?' She frowned at him.

He frowned back. 'So?'

'Well, I'm just saying it must be a lot of pressure. Especially for a young lad like yourself. Not that there's anything wrong being young.' She laughed. 'I was meself once, believe it or not. I don't think people appreciate how hard it is always having to be the one making decisions.'

'I think you're right about that, Eve.' He raised his glass to her in return. 'Want one?' he asked, indicating the bottle of Chivas Regal on the bar.

'Ooh, I wouldn't say no.' She smiled at him and he thought she might have been beautiful once, a very long time ago.

He poured a large measure of whisky into her now empty glass. 'It's a pleasure to meet you, Eve,' he slurred. 'You might just be the sanest person I've spoken to all day.'

'A pleasure to meet you too . . .'

'Jake.'

'Jake.' She smiled. 'A fine name.'

Eve was about to say something else when a figure appeared behind them.

'Can I have a word?' said Paul Carter.

Jake turned around and almost fell off his stool.

'For fuck's sake,' Paul sighed. 'Look at the fucking state of you.'

'You can't speak to him like that, he's the boss,' Eve shrieked.

'Oh, fuck off, love,' Paul replied. 'Are you coming or what?'

Jake's head was spinning as he stood up. He followed Paul into his office and sat down before he fell over.

'Here, have some of this,' Paul said, shoving a bottle of water at him.

Jake drank half of it and placed the bottle on his desk. He might be a bit drunk but who did Paul Carter think he was speaking to him like he was some dickhead?

'What the fuck's the matter with you?' Jake shouted at him.

'Me?' Paul shouted back. 'What the fuck is wrong with you?' He closed the office door and went on. 'You've done nothing but drink and fucking pick fights with everyone for the past two days. My dad nearly lamped you one last night.'

'What?' Jake sat up in his chair.

'You called him a fucking cunt in front of his employees, Jake. You're lucky you're still walking.'

Jake shook his head. He'd been so drunk last night, he didn't even remember that. God, he needed to get a fucking grip. 'What the fuck do you want from me, Paul?'

'I want you to get your fucking act together. Forget about the other night. Pretend it never happened. Tell yourself it was a drunken mistake. I don't care. Just snap the fuck out of this pity party you're throwing yourself. Connor is beginning to wonder whether we've made a mistake going into business with you.'

'What? So, I've been a bit drunk and had a few arguments. That's hardly the crime of the century, is it?' Jake shouted.

'It's not what you've done, it's why you're doing it, Jake. If you can't handle a bit of fucking pressure, then what good are you?'

'Pressure?' Jake snapped. 'This isn't pressure. This is my whole fucking life going to shit, mate.'

Paul stared at him. 'Get a fucking grip, Jake. And thanks, by the way.'

Jake shook his head. 'I didn't mean that. It's just . . . This is a massive deal for me, Paul. As much as I want to pretend the other night didn't happen, I can't. I wish I could just go back in time and not let it happen, because then my life could go back to some sort of normal.'

Paul walked over to him. 'Look, Jake. So, you might be gay. You might be bi. Big fucking deal. I bet half the men on our payroll have sucked a cock or two when they were inside. You don't have to let the world know about it if you don't want to. Nobody needs to know except us if that's what you want. If that's what you're worried about you can trust me – and Connor.'

'Connor knows?' Jake shouted.

'I had to explain why you were acting like such a nutter, didn't I? Besides, I can't keep secrets from him. Listen, have you ever found out about any of the other fellas I've slept with? Did you have any idea I was bi until the other night?'

'No!'

'Well, there you go then.'

Jake looked at him. This man had turned his life upside down and here he was telling him to get a grip. Could he trust Paul? His instinct said he could, but he wasn't sure he trusted himself anymore.

'Look, go home, Jake. Take a long shower. Bang your missus. Get a good night's sleep, and I promise you'll feel much better tomorrow.'

Jake couldn't argue with that advice.

'We have a job to do tomorrow night. Meet us at Eric's gym at seven,' Paul said as he opened the office door. 'Don't be fucking late.'

Chapter 41

'Are you sure he'll be here?' Connor Carter barked at his brother. 'Stop flapping. I told you I had a word with him. He'll be here.'

Just as Connor was about to reply, the door of Eric's gym opened and Jake Conlon walked through, looking sober and well groomed, much to Paul's relief.

'You're late,' Connor snarled at him.

'Sorry. I had to stop at your dad's and have a word. Apparently, I called him a cunt in front of his lads the other night.'

Connor laughed and shook his head. 'I heard about that. You're a braver man than I am, lad.'

'Well, catching my mother walking out of his kitchen half-dressed certainly made him more open to my apology,' said Jake, smiling. 'So, what are we doing tonight, boys?'

'Remember those lads from Kensington who were minding some gear for us?' Connor asked.

'Well, they had a party at the weekend with a load of girls on a hen do from Newcastle, and have now snorted half of it. So, we're going to pay them a visit.'

'Nice,' said Jake.

'Choose your poison, Jake,' Paul said as he indicated the array of weapons on the bench behind him.

The twins chose pickaxe handles and Jake a small wooden mallet that could be easily concealed.

'Let's go then,' Paul said before bounding out of the door.

Connor was always the driver so Jake sat next to Paul in the van on the way to Kensington, their thighs pressed against each other in the confined space. Even through their jeans Jake could feel the warmth of Paul's skin and he tried to ignore the feelings that stirred in him and focus on the task at hand instead. A good scrap was probably just what he needed. It would give him a chance to let out some of the pent-up rage which seemed to be permanently coursing around his body of late.

Paul jumped into the van after his brother and Jake, the adrenaline pumping around his body.

'Fuck!' he shouted as he sat down. 'Let's get out of here, bro.'

Connor crunched the battered old van into gear and started to drive.

'Well, that didn't exactly go according to plan,' Connor said, and laughed. 'Feeling better, Jake?'

Jake shook his head. 'Sorry, lads. I couldn't help it.'

'We were supposed to give them a bit of a slap, Jake,' said Paul. 'Not put them all in hospital for a month.'

'I must have missed the memo,' Jake replied with a grin.

'You're a fucking animal,' said Connor good-humouredly. 'I thought our Paul could be a bit of a savage, but you could give him a run for his money.'

'Whoa,' Paul said as he sat forward and looked over at his brother. 'Let's not get carried away here, Con. Breaking a few bones and stamping on a few heads does not a savage make. I think you forget you're talking about me here.'

Connor shook his head. 'But he did it all on his own, bro. Me and you just stood there and watched.'

'True. You did go a bit Rambo, didn't ya, lad?' Paul said, nudging Jake in the ribs. He opened the glove-box and pulled out an old rag. 'Here, you've got blood on your face,' he said, offering it to Jake.

'Thanks, mate,' Jake said as he took it.

Half an hour later the three of them were back at Eric's gym. Eric had left for the night and they had the place to themselves.

'Can you two get rid of these?' Connor said, handing them the weapons they'd taken with them. 'I'm off to see my bird. See you both tomorrow.'

'See ya,' Jake and Paul chorused.

'Better get going then?' Jake said.

'Don't you think you should get a shower first and change out of that gear? You're covered in blood, mate.'

Jake looked down at himself. 'Shit, yeah.'

'I've got some spare clothes here you can borrow.'

'Thanks,' Jake mumbled.

'No problem.' Paul opened his locker and held out the T-shirt and jogging bottoms he kept in there.

Jake walked towards him. 'I'm sorry I was such a prick about the other night.'

Paul shook his head. 'Don't worry about it, mate. Let's forget about it.'

Jake stepped closer to him and took the clothes from his hand. 'I'd rather not,' he growled.

Paul looked at him, that familiar feeling stirring in his groin.

'Eric doesn't clean up until the morning. The showers in here will be full of pubes and toenails by now. You can shower at my place if you want?'

Jake smiled at him. 'Sounds like a much better idea.'

Chapter 42

People stepped out of Jake's way as he stormed towards the bar area.

'Libby,' he barked. 'Where is my fucking drink?'

She glared at him. She was a stroppy cow, but for some reason his mum seemed to like her and she'd promoted her to assistant bar manager.

'I was busy serving customers,' she snapped at him as she indicated the few stragglers who were already sitting at the bar.

'Fine,' he snarled at her as he took a seat at the bar himself. 'A whisky. Now.'

Libby made pouring him a drink look like a gargantuan effort. Eventually she handed it to him and he took a swig.

'Hi, Jake,' he heard as he became aware of a figure sitting on the stool next to him.

He turned to see the old woman he'd been chatting to the week before. 'Eve?' he said as her name popped into his head.

She smiled, showing a row of perfect teeth, which he suspected must be dentures, given that the rest of her features were so worn and tired.

'Get my friend here a drink too,' Jake barked at Libby.

'Stuck up cow, that one,' Eve said with a sniff as Libby rolled her eyes and went to get the bottle of whisky she'd just put back. 'Don't know why you keep her around.'

Jake shook his head. 'Apparently she's good at her job. Or so I'm told.'

'Pah, she's shite if you ask me.'

Jake laughed. There was something about this old lady that amused him. She spoke without caring if she offended anyone. She seemed to have taken a shine to him, but that was probably because he'd given her a few free drinks. Whatever it was, it was nice to have someone around who looked up to him. Someone who didn't question every fucking decision he made.

Eve was regaling him with a story of how she'd once met and partied with The Rolling Stones, when Jake heard someone else saying his name.

'Jake, I've been looking for you everywhere,' his mum said as she approached.

He turned on his stool to look at her. 'Well, here I am.'

She frowned at him before taking his glass out of his hand. Sniffing the contents, she pulled a face and handed it back to him. 'Is that whisky?' she asked.

He nodded.

'But you don't drink whisky. You hate it.'

'No, you hate it,' he reminded her.

She shook her head. 'What's going on with you? You don't usually even drink.'

He started to laugh. 'Well, now I do.'

'He loves a good whisky, don't you, lad?' Eve butted in.

He watched as his mum looked Eve up and down in disgust, before dismissing her completely. God, were all the women in his life stuck-up cows?

'I'll speak to you tomorrow. When you're sober,' she said tersely.

'I'm sober now,' he growled. 'I've only had a few drinks, for fuck's sake.'

She glared at him then, the way she used to when he'd got into trouble as a kid. 'You become more like your father every day,' she said with a scowl before storming away.

Jake put his glass on the bar. He was nothing like his father. How dare she say that to him? Just because he was having a drink. This was his club and he was entitled to drink in it whenever the fuck he wanted to. Besides, the people in this place drove him to it!

Nevertheless, he bade his goodbyes to Eve and decided to go back to his office. Or maybe he would go and find his mum and see what the hell she wanted him about.

Grace closed the door to her office and sat down. Leaning back, she rested her feet on the desk and rubbed her temples. She could feel a headache coming on and she still had next week's rota to finish before she could go home.

She thought about Jake. He'd been such a moody sod for the past week and she wondered what had got into him. Anyone who spoke to him was liable to get their head bitten off. Even her. And her patience was wearing thin with him. She saw more and more of Nathan in him and it terrified the life out of her. She'd glimpsed a side of him she'd never seen before and it made her wonder how she had gone so wrong with him. Even the drinking was so unlike him; she knew something was going on. Bobby White had backed off, she was sure of that, so what else was making her son so intolerable to be around lately?

Lost in her thoughts, Grace didn't hear the tapping at her

office door. She looked up as Jake walked in.

'All right, Mum?' He half-smiled at her and she was struck by how young he was. For all of his cockiness and his bad temper, he was still a child in so many ways. Her child. For some reason he was in pain and for once she didn't know how to fix it.

'I'm good. How are you?'

He sat in the chair opposite her. 'I'm good.'

'Are you sure, son? You don't seem yourself.'

He smiled at her, no doubt trying to convince her he was fine. 'I'm okay, Mum. Honest. It's just been a rough couple of weeks.'

She smiled at him. He was lying, but she hoped he sorted whatever it was soon.

'So, what did you want me about?' he asked.

'I only wanted to ask about that woman who made the cake for Siobhan's birthday. I want her to make one for Belle's.'

'Oh, her. She's Siobhan's mate. I'll ask her to speak to her for you. It shouldn't be a problem.'

'Thanks, son.'

'If that's everything, I'm going to meet the twins for a drink,' he said before kissing her cheek.

'See you later, Jake,' she said quietly as he walked out of her office. Grace watched as the door closed behind him and shook her head. She'd never seen Jake like this before. Siobhan seemed her usual self, so it couldn't be any domestic between the pair of them that had her boy walking around like the world was about to end. Was it something to do with the twins? The three of them seemed to be inseparable lately, and the more Grace thought about it, the more she realised that Jake's moodiness coincided with him starting to work with Paul and Connor.

Whatever it was, Grace was determined to get to the bottom of it, even if that meant pulling the twins back into line and asking them outright.

Chapter 43

Siobhan cursed as she shook the rain from her umbrella. She'd been enjoying a soak in her Jacuzzi bath when Mel, the cleaner for The Blue Rooms, had phoned to say there was no one at the club to let her in. She'd just come back from a week's holiday and so her own set of keys was in the club safe. It was almost midday and Jake had left at seven that morning to go to Paul Carter's flat for an early business meeting, so he should have been at the club hours ago. Siobhan had phoned his mobile a few times but it just kept ringing out. Grace had keys too but she and Marcus had taken Belle to Chester zoo for the day.

Just as she was about to press the buzzer to Paul's flat, a woman with a pram came out, allowing Siobhan to slip into the hallway. Taking the lift to the top floor, she started to worry about Jake. Where was he? What if he wasn't at Paul's? What if he was in some kind of trouble? She shook her head. He was fine. Probably his meeting ran over and he'd lost track of time.

Rounding the corridor, Siobhan tried to recall which number Paul lived at. She'd been to his flat once before and hoped she could remember which one it was. She had a feeling it was the second from the end. Connor lived on the same floor, but she didn't know which flat was his. As she looked up she saw Jake walking out of the door of the second flat from the end of the hallway. So she was right. She smiled to herself. Just as she was about to shout his name, she saw a shirtless Paul Carter taking hold of Jake's arm and pulling him to his chest. She almost threw up the latte she'd stopped for on the way as she watched in horror while the two of them shared a deep, lingering kiss.

She slipped back behind the wall she'd just rounded as she tried to catch her breath. Dear God. Had she just seen that? It couldn't be. Not her Jake. No way. He was a real hard man. As tough as they came. There was no way. And with Paul Carter? No. It wasn't possible.

Except that she'd seen it with her own eyes. As clear as anything, she had seen her boyfriend kissing another man. What the hell was she going to do? Confront him? Pretend she hadn't seen him and carry on as normal? God, no. She couldn't do that. Could she? What she did know was that she had to get away from there, and she needed some time and space to think.

Taking out her mobile phone, Siobhan sent a text message to Mel telling her not to bother cleaning the club today. Jake would turn up and open up soon enough. Then she tapped out a message to Jake telling him she wasn't feeling well and wouldn't be in to work for her shift that evening. As she got into the lift she started to cry. Why had Jake gone and ruined everything? The bastard. He was just like his father after all.

Chapter 44

Vinnie Black walked into Jake's office with a black holdall and placed it on the desk in front of his boss.

'That's fifty so far, boss,' he smiled weakly.

'Fifty?' Jake shouted. 'You lost me two hundred grand four weeks ago, Vinnie, and you come in here today with fifty. Are you fucking serious?'

Vinnie stared at him open-mouthed as Jake stood up from his chair. 'It's all I could get, boss. I'll get you the rest as soon as I can.'

'And just how do you fucking plan on doing that, Vinnie?' he snapped as he drew closer to him.

Vinnie shook his head. 'I don't know yet. But I will. I promise.'

Jake pushed his face into Vinnie's. He was so close he could feel Vinnie trembling through his tracksuit. 'Do you think I'm some sort of soft touch or something, Vinnie?' he yelled in his face. 'Do I look like I'm a pushover or something? Do you look at me and see some pansy who won't take back what I'm owed?'

Vinnie shook his head furiously. 'No, boss. Of course not,' he stuttered.

Placing one of his large hands around Vinnie's throat, Jake started to squeeze. 'If you don't get me my money back by Friday, you useless piece of shit, I will pull out every one of your teeth and fingernails and feed them to you for fucking breakfast. Do you understand me?'

'Yes, boss,' he wheezed before gasping for air as Jake let go of his throat.

'Good,' Jake said before slapping Vinnie hard across the back of his head. 'Now get out of my fucking sight.'

Vinnie stumbled out of the open door of Jake's office as Paul Carter stepped aside to let him past.

'What the fuck was that about?' Paul asked as he took a seat and started to pour himself a brandy.

Jake glared at him. 'That useless knobhead lost me a fuck-load of money, and he comes in here with fifty grand thinking I'll be grateful or something. Do people think I'm fucking soft or something?'

Paul laughed. 'I don't think they do, mate.'

'It's not fucking funny,' Jake snarled.

'It is a bit funny, seeing you all worked up like this,' said Paul with a smirk. 'Reminds me of this morning.'

'Keep your fucking voice down,' Jake muttered as he closed the door to his office.

'Oh, calm the fuck down, Jake,' Paul said. 'It's only Vinnie. Everyone knows he's not a full shilling. You need to cut him some slack. Even your dad was easy on him.'

'Yeah, well. I can't afford to have people thinking I'm a soft touch.'

'Why? Coz you're really a fag?' Paul winked at him.

'Fuck off,' Jake snarled at him. 'Don't fucking say that.' He'd been doing his best to avoid Paul but he couldn't help himself. He was like a drug. And every time Jake gave in to his urges, he hated himself a little bit more.

Paul stood up from his chair. 'Why not?' he said as walked over to where Jake stood. 'It's true, isn't it?'

Jake shook his head. 'Fuck you,' he said, with less conviction in his voice.

'If you want,' Paul chuckled before pulling Jake to him for a kiss.

Chapter 45

Michael watched Grace as she served drinks behind the bar. It reminded him of when they'd first met in The Rose and Crown. He used to love watching her work. He'd worked there himself for a short while, when he was trying to go straight. But it wasn't long before he'd been caught back up in shady dealings. He wasn't cut out for going legit, not like his brother, Sean, who'd taken to a law-abiding life like a duck to water. His wife, Sophia, and her fiery Italian temper had helped see to that.

Michael supposed his security firm was as legitimate as he was going to get. The business was, at least, but the means by which he and his employees operated within that business were most definitely not.

'Penny for your thoughts,' Grace said as she approached him.

'Funnily enough, I was just thinking about you.' He slipped his arms around her waist.

'Oh, really?' She grinned at him. 'And what were you thinking?'

'How much I enjoyed your surprise visit last night. It was very . . . satisfying.'

'Well, I aim to please, Mr Carter.'

'You certainly do,' he growled. 'Are you coming home with me tonight?'

She shook her head. 'I can't. I need to go home soon. Marcus is going out with his new boyfriend, James.'

'Let me stay with you then?'

'You can't.'

'Why not?'

'You know I don't want strange men sleeping in the house when Belle is there.'

He frowned and pulled away from her. 'So you're saying I'm a strange man?'

'To my daughter you are.'

'Well, let her get to know me then.'

Grace sighed. 'But there's no point. We're going home soon.'

Michael shook his head in annoyance. 'That doesn't mean this has to end, Grace.'

'It does.' She swallowed. 'We knew this was a temporary thing.'

He shook his head and thought about walking away, but then she took his hand and led him to the office they shared. Closing the door behind them, she smiled at him.

'I don't have to be home for an hour. There's no reason we can't make the most of the time we do have,' she purred as she started to unbutton his shirt.

Michael groaned. He should tell her to go home. She was going to break his fucking heart and walk away without a backward glance. As she started to plant soft kisses along his throat he felt his resolve weaken. Running his hands through her hair he pulled her face up to meet his, taking any control he could get, and kissed her so hard he hoped she'd change her mind about ever leaving him.

* * *

Grace was zipping up her dress as she watched Michael putting his shirt back on. She loved looking at his body. She loved the feel of it. She loved the way he kissed her. The way he made love to her. The way he looked at her like she was the only woman in the world. She shook her head. Why was she doing this to herself? She had to leave – soon. The longer she let their affair carry on, the harder it would be for all of them. She wondered what it would be like to stay in Liverpool. To stay with him. To enjoy his coffee-and-peppermint kisses whenever she liked. But she couldn't, as much as she might want to, and it was all her own stupid fault. She had to leave before he discovered the truth. She couldn't bear to see his face when he did. He would hate her. And she would deserve it. She'd been lying to him, and almost everyone else, for over eighteen months.

'I'd better get back to work,' Michael said as she continued watching him.

Grace nodded. 'People will be wondering where you are. Siobhan told me things have been quiet for the past few nights.'

'It's the last week before payday. It's always a bit quieter then. Nothing to worry about. That crank was in here again last night though,' Michael said as he put on his jacket.

'The blonde you threw out the other week?' Grace asked.

'Yeah.'

'Did she behave herself?'

'I suppose. Just got a bit drunk and tried to cop off with the bar staff and the bouncers. She was asking for Jake again. Nothing we couldn't handle though. But I think you should bar her.'

Grace shrugged. 'She's no bother really. She seems lonely. And besides, Jake seems to like her.'

'She's not the type of clientele we want to attract though, is she?' he said as he walked over to her.

'Michael Carter, you ageist old sod.' She laughed. 'I bet if she was thirty years younger and wore miniskirts you wouldn't have a problem with her.'

'I never said that,' he shook his head in exasperation. 'I just meant—'

'Just for that, I'm not going to bar her,' Grace said. 'Unless she's causing a nuisance, then just leave her be.'

'Whatever you say, boss.'

'I'll see you tomorrow?' Grace asked as she picked up her handbag.

'Of course. I'll be here early.'

'So will I then.' She blew him a kiss as she left.

Chapter 46

Jake opened the door to his and Siobhan's flat and saw the light from the television illuminating the wall in the hallway.

'You still up, babe?' he shouted as he took off his coat.

There was no reply and he walked into the lounge to see Siobhan sitting on the sofa surrounded by used tissues.

'Are you okay? You feeling any better?' he asked as he sat down beside her, placing an arm around her shoulder.

She shrugged him off. 'I'm fine,' she said with a sniff.

Probably on her period, he thought, as he got up and went to the kitchen and got a beer from the fridge.

'How was your meeting this morning?' Siobhan asked.

Jake shrugged. 'Fine. The usual. Why do you ask?' He frowned at her.

'Because you never turned up to let Mel in to clean.'

'Oh shit,' he replied. 'I forgot she had no keys. Our meeting ran late.'

'We pay her company a lot of money to keep that place clean, Jake.'

'Is that why you're upset with me?'

'You should have been there.'

'For fuck's sake, Siobhan. I was busy elsewhere.'

'Doing what?'

'Doing fucking business,' he shouted. 'What the hell has got into you?'

'You, Jake,' she spat. 'You just go about your business, doing your thing and forgetting that other people are counting on you. Mel stood in the rain for half an hour waiting for you.'

'Are you kidding me with this?'

'Oh, piss off,' Siobhan snapped. 'I knew you wouldn't care.'

'I don't need this,' he shouted. 'I came home early to see if you were okay and all you've done since I walked through the door is have a go at me.'

'Well, why don't you go somewhere you're more appreciated then?' Siobhan said as she threw a cushion at him, which he ducked to avoid. It collided with a vase on the table instead, sending it crashing to the floor.

'Fine by me,' Jake shouted as he walked out of the room.

Climbing into his car, Jake shook his head. What the fuck was up with women? He started the engine and dialled Paul's number. After a few rings, Paul's voice filled the car.

'All right, mate?'

Jake sighed. 'No. Me and Siobhan have had a massive row. Are you in?'

'Sorry, lad. Me and Connor are on our way to Glasgow.'

'Glasgow?'

'Yep. Seeing a man about some cleaning supplies. We'll be back tomorrow.'

'No worries. Have fun,' Jake sighed.

'I'll see you tomorrow night. My place at eight?'

'Yeah. See you there.'

Jake pressed the button to end the call and scrolled down to his mum's number.

'Hiya, son,' she answered sleepily.

'Mum, can I stay for a few days?'

'Of course. What's wrong?'

'I don't know. Siobhan's on one. I don't really feel like talking about it in the car.'

'Okay. See you soon. Give us a bell when you're near and I'll put the kettle on.'

'Thanks, Mum.' Jake floored the accelerator and sped down Dock Road. Twenty-one years old and still running back to his mum. How fucking pathetic! He punched the steering wheel, the horn blaring out into the darkness as he did. He was Jake fucking Conlon – at the top of his game, and he had nowhere to go except his mum's house. He needed to get himself some new mates, and a flat. Yes, he needed a flat – a bolthole he could go to when Siobhan was in a mood. It would be an investment. His mum was always going on at him to invest his money. So that was exactly what he was going to do.

Chapter 47

Connor Carter wiped the spatters of blood from his brow with his T-shirt before removing the rest of his clothes, and watched as Paul did the same. Together, they tossed their blood-stained clothes and trainers into a pile along with the baseball bats and sledge-hammers they'd used for the job. Taking a rag each, they doused them with alcohol gel, the type they always carried on such occasions, and wiped themselves down, checking each other for any traces of blood, before tossing the rags and the bottle onto the pile. The broken, bloodied corpses of Jock McGrath and Phil McCauley lay side by side on the floor nearby.

Stepping into the hallway of the derelict house, they took clean clothes from the holdall on the floor and dressed in silence. Connor watched his brother closely. He'd had a smile on his face the whole night. It was unnerving. They both enjoyed their work, and took pleasure in being highly skilled at it, and this had been a very lucrative contract for them. But this was not the kind of contentment Connor could currently see plastered across his brother's countenance.

Soon they were both dressed in clean clothes and shoes. If they were stopped for any reason, no one would be able to tell that they had recently tortured and beaten two men to death.

'Ready,' Connor said, and nodded at his brother, who picked

up the jerrycan of petrol, walked back into the house's former sitting room, and proceeded to pour it over the bodies and the discarded clothes. Connor watched from the hallway as Paul struck a match and tossed it into a puddle of petrol before turning around and walking out of the room.

A few moments later they jumped into the old Range Rover and Connor drove away as the flames started to engulf the house behind them.

Paul fiddled with the radio, trying to change the channel, no doubt looking for Radio City, but the old car had an ancient analogue radio so he settled on Smooth FM and sat back in his seat with a smile.

'You're playing a dangerous fucking game,' Connor said as he turned the car onto the main road.

Paul looked at him. 'What are you on about?'

'You know what I'm fucking on about, Paul. Jake fucking Conlon! Of all the people you could fuck around with, you pick him. Why?'

Paul laughed. 'He's gorgeous, and more importantly he's got a knob like a baby's arm holding an apple.'

'He's also our business partner and he's Jake fucking Conlon.'

'And what?'

Connor shook his head. 'I've never seen you like this, Paul. I've never known you see the same bloke more than twice before. But you're seeing Jake nearly every night.'

'What are you getting at, Con? You've been seeing that Kelly bird for weeks. It's not like I'm standing you up or anything, is it? I'm just having a bit of fun. Leave me the fuck alone.'

Connor sighed. 'That's just it, bro. I don't think it is fun.'

'Oh, trust me, it is,' Paul said with a laugh.

'I mean, I think you're in deeper than that. I don't want to see you get hurt. Do you think Jake Conlon would ever admit to being gay?'

'For fuck's sake, Connor. Chill out. We're having a bit of a laugh. That's all. It won't affect business. It won't affect me and you. It's all good.'

'Whatever you say.' Connor went back to concentrating on the road ahead. Whatever his brother said, Connor was worried about him. He saw how Jake and Paul looked at each other and it was only a matter of time before someone else noticed it too. However much Paul tried to convince himself that this was a bit of fun and no one was going to get hurt, Connor knew that things never quite worked out like that.

Chapter 48

Grace opened the door to Michael's smiling face and her heart sank through her knees and hit the floor. 'What are you doing here?' she asked. She was still trying to figure out a way to extricate herself from their casual arrangement, partly because she was enjoying it so much. But the problem was that Michael seemed to view it as anything but casual.

'I was passing, and I thought I'd stop by.' He leaned in and kissed her. 'I missed you today.'

'I know, sorry about that. Marcus had a hangover from hell and I couldn't leave Belle with him in that state. And I figured he deserves some time to himself, he helps me out so much with her.'

Michael shrugged. 'No problem. These things can't be helped. I know you said you didn't want me staying over, but I can visit, can't I?'

Grace felt the heat creeping up her neck. 'Of course you can.'

'So, can I come in then?'

'What? Yes, come in,' she said as she opened the door wider, knowing that she couldn't think of a reasonable excuse to put him off. 'I was just going to start getting Belle ready for bed though. Why don't you wait in the living room for me?'

Ignoring her request, Michael walked into the kitchen to see

Belle in her high chair, covered in banana. 'Hello there, beautiful girl,' he said as he picked her up, not caring that she wiped her banana-covered hands all over his expensive suit.

Belle gave him a beaming toothy smile in reward.

'She must like you,' Jake said as he walked into the kitchen, all suited and booted and reeking of aftershave. 'Not everyone can get a smile off you, can they, Belle?' He gave her cheek a squeeze.

'Aw, she knows I'm her uncle Michael, don't you, sweetheart?' he said.

'Mum,' said Jake, 'I meant to tell you, before Siobhan stopped speaking to me for no apparent reason, I asked her about that mate of hers who makes them cakes. She said just put the order in a couple of weeks before you need it. She can make any type you like.'

'Cake?' Michael asked. 'What's the special occasion?'

'Come into the living room and I'll get you a drink,' Grace said, trying to change the subject.

'It's for Belle's birthday,' Jake answered before disappearing back upstairs to get whatever it was he'd forgotten.

Michael followed Grace into the living room as she took some glasses from the drinks cabinet. 'So when is her birthday then? It can't be far off now?' he asked.

Shit.

Before Grace could trot out her usual lie, Jake walked in and answered for her. 'November twenty-eighth, a month after mine.'

Grace glared at her son's back. She could bloody murder him sometimes. Why, tonight of all nights, had Michael decided to turn up? The very day after Jake and Siobhan had had a massive bust-up and he'd decided to decamp to Grace's house for a few days. Why hadn't she told him to sod off and go back to his girlfriend and work things out like a grown-up?

'A while off yet, then,' Michael said to baby Belle as he kissed her cheek.

'So what have you been up to today?' Grace asked him, desperately trying to steer the conversation in a new direction as she took a wriggling Belle from his arms.

But it was already too late. She could see the cogs turning in Michael's brain. Belle had been born at the end of November and Ben had died in the middle of January. In Harewood, no one really cared when Belle's birthday was. Nobody knew Ben, so the fact that his daughter was born over ten months after his death hadn't occurred to anyone. And to Jake, who paid little attention to such matters, Grace had pretended Belle was two weeks overdue, rather than a week early. Only Marcus knew the truth.

Michael glared at her and she knew the proverbial penny had dropped.

'Jake, can you take Belle for her bath, please?' she asked him.

'I'm going out in a minute, Mum,' he groaned.

'Please, Jake. Just take her,' Grace said as she handed Belle to him.

Sighing, Jake left the room, chatting to Belle as he did.

'She's mine, isn't she?' Michael growled before the door had even fully closed.

Grace nodded. There was no use denying it any longer. She'd known it would come out and had contemplated telling him herself ever since she'd set eyes on him, but she hadn't been able to find the right time, or the right words. It was stupid to think she could keep her secret once she was back in Liverpool, especially as she'd recklessly got herself involved in a relationship with the very man she was trying to keep the secret from.

'I don't fucking believe you, Grace,' Michael barked as paced up and down the room. 'How could you keep this from me? How could you lie to me? To everyone?'

'I can explain—'

He glared at her. 'She's my fucking child, Grace,' he shouted. 'There is no reasonable explanation for you keeping her from me.'

'I thought it was for the best.'

'The best? Who are you to decide what's for the best?' he snapped as he moved closer to her. His face was now only inches from hers, so close that she could feel the heat from him.

'I'm her mother, that's who,' she snarled back at him.

'And I'm her fucking father. Were you planning on ever telling me? You weren't, were you? Is that why you moved to the other side of the fucking country?'

She shook her head. 'I didn't find out I was pregnant until after I'd left. I swear.'

He shook his head. 'I don't believe you. Did you honestly think this wouldn't come out?'

'Michael,' she said, her tone softer now. 'I did this for you.'

'Don't you fucking dare. You did this for you, and only you.'

'You were a married man. How would your wife have felt about you fathering another woman's child? Do you remember what you said to me before I moved away?'

'Don't,' he growled.

'You said you never wanted to see me again. That you loved Hannah and you had to make it work with her. Do you remember?'

'You know that was just the guilt talking. You know I didn't mean it, Grace. And even if I did, do you think that justifies you not telling me about my own daughter? Do you honestly think I wouldn't want to be there for you when you were carrying my child?'

'Don't you think I felt guilty too? Sleeping with someone else's husband. I couldn't bear to cause any more hurt than I already had. I thought I'd never come back here. I really thought it was for the best.'

Michael stood glaring at her, the anger radiating from him like the heat from a furnace. 'Well, guess what? You don't get to decide what's best for everyone. You are not the centre of the fucking universe, Grace. You had no fucking right to keep her from me. I will never forgive you for this.'

'Where are you going?' she sighed as he brushed past her.

'Out of here before I do something I regret,' he growled.

Then he was gone.

Grace sat on the sofa with her head in her hands. What a bloody mess she'd made of everything. She remembered the night it happened as clearly as yesterday. It had been a week since she'd left hospital after Nathan had almost killed her. At least one member of the Carter family usually turned up at various times of the day to check in on her and make sure she was okay. At first she'd found it infuriating, but had soon come to realise that they did it because they genuinely cared about her. After all, she would have done the same for them. It was usually Patrick or Sean, although Connor and Paul had called in a few times too. She'd only seen Michael briefly while she was still in hospital.

When she opened the door to him that evening, he could barely hide the shock on his face.

'Bloody hell, Grace,' he said. 'You look a right state.'

'Thanks, mate.' She laughed. 'Just what a girl wants to hear.'

He stepped into her house. 'You know what I mean,' he said with a nervous laugh.

As they sat down in her living room, she caught him staring at her cuts and bruises. 'It looks much worse than it is now,' she assured him. 'I feel fine. Honestly.'

'I still can't believe what happened.' He shook his head. 'I'm so sorry, Grace. I should have been here.'

'You weren't here because I asked you not to be. You were protecting your family.'

'But I should have been here, protecting you.'

'No, you shouldn't. Just because I pay you—'

'Not because you pay me, Grace. For fuck's sake,' he snapped.

'Okay. Calm down. What's the matter with you?'

'You! I love you, Grace. That's why I should have been here. Don't you get that? Even after all this time?'

'Michael—' she started.

'Yeah, I know. I'm married.'

Reaching out her hand, she stroked his face with her finger-tips. 'None of this is on you.'

'I'm sorry he hurt you,' he said again as he tucked a loose strand of hair behind her ear. His fingers trailed across the bruising on her neck and over her collarbone. 'This looks painful.'

'I told you I feel fine,' she whispered.

Then he kissed her and she didn't stop him. Instead she began undoing the buttons on his shirt. With Jake at uni and no pub to run, she'd been feeling so alone. And Michael was so warm. So familiar. It felt good to be kissed. To be wrapped in his strong arms.

The following morning he'd told her that he couldn't see her again. He loved his wife and he owed it to her to make their marriage work. She'd watched his face, racked with guilt, as he'd retrieved his clothes from her bedroom floor, and had felt sick with shame and remorse. But despite that, his words had cut her to her core.

Grace had moved to Harewood by the time she found out she was pregnant. She fudged the dates and let everyone believe her child was Ben's. When Belle was born, Grace saw Michael in her immediately. She almost went to see him to tell him he had a beautiful daughter, who had his eyes and looked exactly like him when she frowned. But she didn't. It would have ripped his marriage apart – and neither he nor Hannah deserved that.

So she'd kept up her pretence that Ben was Belle's father and hadn't allowed herself to think about the possibility of ever seeing Michael again.

Michael punched the steering wheel of his brand-new Audi. How could Grace have lied to him like that? Kept his own daughter from him? Did she have no respect for him at all? Shaking his head, he started the engine and put the car into gear. He had to get away from Grace's house before he went back in there and did something stupid.

He had been in love with Grace Sumner from almost the moment he met her. There had been a time when he'd thought they might have had something but she'd shot him down in flames. He later learned it was because she'd been in love with Ben McKinley, her ex-husband's best mate, for years. She'd kept that from him too. How many other secrets did she keep from him? It didn't matter now anyway. He wanted nothing more to do with her. He would fight for contact with Belle. She was his daughter and he would be in her life no matter how much Grace might try to stop him.

As he came to a stop at a traffic light he laid his head back on the headrest and let out a long, slow breath. He had a daughter

– with Grace. That had once been something he'd fantasised about. And now it was real. Belle Sumner – as beautiful as her mother. How could he move on from Grace when they had a child together? They were stuck with each other for ever now. As much as he hated to admit it, something about that gave him hope.

Chapter 49

Jake knocked on the door of Paul's flat and waited for him to answer. When he did, he was dressed in just a pair of jeans and Jake had to remind himself that he was there to give him some disturbing news. News that would no doubt change the nature of their relationship once more.

'You're two fucking hours late, lad,' Paul snapped. 'It must have been some family drama.'

'It was,' Jake sighed as he followed Paul inside and into his living room.

'Well?' Paul asked as he handed Jake a bottle of Bud.

'Haven't you spoken to your dad?'

'No. Why?' Paul frowned.

Jake sat on the leather sofa and took a deep breath. 'So apparently Belle is your dad's kid.'

'What?' Paul almost spat out the lager he'd just taken into his mouth.

'It's true. Your dad just found out tonight.'

'Fuck me! But I thought she was Ben's, or even your dad's?'

'I did too. My mum had us all fooled. She and your dad had a thing before she moved to Harewood.'

'Fuck! My dad must be fucking fuming.'

'Oh, he is.'

'What was your mum thinking?'

Jake shrugged. 'Who knows why she did it, Paul? She says she thought it was for the best and she didn't want to cause problems between your dad and Hannah.'

'I think that ship sailed when they . . .' Paul trailed off and Jake was thankful he hadn't finished the sentence. He'd spent the past two hours with his mum, mostly arguing about why she'd done what she did, and why she'd kept it from him. Jake didn't agree with her decision and he never would, but she was his mum, and he supposed he understood she had her reasons. What he was less happy about was the fact that he'd been screwing his baby sister's half-brother.

'You do realise we now have a sister in common?' Jake said.

Paul's mouth was still open in shock. 'What the fuck does that make us then?'

'I don't know. Step-brothers or something?'

'Nah. Your mum and my dad would have to be married for that.'

'Whatever it is, it feels fucking weird.'

Paul shuddered as he took another swig of his lager. 'I feel violated,' he said, and laughed. Jake knew he was only half joking.

'I wish she'd have fucking told me,' Jake snapped.

'So do I, mate.'

'I suppose this means . . . It just feels too weird now, doesn't it?'

'It certainly doesn't make things any less problematic, like.'

Jake swigged the rest of his lager. He could kill his mum for keeping this little secret from him. He would never have got involved with Paul if he'd known. Then he wouldn't be eaten up by shame and guilt every time he looked in the mirror, and so he wouldn't be sitting having this awkward conversation. Why did everything in his life have to be so fucking complicated?

'Hey, at least we know now and not in ten years when we're married with four adopted kids,' said Paul, winking at him.

Jake smiled, but he felt a tightening in his chest that took him by surprise. He had never contemplated for one second the thought of a future with Paul. He was always too caught up in the immediacy of the snatched moments they shared, or busy dealing with his feelings of guilt and shame. And now it was as though it had been offered to him and taken away in the same breath.

Chapter 50

Peering through the spyhole on her front door, Grace saw that it was Sean Carter ringing the doorbell at nine o'clock on a Sunday morning. She'd been up half the night with Belle, who was getting her back teeth through, and she had only just settled her back down. Grace cursed under her breath. What the hell did Sean want? She wasn't in the mood for an argument. She hadn't heard from any of the Carters since Michael had discovered that Belle was his daughter, two days earlier.

Opening the door, she forced a smile in an effort to avoid any unnecessary confrontation. 'What can I do for you, Sean?'

'Can I come in?'

Grace opened the door wider to let him in and he followed her into her living room. Sitting on the sofa, Grace curled her feet beneath her and waited for Sean to speak.

'Michael told me about Belle,' he said.

Of course he had. Sean was his best mate as well as his brother.

'Where is she?' he asked as he scanned the room.

'She's asleep. She's been awake half the night.'

'Is she okay?' he asked, his voice full of concern.

'Yeah. She's just teething.'

'Oh.'

'Are you going to sit down?' she asked, frustrated at him standing over her – in judgement, no doubt.

He shook his head. 'I'm not staying. I just came to say that we want to see Belle. Michael wants to see her.'

'Of course.' She hadn't kept Belle away from them for any reason other than she hadn't wanted them to know Michael was her father. Now that it was all out in the open, she was happy for Belle to spend time with the Carters. They were her family, after all.

'I was hoping I could take her today? Sue's doing a roast. Michael really wants to see her.'

Grace shook her head. 'I don't think that's a good idea. She's not feeling herself today. And she doesn't really know any of you.'

'Well, whose fault is that?'

'I know it's mine, Sean,' she sighed. 'All I'm saying is she needs to get to know you, and Michael, a little bit first.'

'So how do you suggest we do that? Michael doesn't even want to be in the same room as you, and I can't say I blame him.'

'I know that. I don't expect him to.' She didn't particularly want to see him either. 'Maybe Marcus could bring her?'

'Hmm. That could work.'

'Good. Tell Michael that Marcus will bring her for a few hours tomorrow if that suits him. They can arrange between themselves when he wants to see her next. Marcus knows my schedule. And then as soon as she's used to him, he can see her whenever he wants.'

'And she could stay over at his place? For the weekend?'

Grace's stomach contracted involuntarily. She knew Belle would be safe with her father, but she'd only spent the occasional night away from her before. She nodded anyway. It was only fair that Michael got to see his daughter, especially as she'd kept them apart for so long.

'Good. I'll let him know,' Sean said. 'I'd better get going.'

As Grace stood to show him out, he stared at her, as though there was something on the tip of his tongue, but he couldn't bring himself to say it.

'What is it now?' she asked him, although she had a good idea.

'Why did you do it, Grace? You kept her from all of us.'

'I had my reasons, Sean. As I'm sure Michael has told you.'

'But we're her family.'

She sighed. She really wasn't in the mood for this. 'I had my reasons. I'm not going over them again.'

He shook his head. 'You know what hurts the most though?'

'What?'

'I thought you were our family too.'

Then he turned on his heel and walked out. Grace didn't have the energy to follow him. Instead she sat back on the sofa and listened to the sound of the front door shutting. Closing her eyes, she remembered a time when she'd thought she was their family too. But the reality was, she wasn't. As close as they once were, they weren't blood.

Growing up as an only child, without her mother around, Grace had always dreamed of being part of a big family. She'd fantasised about her dad remarrying and having a whole load of children so that she'd have brothers and sisters to play with. Then she would always have someone to lean on – someone to have her back. Then, when she'd met Nathan, she'd dreamed of a house full of children of her own. But he'd ruined that dream like he ruined everything else.

She'd come to accept that it would always just be her, Jake and Belle. Her two beautiful children were a blessing. And they were enough. They had to be.

Chapter 51

Grace groaned inwardly as Connor and Paul Carter walked into her office and closed the door behind them.

'Can we talk, boss?' Connor asked.

Grace sighed. 'Of course, boys. What can I do for you?' Although she already knew the answer. She'd been berated by half of the Carter family so far, including their grandfather, Patrick. The only one of them who had expressed a modicum of understanding was Sean's daughter, Steph, who could appreciate the complex nature of Grace's relationship with her uncle.

The twins pulled up a pair of chairs and sat down opposite her. Connor smiled at her but Paul stared at his feet and shifted in his seat.

'So, I hear we've got a baby sister then?' Connor asked.

'Yes. Good news certainly travels fast, doesn't it?'

'I wish you'd fucking told us,' Paul growled and Connor shot him a menacing look.

'I wish I'd told you too. I really wish I'd told your dad. But I didn't, and here we are.'

'We understand, Grace. My dad is fucking wounded, and we have to take his side – you know how it is. But we get why you did it. Don't we, Paul?'

'Yeah,' he sighed.

'Do you?' Grace raised her eyebrows. 'Well, thanks for that. But I wouldn't admit that outside this room.' She smiled at them.

'Of course we do,' said Paul.

'My dad was married to Hannah,' Connor said. 'She was desperate for kids but he didn't want any. Imagine if you'd turned up pregnant. It would have caused world war fucking three.'

Grace nodded, but the information about Hannah wanting children was new to her. Michael had never mentioned not wanting more kids. He wanted to be part of Belle's life, she knew that for sure. But she supposed it was different once a child was actually born. Live flesh and blood that was a part of you was entirely different from the mere possibility of a child.

'So you're still speaking to me then?' Grace asked.

The twins nodded. 'You've always looked out for us, Grace,' Connor said. 'There was a time you could have fed us to the dogs, but you didn't. Even though we caused you a tonne of shit, you looked after us. We'll never forget that.'

'No, we won't,' Paul agreed.

'Thanks, boys. It means a lot.'

'Any time, boss,' they said in unison.

'Now, where is that wayward son of yours?' Paul asked.

'God knows. I'm surprised he's not with either of you. You all seem to be joined at the hip these days.'

'Well, we're family now, aren't we?' Connor said and winked. Grace saw Paul frown and wondered what that was about. Probably still stinging from not knowing about Belle.

'Well, just take care of yourselves, boys. All of you.' Grace suspected that the three of them had formed an unholy alliance. She wasn't sure yet if that was a good or bad thing. But God help anyone who stood in their way.

'We will,' the boys chimed. 'Later, boss.'

'Later.' Grace smiled as she watched them walk out of her office.

Chapter 52

Connor Carter went behind the bar of The Blue Rooms and helped himself to a large measure of Stolichnaya vodka. Sitting on one of the barstools, he took a gulp before resting his head on the bar.

'We're heading off now, boss,' Billy Murphy, their head doorman, said. 'You coming?'

Connor shook his head. 'I'll hang around for a bit yet. Thanks, lads. Leave me the keys and I'll lock up.'

Billy placed his set of keys on the counter. 'I'll just check the back and make sure there's no one left.' He came out from behind the bar. 'Siobhan's still here, boss. There's a problem with the takings she's sorting out. Want us to hang around?'

Connor shook his head. 'I'll stay until she's finished.'

'Night then, boss,' Billy said before he and the rest of the bouncers filed out of the side door.

Connor poured himself another drink and waited for Siobhan to finish. He wondered if she had her car or whether she'd need a lift home. Twenty minutes later, there was no sign of her so he walked out into the back office to find her head bent over a book.

'Still not able to balance those books?' he asked.

She looked up at him and smiled. 'Hiya, Connor. Sorry to

keep you waiting. But no. There's a hundred quid missing and I can't find it.'

'Leave it until tomorrow, Siobhan,' he said. 'It's late. You should be getting home. We'll find it tomorrow, and if we don't, we'll find the little fucker who took it.'

She sighed. 'I suppose so.'

'Do you need a lift?'

'Isn't Jake with you?'

Connor shook his head and felt guilty for the lie he was about to tell. 'He's still on a job,' he said.

Siobhan looked so upset by that, he almost told her the truth. 'I can take you home,' he offered.

'Well, it looks like I don't have much choice, doesn't it?'

Connor hung his head. He could kill Jake and his brother for this. He'd had the day from hell and had wanted to come to the club and have a long, quiet drink alone, and instead he was having to deal with Siobhan's upset too.

'I'm sorry, Connor,' she said. 'It's just been a long day, and I was hoping that my boyfriend would be here to pick me up.'

'Don't tell me about long days.'

'You too, eh?'

He nodded. 'Fancy a quick drink?'

Siobhan looked at him for a few seconds before agreeing. 'Yeah, why not.'

Half an hour later, Connor and Siobhan were sitting at one of the booths in the club, with a now almost empty bottle of Stolichnaya on the table in front of them.

'You do realise we'll have to get a cab home now?' Siobhan said.

Connor downed the rest of his glass and nodded.

'God, I haven't been this drunk since I was eighteen.' She giggled.

'A drunken eighteen-year-old you. I'd like to have seen that.' Connor smiled at her and she closed her eyes and rested her head on his shoulder. He could smell the expensive perfume she used and it made his groin twitch in a way he knew it shouldn't when he was with the girlfriend of one of his best mates.

'How did you know it was me and not Paul earlier?' Connor asked her, trying to restart the conversation and make her sit up and take her head off his shoulder. 'How are you always able to tell us apart? Not many people can.'

She sat up and looked at him. 'You're much more handsome than Paul,' she said with a grin.

'Fuck off. We're identical.'

'Almost,' she said. 'But you have a nicer smile. Paul is always so bloody cocky,' she snorted.

'Easy. That's my brother you're talking about.'

'Hmmm.' She picked up her glass and finished the remnants of her vodka before wiping her mouth with the back of her hand.

Connor had never seen her looking so dishevelled. She was usually so polished and pristine. It made her look sexier, or perhaps it was the vodka playing tricks with his addled brain. Whatever it was, he was starting to feel things for Siobhan he had no right to.

'Come on, let's get you home,' he said.

Standing up, he pulled Siobhan to her feet.

She threw her arms around him. 'My knight in shining armour,' she said.

Then she kissed him, pushing her tongue into his mouth. He could taste the vodka they'd been drinking. He should have pushed her away, but the alcohol was clouding his judgement.

Besides, kissing Siobhan felt too good and he needed to feel good after the day he'd had. Just another moment, then he'd stop, he told himself. But instead he found them both backing up to the table and before he knew it his hands were untying the belt of Siobhan's wrap dress and she was sitting on the table begging him to fuck her.

Siobhan paid the driver and stumbled out of the taxi. She'd wanted to ask Connor to come home with her but there was every possibility Jake was already there. She walked through the doors to her building and along the corridor to the lift and smiled to herself as she relived the past couple of hours. She'd always been a good girl. She was never the one to go off the rails or take too many chances. She'd always played it safe. Even with Jake – despite who he was, he was a safe choice for her. He was a good provider. They looked good together. She wondered now what she'd been missing out on all her life. Connor Carter was never someone she'd looked twice at. He had a certain charm, but he was a bruiser and she preferred her men with more classic looks.

She'd been so upset when Connor had told her Jake was still on a job. It had taken all of her strength not to laugh out loud and tell him she knew what he really meant was Jake was on *the* job.

Screwing Connor had seemed like a good idea at the time. It was the perfect revenge and a bit of fun. Shouldn't she be allowed a little fun for once?

But what she hadn't counted on was having the best sex of her life. Connor had done things to her that Jake would have never dreamed of. Jake had never given her an orgasm in their whole two years together, and Connor had just given her three in an hour. She felt a flush creeping over her chest and a tightening in her lower abdomen just thinking about it.

Siobhan didn't know how she would look him in the eye next time she saw him at the club, but she knew one thing for sure, Jake could never find out about their little tryst. If he did, there was every possibility he would kill them both.

Chapter 53

Connor ordered two large fried breakfasts from Marie and took a seat opposite Paul at one of the vinyl-topped tables. Marie's café on the Dock Road was a hidden gem. She did the best fried breakfasts for miles and the Carter twins always went there when one or both of them had a hangover from hell.

Paul smiled at his brother as he sat down. 'You look rough, lad. Where did you get to last night?'

Connor shook his head. 'Don't talk so loud, my fucking head is banging.'

Paul laughed as Marie brought over two mugs of tea. 'There you go boys,' she said with a smile. 'Your brekkies won't be long.'

Paul winked at her. 'Thanks, love.'

'So?' Paul asked again. 'Where did you go to get into this state?'

'Only The Blue Rooms,' he answered. 'I just had one too many vodkas.'

'Drinking on your own, bro? You should have phoned me.'

'I assumed you'd be tied up elsewhere,' Connor said sarcastically. 'Besides, I wasn't on my own. Siobhan was there. She had a drink with me.'

'Oh, right.'

Connor hated lying to his brother. They had never kept a secret from each other in their lives, and he wasn't about to start

now. Besides, they knew each other better than anyone. Sometimes
it seemed like they could read each other's mind.

'Anything else happen, bro?' Paul frowned at him.

Connor sighed. 'Yeah. Me and Siobhan . . .'

'For fuck's sake, Con,' Paul said through gritted teeth. 'Are
you fucking insane? That's Jake's missus.'

'Really, Paul? Thanks for clarifying that for me.'

'Jesus Christ.' Paul shook his head. 'What the fuck are you
going to do about it?'

'What do you mean? I'm not going to do anything about it.
It was a one-time thing. A mistake. It won't happen again.'

'Are you sure she feels the same way?'

'Of course she does,' he replied, although he didn't know for
sure. They hadn't really talked afterwards. It had all become very
awkward, very quickly.

Marie brought over their cooked breakfasts and Connor
muttered his thanks before tucking in.

'I don't believe you, Con,' Paul said quietly before spooning
a forkful of beans into his mouth. 'You've put me in a really
fucking awkward position, screwing Jake's missus,' he finished,
once he'd swallowed his food.

'What?' Connor said as his head snapped up. 'Are you fucking
shitting me, Paul?'

Paul glared at him. 'What do you mean?'

'I mean that you two dickheads started this,' he seethed. 'If
you weren't fucking Jake every chance you got, Siobhan
wouldn't have been sat in the club on her own, waiting for
her fucking prince to come home. What you two are doing is
much fucking worse.'

'Worse? Because we're queers? Is that it?'

'Oh, don't be so fucking soft. You know I don't give a shit if you're gay, bi or into fucking horses. But you two are the ones having a full-blown fucking love affair when that poor girl is sitting at home without a clue who her boyfriend really is.'

Paul sat back in his chair. 'Jesus, Con. We've got ourselves into a right fucked-up situation here, haven't we?'

'Jake can never find out, Paul,' he warned.

'You honestly think I'd tell him? You're my brother.'

'I know. I'm sorry. It's just such a fucking mess.'

'Well, we never did like a quiet life, did we?' Paul laughed and Connor laughed with him.

'I need a fucking drink,' Connor said.

'Marie? Two shots of your finest whisky, please?' Paul shouted.

'Strongest thing I've got is coffee, lads,' she shouted back. 'Will that do you?'

'Ah, go on then, you temptress,' he replied.

Paul turned to his brother and gave him a half smile. 'It will be okay in the end, bro,' he said.

Connor laughed and shook his head. 'Remember what Grace always used to say?'

Paul nodded. 'If it's not okay, it's not the end.'

Chapter 54

Siobhan closed the safe in Jake's office.

'I still can't find it, Jake,' she said to him. 'I've gone over the books five times now.'

'It's a hundred quid, babe. Don't worry about it.' He smiled at her and pulled her to sit on his lap. He brushed her long red hair behind her ears and she remembered how loved he used to make her feel. 'Unless you think someone's nicked it?' He raised an eyebrow at her.

'I don't know. Maybe?'

'I'll get one of the lads to check the CCTV.'

Siobhan almost vomited her recently eaten lunch onto his suit. 'No. Don't be silly.' She shook her head. 'I'm sure it's just my adding up. This is all new to me still. I'll go over it again later.'

'If you're sure, babe,' he said before kissing her. 'I feel like I've hardly seen you lately. I'm sorry I've been so busy. Let me take you out tonight?'

It had been so long since they'd been out together. 'Okay. Where?'

'Wherever you like.'

'Can we try that new cocktail bar that's opened on top of the Shankly Hotel?'

'If that's what you want. I love you,' he whispered before kissing her again.

'I love you too, Jake,' she replied honestly. God help her, but she did.

'Are we interrupting something?' Connor Carter said as he walked into the office, Paul behind him. Siobhan jumped off Jake's lap. 'No,' she protested.

'Almost, lads,' Jake said with a laugh.

Siobhan felt her cheeks flush at the sight of Connor, but thankfully Jake appeared to assume she was embarrassed by the twins walking in on them kissing.

'Thanks for getting Siobhan home safe last night, Connor,' said Jake. 'I really appreciate it.'

'Not a problem, mate,' Connor replied.

'Jake, I need to show you some stuff in the van,' Paul said. 'Make sure it's what we agreed on?'

Jake nodded. 'Come on then.'

After Jake and Paul had left the office, Siobhan let out a long breath she felt she'd been holding for minutes.

'Are you okay?' Connor asked her.

'Fine. But about last night—'

'I know,' Connor interrupted her. 'It won't happen again.'

'I wasn't going to say that,' she said, a little hurt that he'd made that decision for both of them.

'Oh, sorry.'

'I was going to remind you about the CCTV. Jesus, Connor, will anyone have seen us?'

He shook his head. 'It only stores the previous forty-eight hours, and nobody would watch it unless there was a reason to.'

'But still . . .'

'Don't worry. I'll take care of it,' he assured her.

Caz Finlay

'Thanks. I've been so worried about seeing you today.'

'I know. We didn't really get a chance to talk. I'm sorry if I took advantage . . .'

'You really didn't.'

'Good. I'm glad you're okay. I'll go and sort that CCTV out. If you need anything else, let me know.'

'I will. Thanks.'

He nodded before leaving the office. Siobhan sat down on Jake's chair and sighed. At least that was over with. He'd sort the CCTV and Jake would never be any the wiser. It seemed they would get away with it. Now, if only she could stop replaying last night over and over in her head, they could all move on.

Chapter 55

Siobhan smoothed the fabric of her dress over her hips and admired her reflection in the full-length mirror. The dress was a new one she'd bought in Cricket a few weeks earlier, which had cost more than two months' mortgage, and she'd been waiting for the chance to show it off. The green was the perfect colour for her complexion. It showed just the right amount of cleavage to be sexy but still classy. The fabric clung to her toned, size-ten figure. It was a pity it was wasted on Jake, she thought to herself.

She had been broken-hearted that morning she'd gone to find him at Paul Carter's flat and seen the two of them kissing. It had taken her days to even look at him again. She'd pretended she had a stomach bug and had avoided him, wondering what to do next. She had taken his phone and his iPad and scoured it for evidence of any other affairs.

She found nothing.

She spent days driving herself crazy. How many men had he done this with? Did he use protection? Surely he would never put her health at risk? She wondered about every time she and Jake had made love. Had he been pretending it was someone else? He'd never been incredibly passionate – he was a quickie-with-the-lights-off kind of man – but she'd thought that was just who he was. Now she knew the real reason.

After a few days of crying and soul-searching, Siobhan put on her big girl pants and decided that Jake and their life together were worth making sacrifices for. She would make sure that she held onto them both for as long as she could. One day, when they were married and had children, perhaps she would tell him that she knew the truth and give him her blessing to pursue a relationship with another man. As long as he was discreet, and as long as he gave her the same freedom. She almost convinced herself that it wasn't as bad as cheating on her with a woman. She was the only woman Jake Conlon loved – she was sure of that, and for now that was enough.

'You ready, Babe?' Jake shouted from the sitting room.

'Coming,' she replied as she picked up her clutch bag.

'You look gorgeous.' Jake smiled at her as she walked towards him. The look in his eye almost had her believing that he fancied her. Perhaps he did? Perhaps he liked both, she thought. He was always attentive to her when they were together. Maybe he was just one of those men who liked to have his cake and eat it?

'You look pretty good yourself,' she said, smiling back. He was dressed in a suit, his expensive shirt open at the collar. He was clean-shaven, which was how she liked him best, although he often sported stubble. His bright blue eyes twinkled as she reached him and kissed him on the lips.

'Let's go then,' he said to her. 'The cab's downstairs.'

Siobhan sat at the table looking out over the Liverpool skyline while she waited for Jake to come back from the bar. They'd had a lovely evening, but she sensed Jake was becoming fed up and wanted to get home. He'd suggested they leave after the next drink, but Siobhan wasn't sure she was ready for the night to end so soon. Maybe she'd propose walking home so they could enjoy a nice stroll through the Albert Dock. She understood why Jake didn't really like drinking in the town centre. He had a club of his own, and he was always wary of who he might bump into. Almost everyone who recognised him wanted to be his best mate.

Siobhan could see the men at the table next to her giving her the once over and was close enough to hear one of them making a lewd comment about 'giving her one'. Just a few months earlier, she would have shot them a withering look and told them to piss off, but tonight it made her feel good about herself. At least someone appreciated the effort she'd made to look good.

Jake returned with her cocktail and a brandy for himself and sat down. The men at the next table continued to get louder and louder.

'Do you mind, lads, I'm trying to have a quiet drink with my girlfriend,' Jake snapped at them.

'All right, sorry, mate,' one of them apologised, while the other two continued laughing.

'If she was my girlfriend, I'd be doing more than having a quiet drink with her,' one of them slurred.

'What?' Jake growled at him.

'Sorry, mate. He's had too much to drink,' said his friend.

'Please don't, Jake,' Siobhan said as she placed her hand on his arm.

Jake turned in his seat to face her. She hated it when he got into fights and he knew it. 'Okay, babe. We'll go after this one, eh?'

She nodded, relieved that he was letting the idiot's comment go.

The three men started arguing amongst themselves then. 'Don't fucking tell me to be quiet,' one of them shouted. 'He doesn't own the fucking place, does he? Look at him in his fucking fancy suit, drinking his fancy cocktails. Fucking tosser.'

Jake stood up so quickly his chair fell over. One of the bouncers came running over to him. 'Is everything okay, Mr Conlon?' he asked. 'Do you want me to throw this lot out?'

'No, don't worry, John. I'll handle it. We're going. Come on.' He held his hand out to Siobhan.

Siobhan stood up and took his hand and he marched the pair of them to the lift. He barely spoke to her on the way to the ground floor.

'Take no notice of those idiots, Jake,' she soothed. 'They're a gang of knobheads.'

Jake smiled at her. 'Are you okay?'

'Of course, I'm fine.'

'Good,' he said as he steered her towards a black taxi. Opening the door for her, he helped her inside before handing her a £20 note. 'I'll be home in an hour, babe.'

'Jake? Please come home with me,' she pleaded.

'I'll be there soon, I promise,' he said as he cupped her chin in his hand and gave her a kiss. Then he closed the cab door and walked back into the hotel.

Siobhan told the driver her address and sat back in the seat with a long sigh.

Jake stepped out of the lift and back into the rooftop bar. The three pricks who had been stupid enough to insult him were still sitting at their table. John, the head doorman, nodded to him as he walked past. The cold and the threat of imminent rain had forced most of the customers inside and it didn't take long for the bouncers to usher the few remaining stragglers into the warmth of the bar.

Jake walked over to the table and smiled. 'Remember me, lads?'

The three of them stared at him as though he had two heads, until the mouthy one who'd called him a tosser a few minutes earlier rose from his seat and squared up to him.

'Do you have a problem, mate?' he snarled in Jake's face.

Jake felt the rage inside him boiling over. He butted him, splitting his nose open and causing him to fall to the floor, howling in pain. Jake was kicking him in the stomach when one of the others jumped on his back. He shook him off easily and threw him to the floor with his mate. Picking up a chair, he used it to hit him repeatedly while the third man backed away and made a run for the door, where he was refused entry by the bouncers. When the second man had stopped moving, Jake returned to the first and grabbed him by his shirt collar. 'Fucking tosser, am I?' he spat in his face. 'You're lucky I don't throw you off this fucking roof, you piece of shit,' he snapped before punching him full in the face.

Feeling some of the anger ebbing away and satisfied that he had done as much as he could in full view of a crowd of people, he stood up and straightened his clothes.

'You,' he shouted at the third man, pointing directly at him. 'If I ever see any of you again, I will shoot the fucking lot of you.' He made his way back to the lift.

Outside, he saw Michael Carter's car waiting for him. John, the head doorman, worked for the Carters' security firm and must have alerted his boss to the situation in the bar.

'You all right, son?' Michael asked him as he handed him a towel.

Jake nodded and wiped the blood from his hands. 'Thanks, mate.'

'Where am I taking you then?' Michael asked.

He thought about going to Paul's; it was where he wanted to be. But he knew Siobhan would be worried about him. More importantly, Michael might wonder why he was choosing to visit one of the twins at this hour of the night instead of going home to his girlfriend. Jake didn't think he had the energy to try and come up with a convincing lie.

'Home,' Jake sighed.

'What happened up there? John said you completely lost it on a couple of dickheads who'd had too much to drink.'

'They were taking the piss, Michael. In front of Siobhan too. I can't have that.'

'I get that. There's a time and place, though, Jake. How many people saw you tonight?'

Jake shook his head again. 'I don't know. But no one will say anything. No one really saw anything. They were all inside.'

'Well, I'll make sure the CCTV disappears too,' Michael assured him.

'Thanks,' Jake said.

'Is there something else going on with you?' Michael asked him, his voice full of concern.

'No, why?'

'You've just been a bit angrier than usual lately, that's all.'

'Nah. I'm the same angry I always am.' Jake smiled. 'I'm good. Honest.'

'Good.'

As Jake let himself into their flat, Siobhan ran over to him, checking him for any injuries.

'Jake. Thank God you're okay,' she gasped. 'What did you do?'

'I just gave them a warning, that's all, babe,' he said. 'It's all good.'

'I was really worried about you,' she said.

'I know. I'm sorry. But I'm fine. Promise,' he lied. He was anything but fine. His once perfect world was falling apart around his ears and there wasn't a fucking thing he could do about it.

'It's late. Come to bed.'

He took her hand and followed her to their bedroom, wishing that he was somewhere else entirely and hating himself for it.

Chapter 56

Grace sat on the giant wooden rocking chair with Belle in her lap. They were reading Belle's favourite story, *Each Peach Pear Plum*. Belle gurgled and Grace smiled at her daughter as she brushed her soft curls from her face. Grace's stomach contracted as she thought about being away from her. Michael had looked after Belle on his own almost every other afternoon for a few weeks and she'd been fine. In fact, she seemed to love her daddy, and she always gave him her biggest, toothiest smile whenever she saw him.

Grace had finally agreed to an overnight stay, but now she was regretting it. What would she do without Belle's beautiful little face, her adorable laugh, her constant gurgles and squeals of delight, for over twenty-four hours? She was contemplating telling Michael she'd changed her mind, but her guilt wouldn't allow her. She had kept them both apart for long enough. It hadn't been fair on either of them and now Grace owed it to them both to allow them some time together.

The sound of the doorbell heralded the end of Grace's seventh re-reading of the story.

'Here's Daddy.'

'Dada.' Belle smiled.

* * *

Michael strapped Belle into her car seat as Grace hovered behind him, watching intently.

'I do know what I'm doing, Grace.'

'Okay. It's just they can be a bit tricky,' she said.

'I'm sure it's not beyond my capabilities. Is her bag ready?'

'Yes. Everything's in there. Don't forget to give her the blue bunny for bed. It's her favourite.'

'I know,' he sighed. 'You told me.'

'Oh,' was all she could say. She'd spent the occasional night away from Belle before, when she'd stayed with this man who could now barely stand to look at her, but that was only when her daughter was being looked after by Marcus. Marcus, whom had known Belle since the day she was born. Sending her off with Michael for the night felt so unnatural. Especially since the twins had told her about him not wanting more kids.

'Are you sure you'll be okay with her on your own?' she asked.

He finished fastening Belle's straps and looked at Grace. 'Are you really fucking asking me that?'

'It's just she's never stayed overnight before. And you're not used to babies. Your kids are grown men.'

'I have nieces,' he reminded her.

'I know. But babies aren't exactly your thing, are they?'

'What's that supposed to mean?' he frowned at her.

'The twins told me about you and Hannah.'

His frown turned to a scowl.

'That she wanted kids and you didn't. Is that why you split up?'

'That's none of your fucking business anymore, is it?'

'No. But don't you see that me not telling you might have been for the best? Can you at least see where I was coming from?

'No, I fucking can't,' he growled. 'Don't you dare use that as an excuse for what you did.'

'I'm not. I'm just pointing out that you didn't even want more kids.'

He picked up Belle's bag and the car seat and brushed past her. 'I didn't want kids with Hannah,' he said brusquely. Then he walked out of the door. 'I'll have her back tomorrow dinner-time,' he shouted as he left.

Michael smiled as his sons came tumbling through his front door, arguing over who was the victor of the fight they'd just had on the front lawn, just like when they were kids. The boys had moved out two years earlier. They'd lived together for a year, before realising they needed their own space and buying separate flats in the same apartment building on Liverpool's waterfront. Michael missed them living at home. They'd moved in with him when they were fourteen, by mutual agreement with their mother, Cheryl. Michael hadn't known who was more relieved at the time, Cheryl or the boys.

Michael carried a gurgling Belle on his hip as he walked down the hallway. 'Pack it in, you two,' he said. 'Dinner's ready.'

'All right, Dad,' they said in unison.

'Hiya, Belle,' Connor said as he took his sister from his dad's arms. She squealed at him as he twirled her high up into the air.

'What's up with you, face-ache?' Michael asked Paul.

'Nothing,' Paul said, frowning as he picked up an apple from the fruit bowl and took a large bite.

Michael watched his son intently. Something was wrong. Paul had always been the quieter twin. He largely kept his thoughts and feelings to himself, but Michael had always been able to tell when he had something on his mind. And today he was sure there was something bothering him. In fact, he'd seemed distracted for a while.

'Seriously, what's up, son?' he asked as he took a seat at the kitchen table opposite him.

'Nothing you can help with, Dad.'

'Try me.'

Paul shook his head. 'It's nothing. I'm fine. Honest.'

'Well, you know I'm always here if you need anything. Anything at all.'

'Yeah, I know.' Paul gave a weak smile. 'Thanks.'

Chapter 57

Michael parked his car on the road outside Grace's house. Taking Belle out of her car seat he chatted to her as he rounded the large gate post and stepped onto Grace's driveway. Looking up, he saw her hugging someone. She was smiling as she kissed him on the cheek. Michael quickly appraised him. Mid-thirties. Well-dressed. Good-looking, he supposed, if you were into that pretty-boy look anyway.

Michael realised he was grinding his teeth as the unknown man walked past him.

'Morning, mate,' he said with a grin.

Michael glared at him. It was 8am. This fucker had quite obviously spent the night and, judging by the huge grin on his face, had been laid too. Jesus. It was the first time he'd had Belle overnight and Grace was busy getting her rocks off. Not that it was any of his business anymore. But despite that, it still pissed him off so much he felt like running after Pretty Boy and punching him in the face.

'Belle,' Grace squealed from the doorstep. Then she ran into the path and took her from Michael's arms.

'How was she?' she asked.

'Great. I'll just get her bags,' Michael snapped.

'Okay.' Grace frowned at him.

* * *

Belle was in her highchair and Grace was making her some porridge when Michael walked into the kitchen.

'She's had her breakfast.'

'Okay, but she was asking for podge.'

'I'll be going then,' he snarled.

'Hang on. Can you at least tell me how she's been? Did she need any Calpol for her teeth? Did she sleep okay? I know you can't bear to be in a room with me, Michael, but you can't completely ignore me.'

'I told you she was great. No, she didn't need any Calpol, and as for sleep I'll bet she had a whole lot more than you.'

Grace frowned at him. 'What the hell are you on about? How do you know how much sleep I've had?'

'Oh, fuck off, Grace,' he snapped. 'He walked right fucking past us.'

She stared at him like he had three heads. 'Who? James?'

'I don't know his fucking name.'

He saw the colour rise from her chest, up her neck and across her cheeks, and realised he was about to feel the legendary wrath of Grace Sumner. 'Not that it is any of your fucking business,' she said quietly as she walked towards him, 'but James is Marcus's boyfriend. They both stayed last night because they came round for a drink and had a bit too much.'

Michael felt the tension slip from his shoulders. He should have known. Pretty Boy wasn't Grace's type at all. And she would never have a one-night stand, let alone rub it in his face if she did. She was many things, but she didn't play those sorts of games.

'Sorry, I thought . . .' he mumbled.

'I know what you thought,' she hissed. 'And like I said, it's none of your business. So, you don't want me, but I can't be with anyone else either. Is that right? I feel like I'm married to Nathan again.'

Michael walked towards her. He was nothing like Nathan. This woman drove him fucking crazy. In a few strides he was standing right in front of her. She squared up to him, glaring at him, daring him to do something.

'God help me, Grace, I wish I didn't want you,' he growled. She blinked at him in surprise and before he could think about the consequences he pulled her to him and kissed her. She felt so good he wondered if he would ever be able to stop.

Grace made the decision for him when she pulled away. 'We shouldn't do this,' she breathed. 'Not here.'

'We shouldn't do this at all.'

Michael bent to kiss his daughter's cheek before walking out of Grace's kitchen.

Why did he let her get to him so much? The sooner she moved back to Harewood, the better for everyone.

Chapter 58

Libby handed Grace a cup of hot coffee as she took a seat beside her in the booth. Grace closed her laptop and turned to give Libby her full attention.

'How's things? Has Maria forgiven you for staying out all night yet?' Grace asked.

Libby shook her head, her blonde ponytail swishing across her shoulders. 'No chance; she's going to keep making me pay for that until at least after Valentine's Day.'

Laughing, Grace took a sip of her coffee.

'Oh God, here she comes,' Libby snorted, inclining her head to indicate Ali, one of the club's barmaids. Ali wasn't exactly a favourite among her colleagues, but she was a hit with the punters – especially the male ones. It wasn't like Libby to comment on such matters though, and Grace wondered what had prompted her sudden dislike of the girl.

'What's she done now then?' Grace asked.

'She's always been a haughty bitch, but since she started screwing the boss she's become bloody unbearable.'

'Jake?' Grace snapped. Surely not? Jake wouldn't cheat on Siobhan, certainly not right under her nose.

'No, sorry. Not our boss. I meant the lads' boss, Michael.'

Grace felt the skin on her face flush instantly. Michael? How could he?

'I thought you knew. You and him aren't still . . . are you?'

'No. No, of course not,' Grace said, shaking her head. Libby, along with the rest of the staff, now knew that Michael was Belle's father. It annoyed her that so many people knew about her business, and the rumour mill had been in overdrive until she, Jake and Michael had put a stop to it. But Libby was one of the few people whom Grace had told the truth. She trusted her and Libby had yet to prove her wrong. She had kept her own counsel even when her colleagues had been desperate for any salacious gossip.

Picking up her coffee, Grace asked Libby about her upcoming trip to Spain to meet Maria's parents. Anything to change the subject. Libby chattered away, but Grace was only half listening. All she could think about was Michael – and Ali. Ali with her long legs and her beautiful smile. What did she expect? That Michael would pine away without her? Of course not. But she at least expected that he wouldn't start screwing one of their barmaids.

Libby's break finished and she headed back to the bar. The club started to get busy so Grace took her paperwork to her office. Hearing giggling as she opened the door, she saw Ali and Michael standing by the desk, his hands on her tiny waist.

'I was just leaving, Grace,' Ali purred as she brushed past Grace and out of the door.

'Sorry. I didn't mean to interrupt,' Grace said to Michael after Ali had left.

'You didn't,' he said, his tone clipped.

'That's not what I've heard,' she sniped.

He laughed. 'Well, I certainly wouldn't be fucking her in our office, would I?'

'Really?' Grace raised an eyebrow at him.

He walked towards her until his body was barely an inch from hers. She could feel the heat radiating from him. Hear his breathing. Smell his aftershave. He was as close to her as humanly possible without touching her, invading every inch of her personal space. She could understand why he was so terrifying to people, but she'd never felt threatened by him in her life. He leaned in close, his lips grazing her skin as he whispered in her ear. 'For you, I made an exception.'

'Well, if you're planning on bringing her to Belle's birthday party, let me know and I'll set another place at the kids' table,' she said breezily. She would never let him know that he got to her.

'Will do,' he said, and smiled before walking out of the office.

Grace sat on the chair, her heart pounding in her chest. Was every encounter with him going to be like that now? She hoped not. She couldn't take much more of the tension.

Chapter 59

Grace was manhandling a tray of hot sausage rolls out of the oven when she heard the doorbell ring. She groaned. Everyone else she'd invited was here so it had to be Michael. She hoped he hadn't brought Ali with him. Grace could do without watching the pair of them fawning all over each other all afternoon. She'd never been a jealous woman, but something about Ali and Michael together brought out the green-eyed monster in her.

'I'll get it, Mum,' she heard Jake calling from the hallway and she shouted her thanks to him. She cursed herself for not making more effort with her appearance, but she'd been tending to visitors all day. Now that Belle's parentage was no longer a secret, every man and his dog wanted to wish her happy birthday and arrange playdates with their children. Placing the tray of food onto the kitchen worktop, she smoothed her hair with her hands and hoped she looked at least halfway presentable as she made her way out into the hallway to greet her newest guest.

Grace was relieved to see Michael had come alone. Well, apart from the five-foot stuffed unicorn he'd brought with him.

'Grace,' he said curtly.

'Everyone's in the back room,' she said. 'We've all been waiting for you.'

'Well, I got a bit caught up,' he said defensively.

'Have to drop your girlfriend off at school?' Grace sniped.

'Oh, fuck off, Grace,' he snapped as he walked past her to the back room.

'Bloody hell, Mum. What was that about?' Jake asked, having watched the exchange. 'I thought you two were trying to be adults about this. You know, for Belle?'

'Oh, don't worry. It's nothing.' Grace sighed. 'He just brings out the worst in me.'

'Don't let him get to you,' said Jake as he put a reassuring arm around her shoulders. 'Come on, let's get back in there.'

It was early evening when Belle finally fell asleep, having crashed from a massive sugar overdose, and her party guests started to leave. Finally, there was only Jake, Siobhan and the Carters left.

'Thanks so much for coming,' Grace said. 'It means so much to me and Belle.'

'Well, we wouldn't have missed it, would we?' Michael said irritably.

'Come on, son. Now's not the time,' Patrick said quietly in his ear as he put a protective arm around his shoulder.

'If you have something to say, Michael, then say it,' Grace snapped, having had enough of him glaring at her and skulking around whenever she was near him.

About to put on his jacket, he threw it onto the sofa in anger. 'Say it! If I say my piece, Grace, then—'

'Then what?' she asked as everyone else in the room froze. No doubt trying to fade into the background while the two of them had a massive row – the kind that had been building for weeks.

'Never mind.'

'Just fucking say it so we can all move on, will you?'

'Move on?' He glared at her. 'Just like that? Pretend you didn't lie to me about my own fucking daughter. That you didn't keep her from me for ten whole months of her life. I never got to see her being born. I never got to hold her when she would have fitted right here.' He held out his forearm and she could see tears pricking his eyes. 'I never got to do any of that because you're . . .'

'I'm what?'

'You're a selfish fucking bitch,' he spat. 'You think of no one but yourself. I'm sorry I ever fucking met you, Grace Sumner. You're no better than that cunt of an ex-husband of yours.' There was a sharp intake of breath from around the room.

Grace sat on her sofa, feeling like he'd punched her in the stomach.

'I think you'd better leave,' Jake snarled at Michael.

'Enough now, son. Let's go,' Patrick said as he guided Michael towards the door.

Grace watched as the Carter family filed out of her sitting room. 'I'm sorry,' Steph mouthed and Sophia gave her a sympathetic glance as she ushered her younger daughters out.

'Cheeky fucker,' Jake snapped after they had left. 'Who does he think he is speaking to you like that? As of tomorrow, I want him out of the club. We can get another firm in.'

'No.' Grace shook her head. 'He was right. About me keeping Belle from him at least. And he's good for the club. You can't throw that away because of his drama with me. This is between me and Michael. Nobody else.'

Jake paced up and down the room and Grace watched him. There was no doubt in her mind that he knew she was right, but he was torn between his loyalty to her and knowing what was best for his business.

Siobhan came in from the kitchen and placed a mug of tea in Grace's hands.

'Are you okay, Grace?' she asked.

'I'm fine. Thanks for the tea.'

Siobhan smiled at her sympathetically.

Grace smiled back. She wasn't fine at all. In all her life, she'd had far harsher insults than 'selfish bitch' levelled at her, and had endured much worse than someone having a bit of a go at her, but with the exception of Ben's death, what had just happened had hurt her more than anything else ever had.

Chapter 60

Michael groaned as he sat up in bed. His head felt like a bass drummer had taken up residence in there and his mouth was as dry as a nun's crotch. The winter sun was blazing through the windows and his body was covered in a thin film of sweat. He hadn't been drunk since he was in his thirties. He hated the feeling of not being in control, but he must have drunk his own body weight in whisky last night. And all because of Grace. Why couldn't he just ignore her? He wanted nothing more than to look at her and not feel anything. But every time he looked at her he was consumed with anger – and the need to grab hold of her and kiss her until he could no longer breathe. How could he love and hate her at the same time?

He couldn't work at the club any more. It was becoming an impossible situation. He couldn't handle seeing her. Even though he spent as little time there as possible, he could never manage to avoid her completely. And then there was that barmaid, Ali, who was always hanging around him. He'd stupidly slept with her a few times – another attempt to forget about Grace – and now she was making out like they were a couple having some sort of epic love affair.

Fuck it all!

Maybe Grace had the right idea, fucking off to the country and cutting ties with everyone. Maybe he should do that?

But he wouldn't leave his boys. Or Belle. She'd only just come into his life and he adored her. Leaving the club would be enough. He'd still let his firm run security, but he'd hand it over to his lads. They seemed to be as thick as thieves with Jake at the minute in any case and he briefly wondered what that was about. He sensed them slipping away from him at times. Perhaps the security game wasn't enough for them anymore? They'd always had their sights on bigger and better things, and they had the balls to take whatever they wanted. He had no doubt they would be branching out on their own sometime soon. He'd miss having them around but he couldn't blame them. They were young and full of ambition. But they believed they were invincible and it worried him more every day.

God, he was getting too old for this shit.

Walking into the en-suite, Michael splashed his face with cold water and then studied his reflection in the mirror. Running his hand through his hair he noticed it was even greyer than the last time he'd looked. No doubt the stress of the last few months. He could blame Grace for that too.

Chapter 61

'**Y**our dad was out of order speaking to my mum like that,' Jake snapped as he stomped around his office. 'In her own fucking house as well.'

Connor shook his head while Paul spun around on Jake's chair.

'Are you two listening to me?' Jake shouted.

'Well, I'm trying my best to drown you out, but you're not making it very easy, to be honest,' Paul replied.

'What?' Jake glared at him.

Connor sighed. 'We learned a long time ago never to get in between your mum and our dad. Just stay out of it, mate. They'll sort it out eventually. Your life will be much simpler if you just leave them to it.'

'I'm sure your blood pressure will thank you for it too,' Paul said with a grin.

Jake shook his head at them both.

'Look, Jake,' Paul said. 'I know she's your mum. I know you feel like you have to protect her honour or something, but I don't think you realise how much of a warrior she is.'

'I know she can look after herself,' Jake said. 'But—'

'But nothing,' Connor interrupted. 'She can not only look after herself, she looks after everyone else too. She has single-handedly saved the arse of everyone in this room. You have no idea some of the things she's done. She is tougher than anyone I know.'

'Why do you think we call her the boss?' said Paul.

'I thought it was just a running joke. A term of affection?'

The twins laughed. 'No, mate,' Paul said as he stood up and put his arm around Jake's shoulder. 'It's because she's the top dog. She always has been.'

'No,' said Jake. 'We're in charge now, lads.'

Connor shrugged. 'We are. Because she's happy to let us run things. But make no mistake, Jake, she is the queen, and we are her loyal subjects. She ensures the wheels are well greased to smooth the way for us. Why do you think she came back here?'

'Because she was bored,' said Jake.

Connor shook his head. 'Don't be daft. Haven't you noticed how much easier your life has been since she came back? How suddenly people are just behaving themselves and not trying to take the piss every five minutes? The club is making more money. Bobby White is being quiet, despite the fact we nicked all his coke. We don't know how she does it, but it's all your mum, mate.'

Jake shook his head in disbelief.

'We thought you knew,' Paul said.

'No,' said Jake. 'I had no idea.'

The rain was hammering the windshield as Jake drove home. The twins had gone to their private men's club, Xcalibur, but Jake hadn't felt in much of a mood to party. He'd pretended to be feeling tired, but he was raging. How could the twins possibly think his mum was the one running things? Is that what she had them all believing? Had she lied to him about the real reason she came back from Harewood? And if so, why? Why had she come back when she did? It made no sense to him.

Jake's knuckles were white as he gripped the steering wheel. He thought about every conversation he'd had with his mum since she'd come back. She'd made him look like a fool in front of everyone. He was the one out there risking his neck and his mum was taking the fucking credit. Well, no longer. It was about time his mum stepped aside and let him have his time in the spotlight for a change. It was nothing more than he deserved.

Chapter 62

Jake was so deep in thought, he didn't notice the man walking into his office. It wasn't until he caught the distinct smell of weed that he looked up and saw the familiar face of Eddie Redman. Jake sighed. What did this prick want?

He'd known Eddie since they were kids, but they'd never liked each other. Eddie was a lowlife, thieving pothead as far as Jake was concerned. He was well known for robbing bikes and mobile phones off schoolkids. He'd come to Jake a while ago, asking for a job, and it had taken Jake all of his strength not to laugh Eddie out of his office. Instead, he'd told him he had nothing going. He hadn't wanted to cause his mum any grief with Sandra, who was one of the few friends she seemed to have left.

'What do you want?' Jake snapped. He was in no mood for visitors, and certainly not for ones he disliked as much as Eddie.

Eddie smiled. That cocky little grin had no right to be anywhere near his face as far as Jake was concerned. What the hell did Eddie Redman ever have to be cocky about?

'I have some news that might interest you, Jakey,' he sneered. 'It's going to rock your perfect little world.'

'Oh, fuck off, you little prick. How did you even get in here?'

'Don't you want to hear what I have to say?' Eddie said, still grinning maniacally at him.

'I have no interest in anything you have to say. Now piss off.' Jake stood so he could personally show Eddie the door.

Eddie squared up to him. 'You're a jumped-up little cunt, you know that? I'm going to enjoy taking half this place from you.'

'What?' Jake started to laugh. 'There's something dodgy in that weed you're smoking, lad, if you think that will ever happen.'

'Really? This place is legally half mine, and I want what I'm owed.'

'What the fuck are you on about?' Jake had really had enough of dickheads today.

Eddie glared at him. 'I thought she might have told you, but obviously you're as clueless as I was. Nathan Conlon was my dad too. Halfy half, *brother*.' He spat the last word. 'It's only fair.'

'What? You need your head feeling. Do you honestly expect me to believe that? You need professional help, lad,' Jake snarled as he moved his face closer to Eddie's.

Eddie shook his head and his cocky smile returned. 'It's all true. Just ask your mum if you don't believe me.'

'My mum?' Jake took a step back. Eddie was fucking batshit. There was no way his mum would keep something like that from him. Would she?

'Yep. Her and my ma have been keeping it from us all along.'

Jake shook his head. This couldn't be true. Eddie was only a bit older than he was. That would mean his dad had got another woman pregnant after he'd married his mum. Just before she got pregnant with him. 'You're a fucking liar,' he shouted.

Eddie started to laugh. 'I don't think so, lad. Nathan Conlon was my dad too. Only I never got to have him around like you did. I never got a fucking penny from him. He owes me. Half of this place belongs to me.'

Jake had had enough. Grabbing Eddie by the throat he pushed

him out of his office and into the hallway. 'I'll put a bullet in you before I ever give you a penny from this place, you lying piece of shit,' he shouted as he pushed Eddie to the floor.

Getting up and dusting himself off, Eddie stared at him. 'Ask your ma about it,' he said. 'I want what I'm owed.' Then he walked down the hallway and out of the club.

Chapter 63

Grace was surprised to see Jake burst into her office. She'd heard a bit of shouting outside, but that was par for the course at The Blue Rooms these days, and she'd been in the middle of sorting out the weekend's banking.

'That dickhead Eddie Redman has just been in here,' Jake barked.

'Has he? What did he want?'

'Half of this place, apparently.'

'What? Is he on glue?'

'He fucking must be because he reckons he's my brother.'

'What the hell's going on in here?' Michael asked as he bounded into the room too. 'Some little prick has just nearly knocked me over walking out of here, and now you two are at it.'

Grace sighed. This was going to be hard enough without Michael getting in on the act too. How the hell had Eddie found out the truth? It must have been Sandra. She was the only other person who knew.

'Is it true, Mum?' Jake snapped.

'Is what true?' Michael asked.

'Yes,' Grace answered, ignoring Michael. 'Your dad was Eddie's dad.'

'What?' Jake screamed. 'And you never thought to tell me this little nugget of information? That fucking ratbag thinks he can walk in here and take what's mine and you never thought to warn me?'

'It wasn't my information to tell, Jake. There was a good reason not to tell you at first, and then, well, the time just never seemed right.'

'Oh, fuck off,' he spat and Grace couldn't hide the shock on her face. He'd never spoken to her like that before. 'You make out like you're always protecting everyone else, Mum. But it's only ever about you.'

She rose from her chair and leaned towards him, her shaking hands planted on her desk for support. 'What the hell do I gain from keeping your father's secret offspring from you?'

Michael laughed in the background. 'Well, you do like keeping secrets, don't you, Grace?'

'Stay out of this, Michael.'

'He's right though, isn't he?' Jake went on. 'Grace Sumner – queen of her own little empire. Only tells us what we need to know, eh, Michael? Always looking out for number one.'

Michael nodded in agreement and Grace felt her cheeks burning with anger. How fucking dare they! After everything she'd ever done for the pair of them.

She grabbed her handbag and stood up. 'Well, you know what? Fuck the pair of you,' she yelled. 'You can all go to hell for all I care. I've had enough of the fucking lot of you.'

Pushing past them as they stood with their mouths hanging open, she walked out of the door and out of the club.

Grace's whole body shook with anger. She expected nothing less from Michael. He was still hurting over his daughter, and he could be a bad-tempered sod at the best of times. But Jake?

She had only ever done what she thought was best for him. She had given up her quiet, peaceful life in Harewood to come back to this shithole and help him out. And he accused her of only thinking about herself. The cheeky little bastard. She needed some distance from him. He was her son and they would work things out when they both calmed down, but she couldn't be around him anymore. She wanted out of this life. She needed to speak to Ivan about some investments and she'd ask Marcus to look after the house until she could find some tenants. Then she was packing up and leaving. She'd be gone by the weekend.

As she drove home, her fury started to give way to sadness. Where had she gone wrong? Why on earth had Sandra betrayed her like that? It was she who'd insisted on keeping Eddie a secret from Jake in the first place, and now she'd gone and landed Grace right in it. Well, that friendship was over. The least Sandra could have done was given her a heads-up. And now Eddie was sniffing around. He was going to end up causing trouble for Jake, Grace knew it. She shook her head. That was Jake's problem now. She was well out of it.

Chapter 64

Grace smiled as she watched Belle playing with her toys on the floor of Marcus's living room.

'She's adorable, isn't she?' Marcus said as he offered Grace a cup of coffee.

'She is,' said Grace. 'Thanks.' She took the cup.

'I can't believe you're leaving in two days,' Marcus said with a pout. 'I'm going to miss you both so much. I don't know what I'll do without you, Grace.'

'I know. I feel the same about you,' Grace sighed. 'It feels like you're the only one I can talk to sometimes. You are the sanest person I know.'

'Dear God, I feel for you then, love. Twenty-five years we've been friends, do you know that?'

'I do. It still feels like yesterday when you rocked up to The Rose and Crown in your ripped jeans and your waistcoat.'

'Well, your fashion sense wasn't much better, if I recall,' he returned good-naturedly.

'God, it was all so simple then, wasn't it?' she sighed.

'Good times. If only we could go back there.'

'If only.'

'I've never found a job I like as much as working at The Rose and Crown. I've never quite fitted in the same anywhere else.'

'Me neither,' Grace agreed. 'We were a good team. The pub in my village is going on the market. The owners are emigrating to Canada. I thought about buying it, but it would be too much on my own.'

'Oh my God,' Marcus shouted.

'What?' Grace almost spilled her coffee. Belle looked at the pair of them in surprise before giggling and going back to her toys.

'I could run it with you,' he said, his eyes lighting up like a toddler's on Christmas morning.

'But you'd hate Harewood. It's nothing like Liverpool.'

'Maybe that's what I need?'

'I don't know,' Grace said. 'It's a completely different way of life. It's quiet and peaceful and—'

'Sounds like just what I need.'

'And what about James?'

'Oh, we're finishing anyway,' Marcus sighed. 'He's obsessed with his dogs. And I just can't compete with labradoodles. I think we could both do with a break from men, don't you?'

'Are you serious?'

'About the break from men?'

'About moving, you twonk!'

'One hundred percent,' he said. 'Let me come with you, Grace. I promise to be a good house guest until I find a place of my own.'

'You can stay as long as you like. The place is huge. But the pub comes with a flat if you want your own space.'

'Sounds perfect.' Marcus grinned. 'Looks like I'd better get packing.'

Grace smiled at him as she drank her coffee. She'd never even considered asking him to move with her. She thought he'd have rather cut off his own arm than move to the country. But it made perfect sense.

Suddenly, she felt brighter than she had in weeks. The fact that both Jake and Michael were no longer speaking to her made the thought of leaving again so much easier. They had been the only people keeping her in Liverpool. Despite that, the thought of leaving them both again broke her heart, but she would do it because she had to. She would make it work in Harewood in spite of them. The next chapter of her life was going to be a good one. She could feel it.

Chapter 65

Eddie Redman climbed the stairs to the fourth floor in the run-down block of flats. He was breathless by the time he reached the top and made a mental note to get himself into better shape.

He walked along the deserted hallway, stopping when he found flat number 418.

Knocking on the door, he surveyed the debris around him while he waited. Most of the flats seemed to be unoccupied and he thought to himself how fortunate that could be for the plan he had in mind.

He was surprised when the front door was opened so quickly.

'Who are you?' The occupant glared at him, a cigarette dangling from the side of her mouth.

'Eddie. I think we have a common enemy, Eve.'

'What?' She eyed him suspiciously.

'Grace Conlon?'

Eve raised her eyebrows. 'That stuck-up bitch from the club?'

'Yeah. And I come bearing gifts.' Eddie held up a bottle of cheap vodka and a bag of weed.

'Well, why didn't you say so,' she cackled as she took the bottle from him. 'Come in then.'

Eddie stepped into the hallway and followed Eve into her stale-smelling flat.

'I'll just get us a couple of glasses. Make yourself at home, lad,' she shouted.

Eddie did as he was told and settled himself into a well-worn armchair. Eve returned a moment later and handed him a glass of vodka. Sitting on the sofa, she studied him closely.

'You remind me of someone,' she finally said.

'Oh? And who's that then?' Eddie asked.

Eve shook her head. 'Can't place my finger on it. It'll come to me.' She took a swig of her vodka and smacked her lips. 'So, what really brings you here then, lad?'

'I'm here about good old-fashioned revenge, Eve. I have some very interesting information to share with you about how we can both get it, and make a fuckload of money in the process.'

Eve laughed. Crossing her legs, she sat back in her seat. 'Well, go on then, lad. I'm all ears.'

It was dark when Eddie finally left Eve's flat. When he'd told her who he was, and shared his idea for a plan to get revenge on Grace, she'd been more than keen to be involved. He'd told her it would take him at least a few weeks to set everything up. He couldn't afford to mess anything up. Everything had to be planned and the timing had to be exactly right.

Eddie realised he'd need some more help than just Eve. He needed a bit of muscle too – just in case. He knew just the right man for the job – a psycho he knew from his estate, Greg Barnes. Greg had always had a screw loose and most people gave him a wide berth. He tortured animals for fun and there had been rumours of sexual abuse allegations involving his younger step-siblings, before his stepmother left with his siblings in tow. Eddie smiled and lit himself a cigarette as he descended the stairs to the ground floor. Greg was the perfect man for the job.

Chapter 66

Bobby White looked at the seven men who stood before him: Liam McGuinness, Harry Bolger, Fat Danny, Alex Callaghan, Franny Hughes, Martin Mitchell and Reuben McBride.

'Tomorrow is the day, boys.' He grinned at them. 'I have reliable information about where our targets will be tomorrow afternoon. And we'll be waiting for them. They won't see us coming. We'll be in two cars. We'll take one of them in each. They're less dangerous apart. I'll be in touch later this evening with further instructions. Until then, fuck off,' he said, smiling at them all. They started to file out of the door.

'Liam?' Bobby called. 'Hang on a minute, lad.'

'All right, boss,' he said.

After the others had left the office, Bobby pulled out a bottle of scotch from the bottom drawer of his desk. 'Fancy one?' he asked.

Liam nodded and Bobby poured them both a drink.

'You feeling okay about tomorrow?' Bobby asked him as he handed him the glass.

'As long as everyone does what they're supposed to, we'll be golden.'

'We need to keep an eye on Reuben and Mitchell. Make sure they don't fucking lose their nerve.'

'One of them in each car, I reckon. We'll make sure they're tooled up. I'll give them a line of coke each beforehand – Dutch courage!'

Bobby took a sip of his whisky. 'And you've sorted out where we'll be taking them, right? Somewhere quiet where we won't be disturbed?'

'Yeah. I checked the place out again this morning. It's perfect. Some fella my uncle drinks with does nights for the security company that looks after it. He said we can use the place for as long as we need.'

'And he can be trusted.'

Liam shrugged. 'Don't know. But he doesn't ask questions. He doesn't know what it's being used for and more importantly he doesn't care. He's just happy to make a few hundred quid for looking the other way. Besides, even if he does open his mouth, there's no link to us.'

'Good work.' Bobby said. 'But your uncle's mate is a loose end that I want tying up. Grace Sumner is a clever woman, and I want *no one* to be able to tie us to this.'

'Whatever you say, boss. I'll sort it. About the job though. I think our best bet is to get it done quickly. Be in and out of the place before anyone has a chance to see us.'

Bobby shook his head. 'You just told me you had the perfect place and we could have it for as long as we need. So, why wouldn't I use that to my advantage? You know quick and clean is not how I operate. The pair of them will suffer first. I want to listen to them plead for their lives, and then I want to hear them beg me to finish them off.'

'But we're not talking about a pair of amateurs here, boss.' Liam frowned. 'These two are serious fucking hard-cases. Given a chance, they'll have the lot of us.'

Bobby glared at him. 'Well, let's make sure we don't give them a chance then, eh?'

'Whatever you say, boss.'

'Good. Now finish your drink and get lost. I'll pick you up later and we can get the stuff we need from my lock-up.'

Liam downed his whisky and walked out of his boss's office and through the bar of the Gin Blossom.

'Bye, Liam.' Bobby's wife, Leanne smiled at him as he approached. He brushed past her, his hands lingering on her waist as he did. 'Bye, gorgeous,' he whispered. 'I'll see you later.'

Chapter 67

M artin Mitchell's hand trembled as held the phone to his ear. 'You'll be picked up from the corner of your road at two. Do not be late,' Bobby White snapped. 'Wear black. You'll be given everything else you need in the car. Do not breathe a word about this to anyone. Understood?'

'Yes,' Martin said quietly.

'What?' Bobby shouted over the sound of traffic in the background.

'I said yes,' Martin replied.

'Good. That's what I thought,' Bobby said before hanging up the phone.

Martin's stomach churned as he poured the water from the kettle into the mug. When Bobby had insisted he be in on the job, he knew it would be more than his life was worth to say no. A request from Bobby was something you didn't refuse.

But Martin was having a severe case of nerves. If he was honest, he was shitting his pants. It had all seemed so easy to give Bobby information to get back at the people who'd humiliated him, but the reality was proving harder to deal with. What Bobby was asking of him was beyond anything he'd imagined. He wasn't sure he had the stomach, or the balls, for it. Martin was well aware that although he liked to present himself as a hard man and run in the same circles as the likes of Bobby White and Jake Conlon, he was actually a coward who preferred to stand on the sidelines and watch others do the dirty work.

His mum had warned him about taking a job at The Blue Rooms and getting involved with Jake Conlon and the Carters, but Martin had thought he knew best. He was a Mitchell – no one would mess with him. How naïve he'd been to think that a name was enough to get him by.

Bobby White climbed into the waiting Range Rover.

'All done, boss?' Liam McGuinness asked.

Bobby nodded. 'Martin will do exactly as he's told. Have you spoken to Reuben?'

'Yeah. He knows the score.'

Bobby laughed. 'Pair of dickheads. They haven't got a fucking clue.'

Liam laughed too as he pulled away from the hard shoulder. A few seconds later he looked over at his boss. 'Do you think people will really believe those two could pull off a job like this?'

'We'll make it look amateur enough. And we'll tell the right people what they need to know to make sure those two are the names in the frame. Grace Sumner and the rest of the Carter clan will be too busy mourning the deaths of their beloved heroes to bother about concrete proof or wondering how that pair of useless tossers pulled it off. They'll just want someone to pay.'

'Whatever you say, boss.'

Bobby stared out of the window as Liam drove him home. He wondered whether Leanne would be back from work yet. He'd been away in Scotland for a few days and although he'd seen her earlier at the bar, he'd missed her. He'd phoned her a few minutes ago but she hadn't answered, which always made him suspicious. If he ever found her cheating on him, he would peel her skin from her body and use it as a rug. Then he would cut off the balls of the bastard she'd cheated on him with and feed him to his dogs.

Chapter 68

Karl Morgan's office was hot and sticky. It was a small room at the back of a sunbed shop, with no windows and little ventilation, and Karl had two fan heaters blasting hot air. Despite the heat, everyone in the room appeared cool and calm. Karl was a well-known hard man. He'd inherited his business from his uncle, a giant Russian named Luka, who had instilled a level of fear surrounding Trident Securities that Karl was still dining out on. As far as Jake was concerned, Karl was a smarmy fat fucker. He called himself a respectable businessman, but in Jake's opinion he was just a thug who had got lucky. He had simply been in the right place at the right time when his uncle got his head blown open with a sawn-off. Nevertheless, he had a reputation as someone you didn't mess about with.

Karl and his firm were Michael's main competition; they'd been rivals since Michael had branched out into the security business, but things had escalated more recently since Michael had taken over security at the club. There had been a few tit-for-tat incidents between the two factions, which had escalated into some of Karl's lads turning up at The Blue Rooms armed to the teeth with samurai swords and a couple of sawn-off shotguns. Despite that, they'd all had their arses handed to them and while Michael's firm had ended up with a few scrapes, most of Karl's crew had been put out of action on a permanent basis.

Despite Michael's firm coming out on top, the fracas had not been good for business and had caused the plod to start asking questions and poking their nose where they weren't wanted. If Jake hadn't had a couple of police officers and some members of the licensing board in his pocket, The Blue Rooms would have been closed down on the spot. With that in mind, they'd decided that the ongoing feud was not good for business and had arranged to meet Karl to negotiate a truce of sorts.

Karl was flanked by two of his heavies – Benji and Maurice. They both sat stony-faced while Michael and Karl discussed the terms of their new agreement. Jake watched all of them intently, looking for any sign that things were about to kick off. He and Michael were searched before they entered the grim little office, to make sure they had no weapons. It was a sign of Jake and Michael's reputations, and the fear they instilled, that they could go to Karl's turf with only each other as backup. The recent bloodshed had caused havoc for Karl. He'd lost some good lads, and, more importantly, he'd lost face. He needed the truce more than Jake and Michael did, but mass brawls with guns and blades didn't fit well with the type of club that Jake wanted to run. The Blue Rooms was becoming the new place to be in Liverpool on Friday and Saturday nights, but no matter how popular a club was, trouble like that would start to scare the punters off. Jake's mum had promoted Siobhan to manager and Jake had to admit that she was doing a great job at it. It gave her something to focus on other than him, and that was one of the many reasons he wanted the place to remain a success.

'So I'll warn my lads off, if you'll agree to the do the same, Michael?' Karl asked.

Michael nodded his agreement. 'I'll see to it personally.'

Karl broke into a grin; it took over his large face. 'Sort us some drinks, Maurice,' he ordered.

The five of them sat in the sticky office drinking cheap whisky and making small talk. It wasn't long before the conversation turned to women. Maurice told them about his wife, Bernie, who'd recently given birth to their sixth child.

'She just pops them out now. No pain relief or anything.'

'And what about you, Jake?' Karl sneered. 'You still knocking off that sexy little redhead from your club? Siobhan, isn't it? Is she still your type?'

Jake's whole body tensed as soon as Siobhan's name was mentioned. And what did Karl mean about her still being his type? 'Fuck off,' he snapped.

'All right, lad. Calm down,' Karl said with a laugh. 'Hit a nerve there, have I?' He looked directly at Jake, challenging him.

In an instant, Jake was filled with rage. He wanted to smash the glass he was holding right into Karl's smarmy face and wipe that smug grin off it permanently. But Michael's hand was on his shoulder before he could move. Michael gave him a light squeeze. It was a subtle gesture, possibly even unnoticed by anyone else in the room, but Jake knew it was loaded with meaning. *Down, boy! Not now!*

Clenching his jaw shut, he forced his mouth into a smile.

Michael put his glass on the table and started to rise from his chair; his eyes did not leave Karl's.

'The Blue Rooms and anyone associated with it are out of bounds, Karl! Make sure your boys know it too.'

Fear flashed momentarily across Karl's face, but his cool facade quickly returned. Showing fear was not a good trait in their line of work. He nodded his agreement and Michael signalled it was time to leave.

'You did good holding your temper in there, lad,' Michael told Jake as they walked towards his car. 'Pricks like Karl will always try and push your buttons. The trick is not to let them. Always better to give them what's owing when they're least expecting it. It's more fun that way.' He winked.

Michael was right, Jake thought. Kicking off in there would have only led to a massive brawl. One he was sure that he and Michael would have won, but it wouldn't have done anything to end the feud with Trident Securities. Sometimes it was hard to control his temper lately, particularly where Siobhan was concerned. He wondered if it was a result of the guilt he felt whenever he looked at her. Whatever it was, he hated the thought that any harm might come to her because of him.

'Let's go and get ourselves a quick drink at the club then. I think we deserve it after not punching Karl in the mouth,' Jake said.

Michael shook his head. 'Another time, Jake. I'm hoping to go and see Belle for an hour before she goes to bed. If your mum will speak to me, that is. Have you spoken to her yet?'

Jake shook his head. 'No.'

'You need to. Before she goes back to Harewood. Don't make me drag you to her house myself, Jake.'

'All right, I'll go and see her tomorrow,' said Jake, relenting.

Michael nodded as they reached his car. 'Good. Now get in. I'm fucking freezing.'

They'd spent longer than expected in Karl's dingy little office and it was late evening when they left. The streetlights overhead had been broken, no doubt by some bored teenagers with nothing better to do, and had yet to be repaired. The result was that it was so dark neither Jake nor Michael noticed the men in balaclavas approaching them. The first thing Jake knew about it was when he felt the searing pain in his skull and heard the sickening thud as he was hit over the head by something hard and blunt.

His ears started ringing. Then everything went black.

Chapter 69

Grace could hear her mobile phone vibrating in her handbag as she sat in the doctor's office holding a squirming Belle on her lap.

'Can you hold her still?' said the grey-haired GP as he tried to look inside Belle's ear.

'I'm trying,' Grace snapped. *Maybe if you weren't such a grumpy old bastard, she wouldn't be so terrified of you.*

'Come on, darling,' she soothed to Belle as she smoothed her curls away from her face. 'Mummy won't let the nasty man hurt you.'

As she walked out of the surgery a few minutes later, with a screaming baby and a prescription for antibiotics for Belle's ear infection, she heard the familiar vibration of her phone again.

'For fuck's sake,' she muttered. It was just after ten and she was supposed to be on the M62 by now. Scrabbling around in her bag with her free hand, she found the phone. Siobhan's name was flashing impatiently on the screen.

'What's so bleeding urgent, Siobhan?'

'Grace,' Siobhan cried. 'Jake and Michael are missing.'

Grace felt as though all of the blood had drained from her body. Even Belle seemed to sense the impending doom, becoming quiet and still.

'What do you mean, missing? For how long?' Grace asked, trying to remain calm, if only for her daughter's sake.

'Since yesterday. They left to go to a meeting at four. I haven't heard from Jake since. I assumed they'd gone for a drink, but then Jake didn't come home, and he's not at your place. He's not with Paul Carter. No one at the club has heard from either of them. What do we do, Grace?' she wailed.

'I'm on my way there, Siobhan. Phone all of the bouncers – their contacts are in the address book in Michael's office – and anyone else you can think of. See if they've heard from them. Can you do that?' she asked, unsure if Siobhan was up to such a task given the state she seemed to be in.

'Yes. Yes. Of course,' she said, sounding relieved that she had something practical to do.

'Phone me if you hear anything. Straightaway, Siobhan!'

'I will,' she said and Grace hung up.

She phoned Marcus and asked if he could meet her at The Blue Rooms and take Belle home. Then, as she drove to Jake's club, she wondered whether Michael's family knew where he was. Had anyone else noticed that they were missing?

Why had Siobhan mentioned that Jake wasn't with Paul?

Grace needed to think.

Fast.

Most of the Carter family, with the exception of Paul and Connor, were annoyed with her for keeping Belle a secret. But Sean was by far the most level-headed of them all, and the one with the most contacts. If she had to choose, he was the one she would want to go into battle with. Besides, if she spoke with him first, he would mobilise the rest of them.

Her heart pounded as she dialled his number. She hoped he would laugh at her and tell her Michael and Jake were sleeping off hangovers somewhere or had even gone home with a couple of strippers. God, anything was better than the alternative.

'Hello, Grace,' Sean said brusquely when he answered the phone.

'Sean, have you heard from Michael? Or Jake?'

'Not for a few days. Why?'

'Apparently they're missing,' she said, although it almost tore her heart from her chest to even say the words out loud.

'What? What makes you think that?'

'Neither of them have been seen or heard from since yesterday afternoon when they went out to a meeting.'

'I'll see if the twins know where they are. Hopefully they've just had a heavy night,' Sean said, but Grace didn't believe that and she knew he didn't either. Michael and Jake didn't really do heavy nights for a start. When people like Jake and Michael went missing, it was usually because someone had made them disappear.

'Where are you?' Sean asked.

'I'm on my way to the club.'

'I'll meet you there in half an hour. I'll phone the twins now.'

'Bring everyone, Sean.'

'Of course. You too, Grace.'

As she drove to The Blue Rooms, Grace phoned every single person she could think of. Anyone who had ever worked for her. Anyone she had ever helped out. Anyone who owed her even the smallest of favours. If they didn't know where Jake or Michael were, then they would damn sure help her to find them.

Sean Carter burst into Grace's former office at The Blue Rooms. Over a dozen men had already assembled there and dozens more were on their way. He made his way over to Grace and sat on the desk beside her, giving her hand a light squeeze as he did.

'The twins are on their way. They're picking up my dad en route,' he said to her before turning his attention to the room.

'Does anyone know anything yet?' he barked.

He was met with a chorus of 'Nope. Not yet.'

'I've sent a few of the lads out to start making some enquiries,' Grace told him. 'No one seems to know who they were meeting with yesterday, although Jimmy seems to think they were headed to the north of the city, don't you, Jim?' Grace indicated the tall, bearded Yorkshireman who was standing near the doorway.

'That's right. Jake phoned me when they were stuck in traffic because there'd been a crash on Queens Drive.'

'He didn't mention where they were going though?' Sean asked. 'Or why Michael was with him?'

'He didn't say, and I didn't ask. If the boss doesn't tell me, then he doesn't think I need to know.'

'Any idea what it was about?' Sean asked Grace.

She shook her head. 'Could be anything where Jake is concerned. Maybe he took Michael along for backup?'

'Is that all we know?' Sean asked.

'So far, unfortunately,' Grace sighed as Patrick and his twin grandsons came almost running into the room.

'Grace,' Pat said as he walked over and pulled her into a hug. 'We'll find them both. I promise you that, girl.'

'I know, Pat,' she said, wishing she felt as confident as she sounded.

As more people started filing into the room, Grace realised that everyone was looking to her to tell them what to do next. It was like being back on top again. Except that she wasn't on top, and she didn't know whether she ever would be again. What if she didn't find her son? Or Michael? God, what if . . .?

It was Patrick's voice that brought her back to the present. 'So what now, boss?' he asked.

Yes, what now, Grace?

'Connor, Paul, take a couple of lads with you and knock on the door of every lowlife you know. Nudge, go and see Ivan Golding. See if he can put some feelers out. Everyone else, scour every drug den, knocking shop, and shithole you can think of. Where were they taken to? It must be somewhere quiet and out of the way. Find someone who knows something. Pat, why don't you pay our old mate Sol a visit? He usually knows what's going on round here. Sean, you and I are going to find that little ratbag Eddie Redman. I doubt he's got the nous or the balls to be involved in this, but we'll see. Keep your mobile phones switched on. As soon as anyone knows anything, no matter how small, phone me, immediately!'

As they all started to file out of her office to follow their orders, Sean handed Grace her coat. 'Come on then. Let's find these fuckers,' he said.

She nodded. They would find who was responsible for Jake and Michael's disappearance, she was sure of that. But would they find Jake and Michael in time?

Chapter 70

Grace stood back as Sean knocked on the door of Eddie Redman's flat. She wondered why he bothered knocking when, five seconds later, he kicked the thing almost clean off its hinges. She followed him down the hall, trying not to gag as the sweet, sickly smell of weed filled her lungs and burned the back of her throat. She stayed behind Sean as he barged into the living room, where a topless Eddie sat on a mouldy sofa, in a cloud of smoke, with two of his crackhead mates.

'What the fuck?' he shouted as he bounced off the sofa.

Sean took hold of Eddie's face in the palm of his large hand and pushed him back down. 'Sit the fuck down, you piece of shit,' he barked.

The two other men tried to get up too and Sean gave them the same treatment.

'The three of you aren't going to move another fucking inch until you tell me what I want to know,' he growled at them, his jaw set like concrete and his eyes as cold as ice. Grace had never seen him look quite so terrifying. Sean Carter had a reputation as one of the most ruthless bastards Liverpool had ever seen, but Grace had only ever known him as her business partner in the restaurants. He'd left his other life behind before she met him, telling her it had almost destroyed him, and now she knew why.

Eddie and his two associates visibly shook as Sean began to ask them questions about Jake and Michael's whereabouts. Grace stood back and watched the master at work. Even his tone of voice had changed: it was terrifying, yet mesmerising to watch.

'Where are Jake and my brother, Eddie?' he growled. 'Don't make me ask you again.'

Eddie shook his head furiously from side to side. 'I don't fucking know what you're on about,' he wailed.

'So you go into Jake's club less than a week ago, you demand money and you threaten him, and you expect me to believe you had nothing to do with their disappearance?'

'It's true,' Eddie stammered.

'Do you think I'm stupid, Eddie? Do I look fucking stupid to you?'

Eddie shook his head again, barely able to look Sean in the face as his two mates cowered beside him.

Sean slapped Eddie across the back of the head. 'Fucking look at me when I'm talking to you, you useless piece of shit,' he shouted.

Eddie raised his head and looked up at his tormentor and Sean rewarded him by smashing his fist into his face, causing Eddie to howl in pain as blood began to pour from his now obviously broken nose.

'What about you two little fuckwits?' Sean asked as he slapped Eddie's two companions across the head.

They both shook their heads too, mumbling apologies to 'Mr Carter'.

Grace had seen enough. These three were off their faces on who knew what. They could barely stand and, judging by the debris around them, looked like they'd been holed away in that grotty little flat for at least two days. They didn't know anything about Jake or Michael's whereabouts. Just as Sean seemed to be starting to enjoy himself, she placed her hand on his arm and whispered in his ear. 'We haven't got time for this. They don't know anything.'

He looked at her and nodded. He gave Eddie a kick in the balls for his trouble as a parting gift. 'Don't you ever threaten anyone I care about ever again, you useless waste of fucking space,' he spat, then he followed Grace outside.

'That went well,' she said sarcastically.

'Useless crackheads,' Sean snarled. 'So where to next?'

'Let's head back to the club and see if anyone else has turned up there with some information.'

Grace glanced at her phone to see if there had been any missed calls or messages as Sean drove away from Eddie's flat in Bootle.

'Nothing yet.'

'We'll hear something soon,' he said reassuringly. 'Someone must know something.'

As though he'd made it happen by some psychic power, Grace's phone started to vibrate in her hand. Looking at the screen, she saw Ivan Golding's name. Swiping right, she answered the call and put him onto loudspeaker.

'Grace. I've got Steven Porter here with me. He thinks he has some information that might be of use,' he said.

Grace nodded. She'd done Steven Porter a massive favour months earlier. Nevertheless, if he was going to come though now for her then she would owe him. 'Put him on, Ivan. You're on loudspeaker.'

'Hi, Grace,' Steven mumbled.

'Steven. What do you have for me?

'It could be nothing, but an alarm went off at one of my properties last night. I get an automatic notification. I phoned the alarm company and they told me it was a fault and they'd sorted it.'

'So?'

'Well, something about it seemed a bit off. It's an old warehouse off Long Lane. The one at the back of Tasker's. No one's used the place for years. I've never had an alarm notification from there before. The alarms have to be reset onsite so how could they have already checked and sorted it when I'd only just had the notification? Anyway, it was late and I didn't want to get into it with them. I was going to check the place myself sometime next week. I thought no more of it until Ivan spoke to me today. It could be nothing, of course.'

'Or it could be the information we've been waiting for. Thanks, Steven.'

'I'm happy to help, Grace.'

Grace ended the call and turned to Sean. 'Head straight there. I'll phone the twins to meet us.'

'We should probably wait for them to arrive before we go in. Who knows what we're going into?'

'I'm not waiting.'

'We could be going into an ambush, Grace. See where the twins are. If they're miles away, we'll find someone who's not.'

Grace phoned Connor and Paul Carter, who were not far from Long Lane, having just been to see some of their contacts in Kirkby.

Ten minutes later, Connor and Paul Carter met Grace and Sean at Long Lane industrial estate. One of the warehouses was derelict but had obviously been broken into recently.

'Let me go first,' Sean said as he edged towards the door.

'Not a chance,' Grace said as she pushed past him. Her son was in there. She was sure of it and she'd be damned if she'd let anyone stand in her way.

Chapter 71

Grace scanned the warehouse for any sign of life. Her eyes were still trying to adjust in the darkness, but the unmistakeable metallic smell of blood flooded her nose and throat. She fought the urge to retch as she desperately scanned the room for Jake or Michael. Sean, Connor and Paul filed in behind her as she heard a noise to her left. She rushed over to find Michael lying on the floor trying to heave himself into a seated position. She reached him quickly and crouched down to look at him. She could barely see his features for blood. He held onto her and she tried to stroke back the hair from his forehead but it was matted with blood. Suddenly, all of their arguing and sniping at each other seemed so petty and meaningless. Any feelings of anger and resentment she'd felt towards him dissolved like sugar in hot tea. All that remained was the love she had always felt for him. Grace blinked back the tears. Michael didn't need her pity right now. He needed her strength – and so did Jake.

'Michael,' she whispered, feeling like her heart would break. 'Where's Jake?'

'Over there,' he croaked as he indicated behind him with his head. Sean reached them and took Michael from her arms as she searched for Jake.

'Over here, Grace,' Connor shouted. He and Paul were sitting on the floor with Jake in their arms, his head lolling backwards between his shoulders, making Grace fear the worst. At that moment she thought she might break down in this dingy, airless room and never get back up again. Running to Jake's side, she held his face in her hands.

'He's breathing,' Paul gasped. 'Phone an ambulance.'

With shaking hands, Grace took her mobile phone and dialled 999. Connor took the phone from her as she took his place by Jake. She pulled him to her. He was covered in blood and had injuries all over his body. But he was alive. They were both alive. Grace swore that whoever did this would pay. She would make sure they felt fear and pain like they had never even imagined. As she cradled her son in her arms, Grace was consumed with anguish and anger. It burned through every fibre of her body and made her heart pound so violently she felt it would explode out of her chest. She rocked Jake in her arms and whispered soothing words in his ear. The thought that she might lose him was too much to consider, so she filled her head with thoughts of what she would do to the people who had tried to take him from her.

Grace had been sitting beside Jake's bed in the ICU for twenty-nine hours. She drifted in and out of sleep and resisted the efforts of Sean and Patrick to get her to go home and rest and change her clothes. She would be here when Jake woke up. It had been touch and go when he'd arrived at the Royal Liverpool Hospital. He'd lost so much blood and suffered so much trauma that he'd died twice and they'd had to resuscitate him. But now he was 'stable'. Critical, but stable. They wouldn't be able to tell the full extent of the potential damage until he woke up. And there was still every chance he might never wake up.

Grace held his hand lightly. Some of his fingers had been broken and she didn't want to cause him any further pain. She willed him to wake up. Surely, if she loved him enough, she could will him back from the brink? But Grace Sumner knew there was no such thing as a happy ending.

Michael had been moved to a ward. He'd lost blood too, but Jake seemed to have suffered the worst of the attack. They'd both fought back. The doctors had said that was clear from the many defensive wounds they had. The police were eager to speak to them both about their assault. Ironically, if it hadn't been for the police, both Jake and Michael would probably be dead. It was only the sound of the police helicopter overhead that had caused their attackers to scarper and leave the pair of them for dead. Whichever little dickhead had stolen a car and driven it through the streets of Liverpool like he was playing real-life Grand Theft Auto in the early hours of the morning had done the pair of them a massive favour. Still, Michael had told the police nothing, of course, and Grace wouldn't either. She would find whoever did this herself.

Michael shuffled down the hospital corridor. Every part of him ached, but he had to see her. He'd thought he was a goner when he'd looked up and seen her in that warehouse. She'd appeared like some angel in the darkness and he was sure he must have been dreaming.

'Mr Carter, you really shouldn't be out of bed,' a nurse admonished him as he walked past the nurses' station.

He glared at her in response and she went back to her paperwork.

When he finally found the ICU, he saw the police officer sitting outside.

'Ready to talk, Michael?' she asked.

'I've already told you I don't know who did this,' he answered.

'Yeah, right. And Elvis is alive and well and working in Primark.'

'How is he?' he asked, nodding towards Jake's room.

'The same,' she replied. 'Still hasn't woken up.'

'And his mum?'

'Still hasn't left his side. I don't think she's even been to the toilet.'

Michael shuffled to the door of the room and peered through the small square window. His heart almost broke when he saw her. Pressing his head against the glass he watched her. She sat so still, her forehead resting against Jake's forearm. He wished he could make it better for her. He wanted to go in there and put his arms around her and tell her it would all be okay. But he didn't know that it would. Jake had taken some serious punishment and had appeared to be the main target of the attack. They'd fought back with everything they had, but they'd been ambushed. He and Jake had been gagged, handcuffed and blindfolded, but despite that Michael knew there had been at least six of them, all tooled up.

Michael didn't know who it was – yet. They'd all worn masks so even when his blindfold had slipped occasionally, he hadn't been able to identify any of them, and he hadn't recognised any voices. They'd barely spoken a word to each other the whole time, which made him think it was someone they'd be able to identify.

'You can go in for a minute if you like,' the police officer said, obviously taking pity on him.

'No, it's okay,' he croaked. 'I'll leave them be.'

Chapter 72

Grace walked into The Blue Rooms and looked at the sea of assembled faces. They had succeeded in finding Jake and Michael two days earlier, and thankfully the pair of them were going to be okay.

She had barely slept in those two days and the tiredness was threatening to overwhelm her. But there was something she needed to do first, and that was find out who had tried to murder her son and her daughter's father. Bobby White would be the obvious candidate, but Grace was sure he would never risk her telling Sol about getting his daughter pregnant. Paul and Connor, who were now standing solemnly by her side, had gone on a violent rampage across Liverpool trying to get answers, but to no avail. Grace knew it was going to take much more than that to find out who had tried to pull off this job. They needed to be smarter than that.

She looked across the room at them all. Everyone who worked for her and the Carters – all waiting for her orders. The weight on her shoulders was crushing. She wondered how much longer she could go on living this life.

'I appreciate you all getting here so early. Speak to everyone you know. Rattle some cages. Bang some heads together. Call in as many favours as you can. Do anything you need to but get me some answers.'

They all nodded and started to file out of the room.

Grace turned to the twins. 'Our biggest lead so far is the alarm company. Steven Porter said something suspicious was going on. I think they were helping whoever did this, or at least turning a blind eye. It's Attak Alarms. They're based in Wavertree. Pay them a visit and see what you can find out.'

'On it, boss.'

'And, boys,' she said as they were leaving. 'Kid gloves today, eh? Let's leave the bull-in-a-china-shop stuff until we actually find out who did this. The police are already crawling all over this. We need to keep this as quiet as we can.'

'Okay.' She was reminded of them in their younger days, when she'd constantly had to rein them in.

Grace had just got home from the hospital when the twins rang her doorbell. She invited them inside and poured them all a large brandy, while Marcus, who'd been looking after Belle all evening, made himself scarce.

'What did you find out?' Grace asked.

'The only person on call on Saturday night was Arthur Smith. He didn't log any problem with the alarm at Porter's warehouse or mention it to the day staff who took over from him. There's no record of any fault.'

'So we need to speak to Arthur then.'

The twins shook their heads. 'We spoke to his boss, Paddy, and Arthur didn't turn up for work on Sunday night, or Monday. So Paddy went to his flat and there was no sign of him. No one can get in touch with him on his mobile. Nobody has seen him in his local. He's disappeared.'

'Does he have any family?'

Connor shook his head. 'Only child. Lives alone. No kids.'

'Shit. Either he's in hiding, or whoever he was working for has made sure he'll never talk. And what about Paddy? Any chance he's in on this?'

'No. He seems legit. Loves his job. Has a young family. Thought Arthur was a bit of a weirdo.'

'So, we're back to square one unless we can find Arthur?'

'Yep,' Paul said.

'I don't think Arthur is going to be found, boss,' Connor said. 'No one to miss him. No one to officially report him missing. He's an old drunk with no life, by all accounts. Easier to off him than spend all that time and effort hiding him.'

'You're probably right. There must be some connection some-where though. How did anyone know what Arthur did and when he'd be working? Stay on Attak Alarms and find out everything you can about Mr Smith.'

'Will do, boss,' the twins said before finishing their drinks.

'I'll catch up with you both tomorrow at the hospital then,' Grace said before showing them out.

Chapter 73

Grace thanked Marcus for the cup of tea as he sat down at Jake's bedside. It was the first time Marcus had visited Jake since his attack and he'd almost turned grey when he walked into the room and saw Jake's swollen and broken body. Grace had sent him to get some hot, sweet teas for them all to give him a chance to compose himself.

Jake had regained consciousness two days earlier, much to Grace's relief and the doctors' surprise. All tests indicated that there had been no permanent physical damage. But Grace wondered how long the emotional scars would take to heal – if they ever did.

'Thanks, mate,' Jake said as Marcus placed his drink on the table next to his bed.

'No problem,' Marcus said softly.

'Have the police been in again while I was out?' Grace asked him.

Jake nodded. 'They're coming in again tomorrow too. Just in case I remember anything in the next twenty-four hours.'

'Don't you remember anything then?' Marcus asked naively.

Jake stared at him. 'Oh, I remember everything,' he growled.

Marcus took a sip of his tea and looked over at Grace.

'Can you think of anything else that might help us find them, Jake?'

He frowned. 'I think I've told you everything, Mum. They hardly spoke so I couldn't recognise their accents. They definitely knew me though. Well, one of them did.'

'What makes you say that?'

Jake shrugged. 'It was the way he kept coming after me. Like it was personal to him. He just wouldn't let up. Even when the others were taking a breather or were just pushing us around, this fella just wouldn't stop laying into me. It was him who broke my fingers. I would have sworn it was Bobby White only he was too short.' Jake winced.

Grace shook her head. 'You've no idea who it was then?'

'Nope. I'll know him when I do see him though. When we were in that warehouse, there was so much blood that I managed to slide one of my hands free, and I almost took the fucker's eye out. I nearly had him. I could feel the back of his eyeball with my thumb, but one of his mates grabbed me and stopped me.'

From the corner of her eye Grace saw Marcus blanching.

'So we're looking for a short, one-eyed man?' Grace tried to lighten the mood for Marcus's sake. 'He shouldn't be hard to find.'

'Well, he wasn't short. Just not very tall.'

'So a man of medium height with one eye? I'll get the boys on it.'

Jake laughed. 'With that description, they'll have him by sundown.'

'I'll have both of his eyeballs sent to you by personal courier, son,' Grace said, only half-joking.

'Do you need anything else bringing in, Jake?' Marcus piped up, no doubt trying to change the subject. 'Anything to read, or I've got a portable DVD player if you want to borrow it?'

'No thanks, Marcus. I've got everything I need.'

'Come on, Marcus, I'll drop you back home. I've got a meeting to go to in an hour. I'll be back straight after though,' Grace said.

'No worries, Mum. I'm not going anywhere.'

'It's good to see you, Jake,' Marcus said as he stood. 'I'd give you a hug but . . .'

'Don't worry, mate,' Jake said with a laugh. 'I doubt you could get to me with all these wires anyway.'

After they had said their goodbyes, Grace ushered Marcus out of the room. He stood against the wall for a moment, leaning his head back against the noticeboard. After a few seconds, he let out a long slow breath.

'Are you okay?' Grace asked him.

He shook his head. 'I'm sorry. I just didn't expect him to look so . . .'

'Awful?'

Marcus nodded.

'He looks a damn sight better than he did a few days ago. Come on, I'll treat you to lunch on the way home.'

Chapter 74

The coffee cups almost slipped from Grace's hands as she rounded the corner and saw Michael walking towards her. His face looked a lot better than the last time she'd seen him two weeks earlier. He was badly bruised, but she could see his features now at least, and was pleased there had been no permanent damage done. Patrick had already told her that Michael was recovering well and would be fine after a few weeks' rest and recuperation. Still, she felt suddenly guilty that she hadn't visited him at all while he'd been in hospital. He had a holdall in his hand so she assumed he was either checking himself out or had been discharged. Probably the former, knowing him.

'Hey you.' He smiled at her.

'Hi,' she said as she felt a flush creep up her neck. 'How are you?'

'Oh, you know me, Grace. Tough as an old boot. I'll be fine.'

'Good. I'm sorry I haven't got round to visiting you.'

'Don't worry about it. You've been with Jake. How is he doing, by the way?'

'Much better now. He's going to have to stay in here for a while. He'll need quite a bit of physio too, but there's been no real lasting damage.'

'Good. Good,' Michael said awkwardly.

'Well, I'd better let you get going. You must be eager to get home.'

'Yeah.' He lifted his bag as if to prove it.

'Belle has missed you.'

'I've missed her too. Can I pick her up later?'

'Of course. She's out with Marcus today, but they should be back by teatime.'

'Okay, thanks.'

'Take care then,' Grace said as she started to walk away.

'You too. And thanks, by the way. For coming to my rescue, I mean.'

'Anytime. I'd better get back to Jake before his coffee goes cold.'

'Yeah, of course. Bye, Grace.'

'Bye, Michael.'

Grace's heart raced as she walked back to Jake's room. Why did everything between her and Michael have to be so bloody awkward? She wished they could go back to the way they used to be. Being in his company had always been so easy. It had always felt so natural. Now, there was no chance of them being anything more than civil to each other. Michael had made it very clear he wanted nothing more to do with her and she couldn't blame him after what she'd done. Although, now they could be in the same room without wanting to rip each other's head off – that was something at least.

'I thought you'd got lost,' Jake said lightly as she walked into his room. She knew he was feeling better when he started giving lip. It got easier each time she saw him to ignore the bandages and the bruises and swelling.

'How could I get lost? I practically live in this place.'

'Yeah, and about that, Mum,' he said. 'I'm going to be fine.

You don't have to be here all the time. You can go home some-times, you know.'

'I do go home.'

'Yeah, last thing at night. Belle will be missing you.'

'I know.' Grace sighed, feeling a pang of guilt for neglecting her daughter. But her other child had needed her.

'To be honest, you're starting to do my head in,' he added with a grin.

'You're a cheeky sod, Jake Conlon.'

'Seriously, Mum. Go home. You can still visit every day. But you don't have to be here *all* day.'

'Okay.' She held her hands up in mock surrender. 'I'll go home if you don't want me around cramping your style.'

They both sipped their coffee in silence until Jake spoke.

'I am sorry, you know, Mum,' he said.

'What for?'

'For the way I acted when I found out about Eddie.'

Grace shrugged. 'Forget about it now.'

'No. I need you to know that I didn't mean any of it. I don't know what I'd do without you. You always have my back, and I should have trusted that you didn't tell me about Eddie for a reason.'

'Jake, maybe I was wrong in not telling you about him. There just never seemed to be a good time. But let's forget about that little ratbag now, eh?'

'Sounds good to me.'

Grace finished her coffee and threw the paper cup into the bin. 'Well, I'm off home then. I could do with a long soak in a very hot tub.' She leaned in to give Jake a kiss and he hugged her unexpectedly, clinging onto her. 'I love you, Mum,' he whispered.

'I love you too, son,' she replied as she wrapped her arms around him and kissed the top of his head. His hair smelled of his favourite designer shampoo – the one he'd insisted on using since the age of fourteen when she'd taken him shopping at Harvey Nichols for his birthday. A wave of relief and happiness washed over her as she realised that her boy was going to be okay, and that she would be able to buy him his favourite shampoo for a long time to come.

Chapter 75

Bobby White eyed his young protégé warily. Liam McGuinness was on edge. The fact that both Jake and Michael were still alive wasn't sitting particularly well with him either, but Liam was getting far too twitchy for Bobby's liking. He trusted the lad, but he'd learned from experience that living on your nerves made you prone to mistakes.

'So, I want you to arrange me a meet with Grace Sumner as soon as possible. You're going to tell her I have some information about who took her kid. I want her to think I'm doing her a favour. Then we'll hang Martin and Reuben out to dry, and we'll be in the clear. This could end up working out well for us. Grace Sumner will think she owes me one.'

'Okay, boss,' Liam said as he avoided Bobby's gaze.

'This is going to work out, as long as you can hold your fucking nerve, lad. You're the one who has been desperate to off Conlon, and now that we've almost succeeded you're acting like a fucking fanny. Get a grip.'

Liam raised his eyes to meet Bobby's. 'I'll sort it.'

'Sort it soon. I want this dealt with before the week is out.'

'Consider it done. I'll get onto it now.'

* * *

An hour later and Liam McGuinness groaned in pleasure as he watched Leanne White's head bobbing up and down on his cock. She was going to be the bloody death of him. Bobby would skin them both alive if he ever found out. Liam just had to make sure he never did.

'Fuck, yeah,' he moaned as Leanne finished him off.

She looked up at him as she wiped her mouth with the back of her hand before giving him an angelic smile. God, she was beautiful. How the fuck had an ugly fat bastard like Bobby ever landed her?

He wrapped an arm around her as she moved up to lie next to him on the bed.

'That was fucking amazing, babe,' he panted.

'You're amazing, Liam,' she said as she kissed his neck.

He pulled her on top of him and brushed a blonde curl from her face. 'I fucking love you, Lea.'

'I love you too,' she said, smiling, but Liam could see the tears in her eyes.

'What's wrong?'

'We have to stop seeing each other. Bobby is getting suspicious.'

Liam shook his head. 'But we're careful. Trust me. He doesn't suspect a thing.'

Leanne climbed off him and started searching the floor of Liam's bedroom for her clothes. 'He's getting twitchy, Liam. I can tell. If he found out about us . . .'

She didn't finish her sentence. She didn't have to. Liam knew. He also knew that Bobby's twitchiness was more likely to do with their recent failed attempt on Jake Conlon and Michael Carter's lives. If only they had finished them off quickly and quietly like Liam had wanted to. But no. Bobby had wanted to teach them a lesson first. He just couldn't resist showing off.

He'd had to make a big fucking show of the whole thing. So instead of leaving two dead bodies in a warehouse, they'd left two live ones. Although one was only barely alive, and Liam had hoped that Jake Conlon wouldn't make it, but he had. That fucking police helicopter turning up had spooked the lot of them and they'd had to bail before the job was finished.

'So, I can't see you again,' Leanne said, bringing him back to the matter at hand.

'I'll figure something out, Lea. I promise.'

'He'll never let me go, Liam.' She started to cry and he jumped out of bed and pulled her to him.

'I'll figure something out,' he whispered.

Liam lay in bed long after Leanne had left, contemplating how his life had turned to shit in a matter of days. Bobby's grand-standing had meant their plan to off Jake and Michael hadn't succeeded. It seemed every criminal in Liverpool, including Nudge Richards, was working for Grace Sumner to find out who was responsible. Despite Bobby's assurances that he could pin the whole thing on Martin and Reuben, Liam wasn't convinced. The pair of them just didn't have the balls or the brains for that kind of job. And now Leanne was getting jumpy. If Bobby didn't suspect anything yet, he soon would if she didn't wind her neck in.

Sooner or later, Liam would be fucked.

There was only one thing for it. He had to get ahead of the game, and that meant making an ally of Grace Sumner.

Chapter 76

Grace had just finished a meeting with Sean Carter and was opening the door to her car when she heard someone calling her name. She turned around to see a man she didn't recognise jogging over the road towards her.

'Grace,' he panted as he reached her.

'Yes.' She eyed him suspiciously.

'I have some information for you.'

'About?'

'About who took your son.'

Grace's heart leaped into her mouth. 'You'd better come inside,' she said as she closed the door to her car and walked back into Antonelli's restaurant.

The stranger followed her inside and she sat at a table near the bar, gesturing to him to sit opposite her. From the corner of her eye, she saw Sean Carter watching the two of them while talking on his mobile phone.

'So, you are?' Grace asked.

He shifted uncomfortably in his seat. 'Liam,' he said as he wiped beads of sweat from his top lip.

'So, who took my son, Liam?'

He looked around him. 'Bobby White,' he whispered.

'And how do you know that?'

'Could I get a drink?' Liam asked as he ran his fingers up and down his throat.

'Of course,' Grace said and signalled the waitress over.

'A glass of water please, Heidi,' she said.

A moment later, Heidi placed a glass of water on the table and Liam took a long gulp.

'So?' Grace went on.

'I know because I worked for Bobby. I still work for him.'

'So, why are you telling me this?' she frowned at him. 'What's in it for you?'

'I'm telling you because he's fucking unhinged, Grace. Going after Jake and Michael Carter like that. He's going to get us all killed.'

'Were you involved?'

'Do you think I'd come here to you if I was?' He shook his head. 'Of course I wasn't.'

'So who was?'

'Bobby and some of his goons. I told him I'd have no part of it.'

'I need names, Liam. Jake said there were at least six of them.'

'Okay. I can get you the names. Bobby wants to meet with you though. He's going to try and pin the whole job on Martin Mitchell and Reuben McBride.'

'Why?'

'He thinks that if he gives you those two, it will put him in the clear, and you'll owe him then.'

Grace laughed. 'Me? Owe Bobby fucking White?'

'That's his plan.'

'But why Martin and Reuben? They're a pair of prize turkeys. What have they ever done to Bobby?'

'Reuben lost him a shitload of money. As for Martin'—Liam shrugged—'he came to Bobby after you fired him, looking for revenge, I guess. Bobby saw an opportunity to use him.'

'Okay. Let's say I believe you, Liam. What now?'

'We need to arrange a meet. With me, you and Bobby.'

'Do you think I'm soft?' Grace frowned at him.

'Of course I don't. But Bobby will have no idea what's going on. I'll be handing him to you on a plate. You can have your backup on standby. Play along with Bobby's little scheme for a few minutes and then have your lads come in and do what they do best,' he said as he wiped his brow with his forearm.

'And what about you?'

'Me? I'll walk away. You won't have any bother from me, Grace.'

'I want the names of everyone involved and I want them tonight.'

Liam looked at her for a few seconds before nodding. 'Okay, I suppose,' he said as he looked around the room again. 'It might take a while though. How do I get them to you?'

Taking a pen from her handbag, Grace wrote her telephone number on a napkin. 'Text me the names by ten o'clock, or I go to Bobby and get them from him myself. And I won't mind telling him who put me onto him either.'

'Okay. Okay.'

'Good. I'd like this meet with Bobby as soon as possible. Meet me tomorrow. Two o'clock. Nudge Richards's place.'

'Nudge's place? Why?'

'Has to be somewhere neutral, or Bobby might get suspicious.'

'Tomorrow at two. It won't be a problem. Bobby won't have a clue. He thinks he's untouchable. But going after your lad, and Michael Carter . . . well, that was just fucking stupid.'

'Hmm,' Grace agreed.

'I'll see you tomorrow then,' Liam said as he stood to leave.

'Tomorrow.'

Grace watched as Liam left the restaurant, pulling his hood up as he walked out of the door. Sean Carter sat down on the chair beside her. 'What was that all about?' he asked.

'He claims he knows who took Jake and Michael,' Grace said. 'Bobby White.'

'Do you believe him?' Sean asked.

Grace looked at him. 'I have no doubt that Bobby White is capable of it. What I don't understand is why he would dare provoke me when I could ruin him with one phone call.'

'But?'

'That guy,' Grace shook her head. 'Something was off with him.'

'Oh?'

'Like, he was really fidgety. But then he was so cocky about how much Bobby trusts him. Said his name is Liam. Bobby's right-hand man is Liam McGuinness, isn't he? So why wasn't he in on it? Would you attempt a job like that without your most trusted employee?'

Sean shook his head. 'Not a chance.'

'And why is he ratting Bobby out now? He must have an agenda of his own, and I want to know what it is.'

'Want me to do some digging?' Sean asked.

'Yes. Find out everything you can about Liam McGuinness. If possible, get me a picture. I want to make sure that was him I just spoke to.'

'Will do. And then what?'

'I've arranged a meeting with Bobby and Liam tomorrow, under the pretence that I think Bobby has some information.'

'What time? I'll come with you.'

Grace shook her head. 'Bobby might get suspicious if I take backup.'

'You can't go in there on your own. What if it's a set-up?'

'It could well be, but I'm meeting them at Nudge's place and he won't let anyone but those two in through the electric gates. Nudge has that metal detector in his portakabin now, so they can't come tooled up, and he'll wait with me until we're sure there's no danger.'

'And then what?'

'Then, I will leave the pair of them alone in a locked room with your delightful nephews. Sound like a plan?' she asked.

'Best plan I've heard all day. I'll get onto the lads now. Let's see what we can dig up on this Liam.'

'Great,' she said as he stood up. 'Let me know as soon as you find out anything.'

'Will do,' he said before kissing her cheek. 'Speak to you later.'

Chapter 77

Liam McGuinness crossed the road and jogged over to his car. He was climbing into the driver's seat when the passenger door opened and a familiar face slid into the seat next to him.

'Reuben? What the fuck do you want?'

'Me? I want to know what the fuck you were doing with Grace Sumner.'

Liam shook his head. He could do without this shit. 'Just fuck off home and wait for Bobby to phone you.'

'Do you think I'm fucking soft? You and Bobby are up to something and I want to know what it is. He fucked up big time letting those two psychopaths live and I'll be fucked if I'm going to take the fall for it.'

'Look, Reuben, Bobby knows what he's doing. So, do me a favour and get the fuck out of my car.'

Reuben smiled at him. 'Does Bobby know what you're doing though?'

Liam frowned. 'What are you on about?'

'I'm not as thick as I look, mate. I've been keeping tabs on you for weeks. Needed some insurance in case things went tits up, didn't I? What do you think Bobby would do if he knew you were screwing his wife?'

Liam's stomach sank. Reuben could fuck up everything for him.

'So tell me what's going on, or I'll tell Bobby all about you and his missus.'

Liam considered Reuben. He'd underestimated him. He should have realised people like Reuben had nine lives. He was a wily little fucker really. Perhaps this could be an advantage? Liam didn't know who to trust any more, but if his plan was going to work, he had to act fast.

'Look, Reuben. Bobby is going to try and pin the whole kidnap on you and Martin. He's meeting with Grace Sumner tomorrow to give her the information,' he said, and watched the colour drain from Reuben's face. This was Liam's chance to start building his own firm, with Reuben as his first, loyal recruit. 'But, if we play our cards right, we can make sure that doesn't happen.'

Reuben licked his lips. 'Okay. Go on.'

Grace took Belle from Sean's arms. He'd called round just as Grace was putting her to bed and Belle had been so excited to see him that she'd refused to go, and had crashed out an hour later sitting on his knee.

'I'll just get her to bed, and then you can tell me what you know,' she said quietly.

She returned to her sitting room a few minutes later to find Sean had made them both a cup of tea.

'Thanks,' she said as she took one from him and sat down on the sofa. 'So, what do we know about Mr McGuinness?' she asked.

'For a start, he's the guy who came to see you today,' he said as he pulled from his pocket a photograph of a smiling Liam behind the bar in Gin Blossom.

'Thought so.'

'Our mate Liam also has a few reasons for wanting his boss dead.'

'Oh? Such as?' Grace sipped her tea.

'Firstly, Liam stole a massive shipment of drugs and guns from Bobby a few months ago. Nudge moved them on for him and Bobby has never found out to this day. But, as you know, secrets like that have a habit of popping up when we least expect it. There's also the fact that Michael and Jake were supposed to die in that warehouse, and they didn't. That would make anyone involved twitchy.'

'Seems enough of a motive for me.'

'I also spoke to Bobby's wife, Leanne. When I mentioned Liam, she got all flustered and started babbling. She's a good-looking woman. Far too good for Bobby. I'd bet one of my restaurants that she and Liam are carrying on behind Bobby's back.'

'What better reason to want to get rid of your boss than the fact you're boning his wife?'

'Exactly. So, you're still going ahead with the meeting tomorrow?'

'Yes. I think Liam believes he's making some sort of alliance with me and I'm going to owe him one. I don't think for one second he gives me enough credit to be able to see through his bullshit.'

'It amazes me how many people underestimate you, Grace.'

'Do you think it's because I'm a woman?' she asked him.

'Probably.'

'Well, it gives me an edge, I suppose.'

'How so?'

'Because they never see me coming, Sean.'

'I miss working with you, Grace,' he sighed.

She looked at him. 'I miss working with you too. Remember the first restaurant we opened? Remember when you thought you were ordering toilet rolls in singles instead of packs of sixteen and we ended up with a stockroom full of bog roll for the first six months?'

Sean laughed. 'I'd forgotten about that. We got our acts together pretty quickly after that though, didn't we?'

'Well, you did. I already had mine together.'

'So modest.'

Grace took another sip of tea and sighed. 'I wish things could have been different, but after Nathan, and Ben, I just had to get away. I couldn't bear being around this life any longer.'

'And now here you are again.'

'It seems I can't escape who I really am. Despite how much I want to.'

'Well, I'm glad you're back. We all are. My dad cried like a baby when you left, you know. I've only ever seen him cry once before, when my mum died. When he heard you'd come back, he was all for turning up at your house the very same day. I had to convince him to give you a few days to settle in.'

Thinking of Pat Carter brought tears to Grace's eyes. 'I love your dad like he's my own, Sean, but it was partly because of him I couldn't bear to stay. Every time I looked at him, all I could think of was what Nathan did to him, and the guilt was unbearable.'

'But that wasn't your fault, Grace.'

'You've changed your tune,' she retorted, remembering one of the arguments they'd had after her ex-husband had tortured and almost killed his father.

'I was angry. You know I didn't mean any of it.'

'I know.' She patted his arm.

'Were you happy out there in the middle of nowhere?'

'Yes. I was. At least I thought I was. Now I'm not so sure. It was certainly easier there anyway.'

'Why did you really come back then?'

'Because Sol Shepherd phoned me and told me Jake was in trouble. He said Jake would end up dead if I didn't get back here and *get my house in order*.'

'Well, it seems he was right about that.'

Grace stifled a yawn and Sean took it as his cue to leave.

'I'd better get home or Sophia will worry where I've got to.'

'Of course, give her my love, won't you?'

'Will do.' He gave her a kiss on the cheek before standing up. 'I'll see myself out – stay here in the warm. Let me know if you need anything tomorrow.'

'I will.'

Grace listened as Sean closed the front door. She shut her eyes and thought about the following day. The twins were on a job for her in Scotland and she'd asked them to cut it short and meet her at Nudge's scrapyard at half past two, fifteen minutes after her meeting with Liam and Bobby.

She was counting on the arrogance of Liam and Bobby to ensure that they had no idea she was onto either of them. If they did find out, Nudge had a semi-automatic in his filing cabinet and would use it if he needed to.

At exactly five minutes to ten, Grace saw the text from the unknown number flash up onto the screen of her phone. Five names.

Martin Mitchell
Harry Bolger
Danny Woods
Alex Callaghan
Franny Hughes

Grace smiled. Along with Bobby White, that was the six men responsible for Jake and Michael's kidnap. *At least six*, they'd said though, which meant she hadn't discounted Liam's involvement. She was sure Bobby wouldn't have attempted such a big job without Liam by his side.

Chapter 78

Liam started the engine of his car and pulled away from the kerb. He glanced sideways at his boss, who was grinning like a Cheshire cat.

'This time tomorrow, Reuben and Martin will be pushing up the daisies and we'll be in the clear, lad,' Bobby said with a chuckle.

'What if they talk?' Liam asked. 'What if they mention our names?'

Bobby started to laugh. 'Well, that's the genius of my plan. We're going to offer to find Martin and Reuben for her. Then when we deliver them to her, not only will she be eternally grateful, but we'll make sure they're incapable of telling her anything. It's fucking genius.'

Liam shook his head. Bobby had no fucking clue. He didn't know Grace Sumner at all. There was not a chance in hell she'd leave the handling of whoever she believed to be involved in her son's kidnapping to anyone else, least of all someone she barely knew.

Bobby White smiled as he entered Nudge's portakabin and saw Grace Sumner sitting at Nudge's desk, waiting patiently for him. He was going to play her like a fiddle and she had no fucking clue. She'd be so grateful to him that she'd never consider blabbing to Sol Shepherd about the little mishap with his daughter. Nudge Richards stood behind her, leaning against his filing cabinet. Nudge was a huge fucker, and he could handle himself, but he was no threat to Bobby and Liam if things went south. Liam had a small arsenal in the car that was within a minute's reach should they need it. Nudge had annoyingly installed a metal detector in his portakabin a few months earlier and had made sure it was a widely known fact. It had had the desired effect and stopped people turning up at his gaff all tooled up.

'Hello, Grace,' Bobby said as he approached the desk.

'Bobby.' She nodded at him, her face set in a grimace. He supposed the upcoming topic of discussion was not particularly pleasant for her to hear.

'Tea?' Nudge asked.

Noting that Grace already had one in front of her, Bobby nodded. 'Yeah, why not?'

'Not for me, thanks,' Liam said.

'I hear you have some information for me?' Grace asked him.

Bobby took a seat on one of the chairs opposite her and indicated for Liam to do the same. 'Yeah, I do. I know who took your lad.' He stared at her, trying to gauge her reaction.

'How do you know that? And why would you tell me if you did?'

'I know we've had our differences, Grace, and you know I'm no fan of your son, but I am a generous man. And if I have information you need, I think it's only fair I share it with you.'

'And in return?' She eyed him suspiciously.

'Well, I think we can agree a "you scratch my back and I'll scratch yours" kind of arrangement.' He'd rather not reveal to Liam, or Nudge, that she had some information about him he hoped she'd never disclose. He trusted she was shrewd enough that he didn't have to spell that out to her.

She looked at him, probably considering whether he was telling the truth. He was a pretty good actor, but he knew this was the critical turning point of their meeting. If she suspected anything now, he would give Liam the nod to go to the car and Grace and Nudge would both meet with an untimely demise.

Nudge broke the tension by placing Bobby's tea on the desk in front of him and Grace sat back in her chair, her shoulders slumped in defeat.

'Okay, Bobby,' she sighed. 'I've been drawing a blank myself, so tell me who did it.'

'Reuben McBride and Martin Mitchell. Can you believe a pair of fuckwits like that planned and executed the whole thing? But I have it from a very reliable source that it was them.'

'Not just them though?' Grace frowned and for a split second he thought she was onto him until she went on. 'They must have roped some other idiots in on it with them. They couldn't have handled it on their own. Besides, Jake and Michael said there were at least six of them.'

'Of course. Well, I have no doubt me and Liam will be able to get all of the names for you by the time we've finished with the pair of them.'

'You and Liam?' She raised her eyebrows at him.

'Yeah. We could find them no problem, couldn't we, lad?' He turned to Liam who nodded his agreement. 'You must have your hands full with being up and down the hospital to see that lad of yours. We'd be more than happy to round up the pair of them for you.'

'You'd do that for me?' she asked, a smile tugging at the corners of her mouth.

'Yeah, of course.' Bobby smiled back at her, knowing he'd won her over.

'You know what, Bobby? That would be a massive help. The Carter twins would usually sort that stuff out for me, but they're away on a job. If you two could find Martin and Reuben for me, I'd be eternally grateful.'

'Then consider it done,' he said as he picked up his mug of tea and raised it in a toast. He laughed to himself as Grace did the same.

Grace drained her mug and put it on the desk in front of her. 'I'm really pleased you came to see me about this, Bobby. You have no idea how much it means to me to know who took my son. I'd better call off the search before anyone else gets hurt. Some of Michael's bouncers have been making enquiries for me, and you know how much they all enjoy a good scrap. They're just on their way to Karl Morgan's place. If I ring them now, I might just avoid world war three, eh?' She grinned as she reached into her coat pocket and took out her mobile phone.

'You won't get a signal in here, love,' Nudge piped up. 'Something to do with the metal detectors, I think.'

'Oh,' She frowned. 'I'll just nip outside. I'll only be a minute. Then we can discuss your fee, Bobby.'

'My fee?'

'I assume you usually charge for your waste disposal services? I want all six names, and I want all of them dealt with.'

'Yeah, of course. If that's what you want.'

Bobby watched Grace as she walked out of Nudge's portakabin and resisted the urge to burst into laughter. Not only had he just pulled a fast one on Grace Sumner herself, but she was going to pay him to take out the only people who could tie him and Liam to the crime. He sat back in his chair and grinned at Liam, who looked back at him with a mixture of amazement and awe.

Grace watched as the hulking figures of the Carter twins made their way across Nudge Richards's scrapyard towards her, baseball bats and hammers swinging loosely by their sides. They were a terrifying sight, particularly in the darkness. She smiled at that thought.

'Thanks for coming, boys,' she said.

'Of course, Grace.'

'Why have we brought our little friends here?' Connor asked, lifting the weapons from his side. 'Nudge hasn't been a naughty boy, has he?'

Grace shook her head. 'Nudge? Behave yourself. Nudge is a soldier. Bobby White and Liam McGuinness are in there.' She pointed to Nudge's portakabin. 'The two of them are each under the illusion that I've fallen for their bullshit. Bobby thinks I believe he's here to tell me who was responsible for taking Jake and your dad. He's trying to pin it all on Martin Mitchell as well as some poor bastard named Reuben McBride. Do you know them?'

'Martin worked at The Blue Rooms for a while, didn't he? And I've heard of Reuben,' Connor said. 'He used to be into armed robbery. My dad had a run-in with him years ago. Caused him some problems with his hearing if I remember correctly. But they were always sound after that.'

'Well, little does Bobby know that his right-hand man, Liam McGuinness, has already thrown him to the lions and fingered him for the job. So, Liam thinks he's here to set up Bobby. But I know the pair of them were in on it together. I told them I was stepping out to make a call and they're waiting patiently for my return.'

'Stupid fuckers,' Paul growled.

'I warned Bobby to stay away from Jake, but he wouldn't listen.'

'What's the situation in there, and what do you want us to do, boss?' Connor asked.

Grace had been adamant that she was out of this game, so that no more deaths would be on her hands. But someone had taken two of the people she loved most in the world, and now all bets were off.

'They have no weapons on them. They don't suspect a thing. So, do whatever you want, boys,' she smiled. 'Be as creative as you like. No one can hear for miles around here. Nudge said he'll send a clean-up crew in first thing tomorrow. But try not to get any blood spatters on his Constable knock-off. It's hanging above the tea urn. Liam has given me the names of the others involved,' she said as she handed them a piece of paper with the five names written on it. 'Once you've dealt with that pair, pay this lot a visit too.'

Connor and Paul nodded, their faces impassive. In the past, an order like this would have had them giddy with excitement. But they'd grown up a lot, and those two fuckers in there had kidnapped and tortured their dad.

'Just make sure none of them are ever found,' she said. 'I don't want this coming back on any of us.'

Grace pulled the collar of her woollen overcoat up over her neck as she exited the scrapyard into the deserted street outside. The air was chilly and the wind blew empty crisp packets and pages of old newspapers around her feet. Snowflakes had started to settle on the ground, covering the earth with a flimsy veil of white. She walked to her car, eager to reach the warmth of its interior.

At twenty-two years old, Connor and Paul Carter had already sealed their reputations as ruthless individuals. In the six months since she'd been back, Grace had learned that they were able to inflict the type of suffering few men were capable of, without even breaking a sweat. Despite their youth, they were calm and level-headed in the most extreme situations. They had witnessed, and inflicted, the type of punishments that would have relieved some of the hardest men she knew of the contents of their stomachs.

So, while Grace would have liked to do those two muppets in herself, she had other places to be. This was to be her last order. As she pulled out of the deserted car park to make her way home to her warm, comfortable sofa, Grace had every confidence that Bobby White, Liam McGuinness and their co-conspirators would suffer, and that no trace of them would remain by morning.

Paul watched intently while beads of sweat ran down Liam McGuinness's forehead as he anxiously eyed the two men standing before him. Liam couldn't move – he was bound to a chair with gaffer tape. He'd started shouting that they'd got the wrong man, that he and Grace had a deal, when Paul had grabbed him and taken out both of his kneecaps. Bobby had spewed fury at Liam as he was taken down by Connor. They'd strapped Bobby to a chair too, but despite that, he glared at them defiantly. In different circumstances, Paul might have admired him. Going down with some dignity. Unlike Liam, who'd thrown Bobby and the rest of their accomplices under the bus, cried and then pissed himself.

Connor was doing most of the talking. He usually did. Paul was happy to let him; he preferred action to words. Leaning down until he could look directly into Liam's eyes, he saw the pure terror there. It reminded him he was at the top of his game. He wondered if they had seen a similar fear in his father's eyes. No. Not a chance. Michael Carter was as hard as fucking nails. What about Jake? Had he been afraid? They'd tortured him. Beaten him so badly he'd almost died. These pricks had no idea what Jake meant to him. But they soon would.

Connor had stopped talking and Paul decided they had given their captives enough of a reprieve.

'You made a big mistake messing with our family,' Paul said.

'Your dad cried like a fucking baby,' Bobby snarled as Connor ripped the tape from his mouth.

'Shut up, will you?' Liam snapped. 'Just shut the fuck up.'

'Did he really?' Paul asked, pushing his face close to Bobby's. 'Did he?' he spat.

Bobby nodded. 'A big fucking—'

Before Bobby could finish his sentence, he let out an almighty howl as Paul bit his nose clean off. Bobby stared at him in horror as he spat it onto the floor. Liam's eyes widened as Paul wiped Bobby's blood from his mouth. 'That's just for fucking starters, boys.' He grinned.

Paul smiled at his brother before turning his attention to Liam, who'd now closed his eyes, as though it might offer him some protection from what was about to happen.

'Open your eyes, son. You're going to miss the show,' Paul laughed.

Then Liam shook his head before he felt the first blow of the hammer as it smashed his ankle into pieces.

Chapter 79

Jake winced as he tried to prop himself up in bed. He wasn't expecting a visitor so late in the night. It wasn't allowed. But he was in a private room and most of the people he knew could persuade anyone they wanted to look the other way when necessary. He smiled. He'd been wondering when this particular visitor would make an appearance. He was the one person he'd been desperate to see.

Paul Carter approached his bed and sat down beside him. 'I'm sorry I haven't been in before now. But your mum was here, and Siobhan . . .'

'I know. You don't have to explain.'

'How are you doing?' Paul asked.

'Never been better.' Jake grimaced.

'Stupid question.'

'Everything fucking hurts, mate,' Jake said as he closed his eyes. 'Even breathing feels like a fucking effort.'

Paul placed his hand over Jake's. 'I thought you were a goner, lad. When we carried you out of there . . .'

'So did I,' Jake rasped.

'It nearly fucking killed me – seeing you like that, and having to pretend . . .'

'I thought I'd never see you again,' Jake said and closed his eyes quickly before Paul could see the tears forming there.

'You've got to tell her, you know. It's not fair. On either of us.'

'I know.' Jake swallowed. 'But it's not that easy, Paul. Just give me some time.'

'I'd better let you get some sleep,' Paul said and stood up.

'No. I'm fine,' Jake said as he grabbed Paul by the arm. 'Stay for a bit.'

'Okay. If you're sure?'

'I am. I've been waiting to see you for ages. You can't go yet,' he said as he pulled Paul towards him.

Michael smiled at the nurse as he approached the nurses' station. 'I'm here to see Jake Conlon,' he said quietly. She waved him past.

Michael could hear muffled noises as he pushed open the door to Jake's room and wondered who else was visiting Jake at this hour of the night. He wished he'd knocked when he walked in and saw his son Paul half-naked and straddling Jake.

The pair of them looked up as he entered and Paul scrambled off the bed. 'Fucking hell, Dad. Don't you knock?'

Michael shook his head. 'I didn't think I'd need to. I fucking knew it. I knew something was going on with you two. Although, if I'm honest, I didn't think it was this. Jesus Christ, son.'

'Dad, we can explain,' Paul said as he started to put his shirt on.

'Really? Can you?'

'Michael, listen,' Jake started.

'Listen to what, Jake? How you two have been sneaking around behind everyone's back?'

'Well, to be fair, Dad, it's not really anyone's fucking business but ours, is it?' Paul snapped at him and Michael took a few steps towards him. His son was one of the most feared men in the country, but he'd be damned if he'd let him speak to him like that.

'I think it's Siobhan's business, don't you?' he barked.

'Well, yeah,' Paul agreed, running his hands through his hair as he sat on the chair beside Jake's bed.

'But that's my responsibility, not Paul's,' Jake said.

'You're not wrong there,' Michael said before taking a seat beside his son.

'Look, what are you two actually playing at here? Is this a bit of a fling, or is it something more? Because if it's more—'

'What?' Jake demanded. 'What if it is more? Can't handle your son being gay, is that it?'

Michael glared at him. 'What? Don't be so fucking ridiculous. I've known about Paul since I walked in on him having a wank to *Top Gun* when he was fourteen.'

'Thanks for that, Dad,' Paul muttered.

'But if it is more,' Michael went on, 'you need to tell Siobhan – and your mother.'

'We don't know what it is yet, Dad,' Paul said.

'I hate lying to your mum, Jake,' Michael said. 'You know she won't care one way or another if you're gay. But she'll go nuts if she finds out we've all been lying to her.'

'She'll care about me cheating on Siobhan,' Jake reminded him.

'But her priority would still be you. It always is.'

'Just give us some time to figure this out,' Paul said.

'Whatever. I don't need this shit right now. Can I see you outside?'

Paul sighed. 'I'll be back in a minute,' he said to Jake.

Michael looked at his son and his heart broke for him. Paul was never going to find happiness with Jake Conlon, but he had learned a long time ago that he had to let his sons live their own lives.

'I came to tell Jake that Bobby and the others had been dealt with. But I suppose you've already apprised him of that fact. I assume you were there?'

Paul shrugged. 'Of course I was. We wouldn't let anyone else sort it, would we? You're our dad.'

'You're good lads. I'm proud of you, son.'

Paul smiled at him and shook his head. He had always found it difficult to accept genuine praise. 'Thanks, Dad. And look, don't worry about what you just saw. I'll sort it out.'

Michael put his hand on Paul's shoulder. 'Please be careful, son.'

Paul frowned at him. 'I always am.'

Chapter 80

Siobhan smiled as she held the white piece of plastic between her fingertips. Her stomach fluttered with excitement.

Two lines.

Positive.

She'd stopped taking the pill two months earlier, and had even bought some of those ovulation tester strips, just to make sure she was pouncing on Jake at exactly the right time. She knew he'd never refuse her. Even if he was tired or not in the mood. Probably the guilt, she thought to herself. He would do anything to keep her sweet and make her happy.

She knew he loved her, in his own way. She loved him too. She loved the lifestyle he afforded her. The lifestyle he would provide for their children. She loved Grace, and Belle. She loved working at the club, especially now she was the manager. And one day soon, she would become Mrs Siobhan Conlon, and she would have the world at her feet. Siobhan tried not to think about the possibility that this baby was Connor Carter's. After all, it had been one night. One memorable, stupid night. This was Jake's baby, she knew it.

Growing up on a council estate in Seaforth, she'd worked hard to get a scholarship to St Mary's College. She'd done well in her GCSEs and A Levels and had secured herself a place at Liverpool

University. But she'd always been the one with the hand-me-down clothes. Any designer gear she owned had been carefully sourced by her mum from charity shops or car boot sales. She was popular enough and had been invited to parties and sleepovers – invitations she could never reciprocate because she was too ashamed of her mum and dad's small terraced council house. She was always the poor friend and she wandered through her teenage years awestruck by a wealth she longed to have a taste of herself. Her friends' parents owned massive detached houses in Crosby and Southport, had brand-new cars and designer handbags and shoes. It was a world that Siobhan could only ever participate in from the edges. She could touch it, but she could never hold it in her grasp.

Until she'd fallen in love with Jake Conlon.

He had opened doors for her that she couldn't guarantee her education ever would. He lavished expensive gifts upon her and treated her to spa days in high-end salons. Money was no object to him. He even gave her parents the money to buy a nice little semi in Waterloo. Whatever she wanted, he gave her. No matter how expensive or seemingly insignificant.

She and Jake were going to be a proper family. He would ask her to marry him once he found out about the baby – he was traditional like that. Then she would have everything she'd ever needed.

Siobhan Davies had it all worked out. She could see her life unfolding in front of her and liked what she saw.

Chapter 81

Jake laughed as the nurse told him another funny story about one of her patients. He knew she was flirting with him, but he didn't care. He had no interest in her that way, but she was a welcome distraction. Paul was continuing his late-night visits and Jake had been going over and over their conversations in his head all day. Paul was getting restless. He wanted more from Jake than he could give. It wasn't easy for him even to admit he had feelings for Paul. To admit that to anyone else felt completely terrifying and unnatural to him.

What he had decided was that he needed to end things with Siobhan. It wasn't fair to keep stringing her along believing they were going to live happily ever after. She was due to visit soon and he'd finally worked up the courage to tell her that he wanted to end things. The guilt had been eating away at him for months. Trying to divide himself between two people, all while being terrified that his secret was going to be uncovered, was exhausting. He couldn't do it anymore. Almost dying had made him re-evaluate what was important in his life. He wanted to spend every minute with the person who had come to mean more to him than he'd dare to admit. Without Siobhan tying him down, waiting for him to come home every night, he could do that much more easily. He could screw enough of the women who constantly threw themselves at him to convince everyone he was a hot-blooded, straight man.

He and Paul were best mates, nothing more – at least that was how it would appear. Life was too short to spend it with the wrong person. And he didn't want to lie to Siobhan any more; he didn't want to hurt her any more than he had to. He loved her, but like a best friend or a sister, not like a boyfriend should. And she deserved someone who worshipped her.

He hoped Siobhan wouldn't take it too badly. But who was he kidding? She was going to be heartbroken. Confused. Angry. He wouldn't blame her if she hated him.

The nurse was just leaving as Siobhan walked through the door. 'Bye, Jake,' the nurse said, fluttering her eyelashes at him. Siobhan grinned at him and rolled her eyes. She was never jealous of other women. That was another one of the things he loved about her. Despite what he was about to do to her, he hoped they would be able to be friends one day.

'Hiya, babe,' Siobhan said and kissed him on the cheek.

'Hiya,' he replied, forcing a smile as his stomach did somersaults. Could he really go through with this?

'I have some news for you.' She beamed at him and he remembered how much he loved her smile. She could light up a room. Could he really break her heart?

'What's that?' he asked her.

'I'm pregnant.' She grinned as she held out a pregnancy test for him to see.

He took it from her and looked at it. Not that he even knew what he was looking for.

'Two lines,' she said. 'That means it's positive.'

Jake stared at her, blinking, while he thought of the appropriate reaction. So many thoughts thundered around his head.

Wasn't she on the pill? This was the worst timing ever. How could he break it off now? Jesus Christ, he was going to be a dad! They'd never talked about kids. He didn't want kids. Not now, anyway. And not with Siobhan. What the hell was he going to do?

'Jake, I know we didn't plan this. But aren't you happy for us?' She stared at him, her green eyes wide and brimming with tears.

'Of course, I am, babe,' he lied as he held out his hand to her. 'It's just a surprise. I thought we were covered, you know?'

'We were. But the pill isn't one hundred per cent effective. Accidents happen all the time. But it's a good surprise, isn't it?'

Jake nodded feebly. If he didn't feel so guilty, he might have told her that no, it wasn't a good surprise at all. But she had completely blindsided him. He had spent the whole day psyching himself up to have one difficult conversation, and she had started an entirely different one. He needed time to think. He felt like the walls were closing in on him. 'Come here,' he said as he put his arm around her and kissed her forehead.

Siobhan sat next to him on the bed and snuggled into him. He rested his head on hers, her long red hair feeling soft against his cheek. He could smell the expensive shampoo she used and the perfume she wore and it reminded him of how, when he was a kid, he would sneak into his mum's bed whenever he'd had a bad dream. He would cuddle into her and he always felt safe. There were no monsters that could get to him then, not even the one he called Dad.

How could Jake be a dad? It was hard enough keeping himself and Siobhan safe, never mind a tiny, helpless little human too. While he hoped he'd be a great dad one day, in the very distant future, he didn't exactly have the best role model. Who knew if he was even up to the job? One thing he did know was that he couldn't end things with Siobhan now. If she chose to keep the baby, he'd have to stay with her. If he couldn't convince her otherwise then he was stuck. Did he even have the heart to try and convince her otherwise? She looked so bloody happy.

This was going to mean the end of his secret meetings with Paul. No matter how much it would kill him to end it, he would have to prioritise Siobhan and the baby.

They were his future.

Not Paul.

Maybe it was for the best? Jake swallowed the bile rising in his throat. He knew it wasn't. He knew that Siobhan's little revelation had fucked everything up and things would never be the same again.

Chapter 82

Jake had been lying awake waiting for his usual nightly visitor. Paul never arrived at the same time. He called whenever he'd finished whatever job he'd been on. He and Connor had taken up the mantle of running their newly found empire while he was in hospital. Tonight, when the door of his room opened and the light flooded its interior, he didn't feel the familiar rush of adrenaline. Instead he felt sick. Like his stomach had dropped through the floor. Jake had spoken to Paul before Siobhan's earlier visit and her bombshell, and told him he was ending things with her, convincing him that it was all he could offer him for the time being.

'How's the wounded soldier today?' Paul smiled at him as he walked towards his bed.

'Okay,' Jake sighed as Paul bent to kiss him.

'Was it that bad? Did she take it okay?' Paul asked.

'Siobhan's pregnant,' Jake said. There was no use pretending for a minute longer. It was like ripping off a plaster. It was going to hurt like hell, so better get it over with as soon as possible.

'Fuck! Were you trying?'

'Of course we fucking weren't.'

'Then how is she pregnant? Isn't she on the pill or something?'

'Yeah, but she says these things can happen.'

'And you believe her?' Jake stared at him.

'Are you saying she did this on purpose?'

'Wouldn't be the first time a bird has done that when she sensed things were on the skids.'

Jake scowled at him. 'Firstly, she has no idea that we're *on the skids*, and secondly, Siobhan's not like that.'

'Oh, come on, Jake. Before you ended up in here, you were spending more time with me than you were with her. Do you think she didn't pick up on something being wrong? She is much smarter than you give her credit for.' Paul sat on the chair beside Jake's bed and ran his hands through his hair.

'Even if she did, which she didn't, I told you, she's not like that.'

Paul stared at him. 'Let's face it, Jake. No one really knows anyone, do they? All we can do is trust that people will keep the promises they make us.' He stood up and started to walk out.

'I didn't fucking ask for this, Paul,' Jake shouted after him.

Paul turned and walked back to him. 'But what are you going to do about it?'

Jake shook his head. 'What fucking choice do I have? She's having my baby.'

'Are you sure it's even yours?' Paul asked him in all seriousness.

Jake glared at him. 'What the fuck do you mean by that? Of course I'm fucking sure, you cheeky cunt.'

'I'm just saying. I bet she never thought you'd cheat on her either. People cheat. They lie. It's human fucking nature.'

Jake shook his head. 'No. She wouldn't. I know her.'

'Looks like you've made your mind up then.'

Jake placed a hand on Paul's arm. 'I wish I could change it. I'd ask her to get rid of it if I thought she would, but she's over the fucking moon. There's nothing I can do about it now. I have to at least try, Paul. It's the least I can do.'

'Whatever.' Paul shook his head. 'This was never going to work long-term anyway, was it? We're practically fucking related.'

Jake forced a smile. His insides felt like they were being pulled through a meat grinder. Why was everything so fucking complicated? His feelings for Paul and Siobhan and their baby all swirled around his head until he had no idea what he felt for anyone any more.

'I'd better get going,' Paul said before turning around and walking out of Jake's hospital room.

Jake watched him go and resisted the urge to call him back.

Closing his eyes, he tried not to think about how much he was hurting and instead focused on his unborn child. Would it be a boy or a girl? Would it look like him, or like Siobhan? God, his mum was going to be beside herself with joy. Maybe this was enough to make her stay in Liverpool?

He hoped so.

He needed her now more than ever.

Chapter 83

Connor was sound asleep on his sofa when he heard the banging on the door to his flat. Groaning, he heaved himself up and went to answer it. Looking through the spyhole, he saw it was Paul.

He unfastened the bolts and opened the door.

'Don't you answer your fucking phone, Con?' Paul pushed past him and into the sitting room.

'Do come in,' Connor said sarcastically as he followed his brother. 'I was asleep. What's so fucking urgent?'

Paul paced up and down the room. 'I've got something to tell you.'

Connor sat down on the sofa. What the hell had happened now? His life was becoming like one long fucking soap opera lately. 'What now?'

'Siobhan's pregnant.'

Connor's heart sank. He chewed his bottom lip while he calculated how long it had been since he and Siobhan had had sex.

'Doesn't mean it's mine,' he offered.

'Doesn't mean it's not either. Did you two use anything?'

Connor shook his head. 'It wasn't exactly planned, was it?'

'You were in a fucking nightclub. Every toilet has a condom machine. Fucking hell, Con!'

'Well, we obviously weren't thinking straight or it would never have happened. I assumed she'd be on the pill or something.'

'Jesus,' Paul said as he sat on the sofa beside his brother. 'This is all kinds of fucked up.'

Connor ran his hands through his hair. 'I know. What has Siobhan said? Did she tell Jake the baby was his?'

Paul nodded.

'Well, there you go then. It must be. She'd know the dates and stuff, wouldn't she?'

'I don't fucking know,' he said. 'I do know that Jake was ready to finish things with her, and then she hit him with becoming a daddy, and now he's convinced he'll have to marry her or something.'

'Look, Paul. I'm sure the baby is his. It must be. Maybe this is for the best? You and Jake are not exactly right for each other, are you? We've got a sister in common for a start. That makes us almost fucking related. You needed to put a stop to this sooner or later. Now we can all get on with our lives and pretend this never happened.' Connor tried to be the voice of reason in a sea of chaos.

Paul sat back against the sofa and sighed. 'You're probably right. But . . .'

'But what?'

'I love him, Con,' Paul whispered.

Connor had suspected for a while that his brother's feelings for Jake ran much deeper than he'd let on. But there was no happiness to be had for him or Jake if they continued to pursue a relationship together. For one thing, Connor suspected it would be a cold day in hell before Jake would admit to being gay. The sooner they both accepted it was better to end it, the quicker they could move on. Taking hold of his brother by the neck, he pulled him in for an awkward hug. 'It'll all be okay in the end, bro,' he said quietly.

Paul nodded. 'And if it's not okay, it's not the end, eh?'

Chapter 84

Connor Carter rang the buzzer to the entrance of the expensive waterfront apartment block. It was similar to the one he and Paul lived in, and only a fifteen-minute walk away.

'Hello?' Siobhan answered the buzzer.

'Siobhan, it's me. Can I come up?'

'Connor, I was just on my way to bed. Can it wait?'

'Not really,' he replied.

The door clicked open and he made his way inside.

Siobhan was waiting for him at the door of her and Jake's apartment by the time he got there. 'Come in,' she said as he reached the door.

He followed her into the open-plan sitting room.

'What's so important?' she asked him.

'I heard your news.'

She sat down on the sofa and put her head in her hands. 'Bloody hell, news travels fast. I only told Jake yesterday.'

'Is there any chance it's mine, Siobhan?' he demanded.

She stared at him, her pale cheeks flushed pink, and shook her head. 'No.'

'No? You're sure? How far are you?'

'What? Why does that matter? This is Jake's baby, Connor.'

'Then tell me how far gone you are.'

'Just a few weeks,' she said as she pulled her silk robe tighter around herself.

'So, it could be mine then?' He shook his head and sat in the armchair.

'We had sex once, Connor. This is Jake's baby. Please get it out of your head that it might be yours. Don't you dare ruin this for me.'

'I don't want to ruin anything for you, Siobhan. But I also don't want any comeback from this.'

'What do you mean?'

'I mean, when this baby is born, I hope you're not going to have some crisis of conscience and tell Jake what we did.'

'I won't. Me and Jake are going to get married. What you and I had . . . what we did . . . it was just a bit of fun, wasn't it? There's no need for anyone to ever find out.'

'I'm glad we're on the same page.'

'We are. Now, can I go to bed please? I'm tired.'

'Of course,' he said, standing up to leave. 'Take care of yourself, Siobhan.'

'I will. Thanks.'

Siobhan waited to hear the front door closing before she picked up the cushion and screamed into it. The cheek of Connor Carter moralising to her! Did they all think she was bloody stupid? How she would love to tell them all that she knew about Jake and Paul's disgusting little secret. God, she wished she could see the look on their faces. Well, one day she would tell them. But not until she had Jake exactly where she wanted him. He would regret taking her for a fool. They all would.

And how the hell did Connor know already? She supposed Jake had panicked and told Paul who'd then told his brother.

Although perhaps Jake telling Paul was a good thing, she told herself. Maybe he had finally broken off their disgusting little affair. She hoped so. She needed Jake's undivided attention now that she was carrying his child. She would demand it. If he thought he could go swanning off to be with his boyfriend any time he fancied, he had another think coming.

Chapter 85

Marcus Holden staggered out of The Goose and Duck in Stanley Street. He waved goodnight to the bouncers, who knew him well as he was a frequent customer. Not like the fella he'd just bumped into. It would have been funny if it wasn't so bloody tragic. The man was a raging homophobe and there he was, peddling his dodgy ciggies in a gay bar. But that fact now paled into insignificance. As soon as he'd seen him, Marcus knew what he'd done.

Marcus had sat with Grace by Jake's bedside when he'd told them about coming to in that warehouse. He'd been beaten up and bound but had managed to free his hands and he'd almost gouged out one of his attackers' eyes. Marcus remembered the conversation so well because he'd almost vomited up his latte at hearing the vivid description and the image had been ingrained into his brain ever since. Sometimes he forgot that Grace was part of this other world that he knew nothing about. She had been such a sweet, naïve girl when he'd met her, and he still saw that in her. Maybe that was what he wanted to see.

Marcus cursed as he checked his mobile phone for a signal and realised his battery had died. That was what he got for taking selfies and posting them on Snapchat all night. His friends had left earlier but he'd hung around talking to the bar staff and some of the regulars whom he knew well. He'd be leaving for Harewood in a few days and wanted to soak up as much of the fabulous Liverpool nightlife as he could before he left. He wasn't sure how much of a gay scene there'd be in Harewood. Maybe he would start one!

He looked around for a taxi, but it was the early hours of the morning and most of the clubs and pubs had let out hours ago, so there were no cabs to be found. It was freezing cold, but he'd had plenty to drink and the alcohol gave him a warm buzz as he started to walk home. He didn't live far from the city centre and as soon as he got home he'd phone Grace and tell her he'd found out who really kidnapped Jake and Michael. He felt a little thrill of excitement at the thought of it. Who would have thought that he, Marcus Holden, would be the one to crack the case? Grace would be so proud of him.

Marcus was only two streets away from his flat when he heard the footsteps behind him. He'd been sure he was being followed but every time he turned around there was no one there and he'd put it down to adrenaline, alcohol and his over-active imagination. But he'd definitely heard those footsteps.

Spinning around on his heel, he saw him – the closeted homophobe himself. 'Why are you following me?' he slurred.

'I wanted to buy you a drink, Marcus. Why did you dash off?'

'I needed to get home. I'm tired,' he replied.

'Is that all?' he said as he approached. 'You ran out of there in a hurry when you spotted me.'

'I was surprised to see you in a place like that.' Marcus spoke nonchalantly, but his heart began to race. The alcohol was wearing off rapidly and he started to feel the biting cold through his thin shirt. The hairs on his forearms stood on end and he knew he was in danger. He wondered what Grace would do. She would brazen her way out of it. He could too. Fight or flight, Marcus, he thought to himself. What are you going to do? He knew this fella was a coward; Grace had told him so.

'I know what you did,' Marcus said.

'Is that so?' He frowned as he approached.

Marcus nodded. He wasn't going to back down. He was half a foot taller than this vile scumbag and he was sure he could take him in a fight.

Marcus flinched as the other man moved to within inches of his face. Mentally chastising himself, he stood firm. He was going to front this out. It seemed his tactics were working as he watched his would-be assailant start to back away. But why was he smiling? This wasn't funny.

It was a few seconds before Marcus felt the warmth spreading across his stomach. He looked down and was horrified to see his favourite white shirt was now stained crimson. He glanced up and saw the glint of the metal blade in the streetlight as his attacker pocketed it and began to run off into the darkness.

Suddenly Marcus felt weak and nauseous. He no longer had the energy to hold himself up and stumbled to the ground. Dear God, he'd been stabbed. He needed an ambulance. Fumbling for his phone, he managed to pull it free from his pocket.

'Fuck,' he spat as he saw the blank screen and remembered his dead battery. He tried to call out but felt like he was going to choke every time he tried. He could taste the blood in his mouth and wondered whether he was going to die in this dark alleyway. He could see his flat from where he lay on the ground. Help was so close, but so far away. He'd never been a believer in God, but he prayed anyway, that someone might find him before it was too late.

Marcus was drifting in and out of consciousness when he saw the figure coming towards him. Maybe there was a God after all.

Chapter 86

Michael stood in Grace's living room with his hands in his pockets, and she stared at him as though he had three heads. Surely she'd misheard him. Because if she hadn't, then he'd just told her that her best friend in the whole world had been murdered. Stabbed in the stomach and left to bleed out in an alley like some stray dog.

'Are you playing some kind of sick joke?'

Michael shook his head. 'I'm so sorry, Grace,' he said softly.

'No. I don't believe you. Whoever told you has got it wrong, Michael. There's no way it could be Marcus. There just can't.' She started to stammer.

Michael walked over to her and placed his hand on her arm. 'It's him. I saw him myself.'

'No, he's moving to Harewood with me. We're going to open a pub, Michael. We're . . .'

Then Grace heard a terrible wailing sound and wondered where it was coming from until she realised it was from her.

This couldn't be happening. After everything else. Not Marcus. She felt her knees buckle and Michael caught her before she hit the floor. He moved her to the sofa and pulled her into his arms. She clung to his jacket, her fingernails clawing the expensive material.

Her heart felt like it had been ripped from her chest. Marcus was gone. She would never laugh at one of his snarky comments or sarcastic quips again.

Grace started to weep then. Slow, silent tears, which ran down her face in a constant salty stream, dripping onto the sleeve of her jumper. When she could finally speak and the tears started to subside, she felt the anger surging in her chest.

She looked up at Michael. 'Who did it?'

'It was a random mugging, Grace. Probably some crackhead looking for his next fix. It was nothing to do with us. Let the police handle this one. You've been through enough.'

'My best friend has just been murdered like a dog and you expect me to let the police handle it?' she cried. 'Are you fucking serious?'

'The police will find whoever did it. He left his prints all over the scene,' Michael said softly. 'This one's not on you.'

Grace blinked at him and realised he was being serious. Michael Carter, the voice of reason? The world really had gone mad.

She couldn't bear to think about it any longer. Resting her head on his chest, she began to sob again.

Michael held onto a weeping Grace and felt like his heart was going to break. He had never seen Grace Sumner vulnerable in her entire life. She was always so stoic. The one everyone else looked to for guidance. The calm in a sea of chaos.

As she continued to sob, he pulled her onto his lap, wrapping his arms around her. 'I'm so sorry,' he whispered.

He hated to admit that he enjoyed the feeling of protecting her, of making her feel secure. It was a powerful aphrodisiac. She clung to him then, like a limpet. He stroked her hair and kissed her forehead. Then he just held her there for hours until she was spent and he thought she must have no more tears left to cry.

Grace woke on the sofa. Her head felt like it was stuffed full of candyfloss and her eyes stung. For a glorious moment she forgot that Marcus was gone. Then it all came rushing back to her, her grief washing over her like a tsunami.

Voices from the other room distracted her and she remembered that Michael had stayed the night. He must have seen to Belle. It wasn't just his voice she heard though, there was another too.

Grace walked into the kitchen and saw Marcus's mother, Val. Grace had lost her best friend but Val had lost her son. Grace couldn't even imagine what she was going through.

'Grace,' she said as she walked into the kitchen, her face wet with tears.

'Hi, Val.' She watched as Val's face crumpled like yesterday's newspaper.

Walking over to her, she pulled her into an embrace. 'I'm sorry, Val,' she soothed. She knew then that she had to be strong for her, and for everyone else. There was no more wallowing and feeling sorry for herself. She had loved Marcus Holden like a brother, but he was gone, and the world had to keep moving on.

She remembered Michael was in the room. Releasing Val from her embrace, she asked Michael, 'Would you mind taking Belle for the day, please?'

'No, of course not. I'll keep her for as long as you need.'

'Thanks,' she said.

There was so much to do. The funeral would need to be

arranged and Val wasn't good in a crisis at the best of times. Grace would make sure that her friend had the best send-off Liverpool had ever seen. Then, as soon as his funeral was over, she was leaving Liverpool for good.

Chapter 87

Grace hadn't seen DI Tony Webster for a long time. She hadn't had cause to call on his services and the truth was she could hardly stand the man. There was nothing worse than a dirty copper. So she was surprised to see him walking up the driveway of her house.

She opened the door before he had a chance to ring the doorbell and disturb Belle's afternoon nap. 'What can I do for you Tony?' she asked.

'I need to talk to you, Grace. It's about Marcus.'

Grace blanched at the mention of her friend's name but she allowed Tony into her house and he followed her into the living room. She stared at him, waiting for him to tell her what he knew. The last she'd heard, they'd found Marcus's killer. But she didn't press him because she knew he enjoyed the illusion that he was in charge. He got prickly when she reminded him who really called the shots, and on this occasion he obviously had information that she wanted.

Tony cleared his throat. 'The prints all over the murder scene didn't belong to the murderer,' he said.

'What?' she snapped. 'Who did they belong to then? Why were someone's prints all over the scene if they didn't kill him?'

'They belonged to some kid from the care home near town.

He'd run away and was on his way back when he came across Marcus's body. Seeing the possible opportunity to stay on the run a little longer, he went through Marcus's pockets and took his wallet and mobile phone. He says he didn't stab him.'

'And you believe him?'

'We have no reason to believe was lying.'

'Well, not being done for murder is a pretty fucking big one, isn't it, Tony?'

Tony's face reddened. Despite being as bent as a nine-bob note, he prided himself on being good at his job. 'What I'm about to tell you next is crucial to the investigation, Grace. But I thought you'd want to know.'

She blinked at him, waiting for him to go on. When he didn't, she remembered that they were not friends. He wasn't there as a favour to her.

'How much?' She smiled through gritted teeth.

'The usual is fine,' he said quietly. She hoped he felt embarrassed exploiting her grief but doubted he knew the meaning of the word.

'Of course. I've got it in the safe. I'll get it for you before you go.'

Tony nodded. 'Marcus was still alive when the kid found him.'

'What?' she shrieked. 'And he just left him there to die?' Grace was furious. She knew that Marcus had lain dying in that deserted alleyway for hours before an amorous young couple had stumbled across his cold, lifeless body. 'He deserves to go down for murder anyway.'

'You know that's not how it works. He'll be done for theft from the person, but it's not a crime not to seek help for someone.'

'No, but it's fucking reprehensible. All he needed to do was phone 999. The little shit could do with a good bloody kicking.'

'He's only thirteen, Grace.'

Grace shook her head in despair. She drew the line at going after kids.

'So there goes your theory of a mugging gone wrong then! Anyway, what makes you so sure this kid didn't do it?'

'Two things. Although we found Marcus's blood on his clothing, it was minimal. There were no blood spatters consistent with the attack. And more importantly, Marcus told him who his attacker was.'

Grace stared at him in disbelief. 'What? Who?'

'Reuben McBride.'

Grace felt like she'd been kicked in the stomach. She fought the urge to vomit all over Tony's designer shoes. Reuben McBride's name was popping up all over the place and she wanted to know why. 'Reuben? But why?'

Tony shook his head. 'No idea. We haven't lifted him yet. We only questioned the kid this morning. So you might want to get to McBride before we do.'

Grace nodded. She would get to him, and she would make him sorry he'd ever been born.

After pocketing his money, Tony turned to Grace as he was leaving. 'The kid mentioned something else Marcus said. It doesn't make any sense. He was probably delirious by then.'

'What?' Grace asked. 'Anything might help.'

'He said "eye patch".' Tony shook his head. 'Mean anything to you?'

Grace shook her head. 'Eye patch? What about an eye patch? Reuben had one?'

'Don't know. The kid said he never said more than that.'

Grace sighed. Tony was right, it wasn't much help at all.

* * *

Grace made herself a cup of strong sweet tea after Tony left. She had to think. She needed to find Reuben McBride before the police did. She had to know why he'd killed Marcus. It didn't make any sense at all. Reuben was a thief. He used guns when the occasion called for it – he didn't just go around stabbing people for no reason. At least he never used to. His latest thing was hijacking lorries full of contraband before they could be delivered to their intended destination.

Grace couldn't bring the Carters in on this one. The twins were in Essex on a job and things had been awkward between her and Michael since the morning after Marcus had been killed. She'd spent most of that night on her sofa in Michael's arms but they had barely been able to look at each other since. He would never forgive her for hiding Belle from him, and she would never expect him to. Jake was still in hospital, although he was threatening to discharge himself with every day he grew stronger.

None of them could help her with this. But there was one man who might know where Reuben McBride was. Taking her phone from her pocket, Grace phoned him.

'Hello, stranger.' John Brennan's voice was as bright and cheery as ever.

'John, I need your help.'

'Of course. What is it?'

Two hours later, Grace had dropped Belle off with Libby for the evening and was in John Brennan's car on the way to Reuben McBride's lock-up. John and Reuben ran in the same circles. Reuben had never been stupid enough to try and knock off one of John's lorries, but he'd tried it on with most of John's competitors.

Grace and John waited patiently until they saw a car pull up and watched as Reuben manoeuvred himself out of the driver's door. He looked around him as he walked to his lock-up, but he didn't notice the car parked across the street. Reuben opened the heavy steel shutters and disappeared into the darkness of the building. Grace and John strode quickly across the street and slipped inside the unlocked door. John pulled the shutters down behind them so they wouldn't be disturbed.

Startled by the noise, Reuben spun on his heel. The only light was from a dim bulb swinging from the ceiling but Grace was sure he recognised his intruders. She was surprised to see that Reuben was in fact wearing an eye patch – so the kid had been telling the truth after all.

'What do you two want?' Reuben snarled, trying to feign outrage, but Grace could see his hands shaking. Reuben McBride thought he was a hard man, but he was a coward. He didn't have the brains to earn his own money, which was why he stole other people's. He relied on a hired team of mindless thugs to do most of the donkey work. With paid muscle behind him, he gave as good as he got. But one on one, he was a gutless wonder. And two on one, he was a quivering wreck. Especially when one of those two people was six foot three, almost as wide as he was tall, and swinging a base-ball bat – all while smiling directly at him.

'We know you killed Marcus,' Grace said. 'Tell me why and I'll ask him to go easy on you,' she said inclining her head towards John.

'I didn't kill anyone.' He shook his head furiously.

'You didn't stab him in the stomach and leave him to die in an alleyway then? No?'

Grace walked towards him. 'He was my best friend. He was a good man. He was worth ten of you, you useless piece of shit.'

'I didn't do it.' His legs were shaking so much, he was struggling to stay upright.

'We know you did. Somebody saw you,' she lied. 'They even described that eye patch you're wearing.'

He stared at her like a lamb being led to the slaughter. He knew he wasn't getting out of the room alive. 'He was a fucking queer,' he spat, obviously deciding on a change of tactic.

Grace slapped him across the face with the back of her hand and he fell to the floor. 'How fucking dare you,' she screamed. 'Is that what this is about? Because he was gay?'

Reuben continued to stare at her, blinking as his eyes started to water.

'No,' Grace shook her head. 'You're a homophobic little prick, but you wouldn't kill someone because of that. There must be something else.'

'No,' Reuben shook his head again. 'The dirty little fag came on to me, so I stabbed him.'

Grace fought the urge to laugh. 'Marcus came on to you? Come off it, you horrible little cunt. He had more class in his little toe than you have in your whole body. There's something you're not telling me. Would you like me to ask my colleague here to extract the information from you instead?'

John Brennan, who'd remained silent, stepped forward into the light. His shadow fell ominously across Reuben's body as he cowered in fear.

Grace watched him. Why wouldn't he just tell her and make it easier on himself? Nothing was worse than murdering her best friend, and he'd just admitted that. Reuben started to stand up, straightening his eye patch, which had been knocked slightly askew when Grace slapped him. Then she remembered something and wondered how she could have been so bloody stupid.

Jake and Michael had fought back when they were attacked. They had been unable to identify their masked attackers and had been struck from behind by a group of men. They'd lashed out, hitting anything they could. But Jake had told her how he'd managed to grab one of them and had almost succeeded in gouging one of his eyes out.

'You took my son,' she said to him.

John looked at her and raised his eyebrows and she nodded.

'Bobby and Martin were telling the truth. It was you. Marcus must have found out somehow.'

Reuben started to shake his head again and Grace noticed that he had pissed himself.

'No, it was them,' he said, his voice cracking as he spoke.

'That's why you've got that eye patch. Jake almost took your eye out. He told me.'

Reuben hung his head in defeat. He knew the game was up. 'It wasn't me. It was Bobby,' he cried as he sank to the floor.

Grace had seen enough. 'He's all yours, John,' she said before pulling up the shutters and returning to the safety of John's car. She should have done Reuben in herself, but she just didn't have the stomach to beat someone to a pulp. She never had.

John emerged from Reuben's lock-up ten minutes later. Grace noticed he'd removed his gloves and no longer had the baseball bat with him; he had left them behind as she'd told him to. The flames were already starting to spread out of the lock-up, into the oxygen of the night air.

'That didn't take long,' Grace said as he climbed into his car.

'Nope.'

'Did he tell you anything else?'

John started the engine and started to drive. 'He owed Bobby a lot of money after Jake and his firm stole the lorry full of Bobby's drugs that Reuben was driving. As for Michael, he was in the wrong place at the wrong time, but Reuben saw it as his opportunity to get his revenge for what happened years ago – something he holds you responsible for too by the way – and what better way to get to you than through Jake?'

'What? But that was all sorted years ago,' Grace said, recalling how Reuben had once bounced into her office and threatened her after Marcus had had him thrown out of the pub. As a result, Michael had given him a good hiding, which had left him deaf in one ear.

'Some people can really hold a grudge.'

'But why not just kill them? Put a bullet in their heads? It would have been so much easier. Why the need to take them somewhere and torture them?'

'That's the way Bobby White operated. They were supposed to kill them but they got scared off. The kidnapping and torture were Bobby's way of sending a message that he was the top dog.'

'And Marcus?'

'He saw Reuben in some gay club in town and when Marcus saw the eye patch, he must have put two and two together and realised what he'd done.'

'Reuben in a gay bar?'

John nodded.

'Maybe that explains why he was such a homophobe then.'

'Probably,' John agreed.

'Marcus always was too clever for his own good.'

'He always seemed like a good bloke.'

'He was,' Grace said as she rested her head against the window. 'He was the best.'

They spent the rest of the drive to Grace's house in silence and Grace wondered how much more she could take. It was less than a week before her move back to Harewood and she couldn't wait.

Chapter 88

Grace took Belle from Michael's arms.

'Hi, Mama,' Belle giggled.

'Hey, Baby. I missed you,' she said as she hugged her daughter tightly.

'Peppa. Peppa,' Belle squealed.

Grace and Michael laughed. 'Okay, Peppa,' Grace said.

As Belle sat on the sofa between them watching television, Grace looked at Michael. There were no outward signs of his recent ordeal now. His face was unblemished, and he looked as handsome as ever. Grace had told him all about Reuben McBride's involvement and how she and John had dealt with him. He turned and caught her watching him, making her blush.

'So you're really going back then?'

'Yes, on Monday. It's my last day at the club tomorrow, and then I'll pack at the weekend.'

'Are you sure you want to leave?'

'Jake's out of hospital now. He and Siobhan are settled. The club is sorted. Marcus is gone. There's nothing keeping me here anymore.'

'I suppose not.'

'About Belle. I thought every other weekend would be a good

start? You could pick her up, or I could drop her off? Whatever works best.'

Michael nodded. 'That would be great. I'll pick her up when I can. I'm sure we can figure it out.'

Grace nodded and absent-mindedly picked at the hem of her shirt.

'I'll pick her up tomorrow morning, if that's okay? And bring her back Sunday?'

'Yes, that's great, it will give me plenty of time to tidy up loose ends and pack.'

'Great,' he said as he stood up. 'I'd better get going. I'll see you both in the morning then.' He bent to kiss Belle. 'Bye, gorgeous.'

'Bye, Dada.' She smiled at him.

'Bye, Grace,' he said and walked out of the room.

Grace pulled her daughter onto her lap and cuddled her, blinking back the tears as she did so. What had she expected? That he would beg her to stay?

Of course he wouldn't.

He had loved her once, but that felt like a lifetime ago now.

Wiping her eyes, Grace planted a kiss on Belle's head. Moving back to Harewood, and away from the chaos of Liverpool, was the best thing for her and Belle. They would both be fine. They were Sumners, they would be better than fine.

Sitting in his car, Michael looked up at Grace's house. He'd left a few minutes ago and couldn't bring himself to drive away. In four days' time she'd be leaving again, this time for good, and taking his daughter with her. Grace would be fair over contact, he knew that. She wasn't a vindictive woman, and she always put her kids first. But it wasn't the same as being able to see her whenever he wanted to. Realising he'd better drive home soon before Grace looked out and saw him still sitting there, he started the engine and pulled away from the kerb. If only there was some way he could make her change her mind.

Chapter 89

The glare of the winter sun made Grace squint as she stepped out of The Blue Rooms for what she hoped was the final time – at least for a long while. She'd got all of the paperwork in order and handed everything over to Siobhan and Libby. They, along with Michael, would keep the place running smoothly for the next month or so, until Jake was well enough to return.

She was reaching inside her handbag for her sunglasses when she felt a hand grab her arm by the elbow. Suddenly she was flanked by two men, only one of whom she recognised. Eddie Redman! He was becoming a massive pain in her arse. The other man was shorter and stockier than Eddie and he stank of sweat. Grace was about to give the pair of them a mouthful when she felt the sharp metal nudging at her ribcage through her clothes.

'Just keep walking,' Eddie growled. 'Don't make a scene or I will slip this knife inside you quicker than you can open your mouth to scream.'

Grace's adrenaline kicked in and she began to weigh up her options, calculating how many steps she'd have to take before she reached the sanctuary of the club. Twenty, maybe twenty-five? If she screamed, was anyone around to hear her? No. It was late afternoon and they were all inside by now. Eddie and the unknown man had a firm grip on her arms. She was trapped.

She had no option but to comply. Together, the three of them walked to the waiting car. The engine was running and Grace could see cigarette smoke curling out of the driver's window. Someone was already in the car.

It was a woman.

As she drew nearer, Grace saw it was the crazy woman, Eve, who'd been barred from the club a few months earlier. She almost burst out laughing. What the hell were these three amateurs up to? Surely they weren't going to kidnap her? Grace Sumner? No. They wouldn't dare.

Would they?

As Eddie and his accomplice manoeuvred her into the back seat of the old Ford Mondeo, she realised that they were.

When she was ensconced between Eddie and the man whose stench was becoming increasingly nauseating, Eve put the car into gear and began to drive.

'Where the hell are you taking me?' Grace snapped.

She felt the blade Eddie was still holding at her side dig into her ribs a little more and was sure he'd drawn blood this time.

'Shut the fuck up,' he snarled.

Eve started to cackle in the front seat. 'You're going to get what's coming to you, bitch,' she said between taking drags of her cigarette, which Grace could smell was laced with weed.

'She's going to get more than that,' the stench sneered as he ran a podgy finger along Grace's neck towards her chest.

'Fucking stop it, Greg. We get the money first,' Eddie snapped. 'Then you can do what you want with her.' He started to laugh and the other two joined in. The three of them were stoned off their faces, Grace could tell, but she was at their mercy for now. She knew now that they wanted money. Well, she could get them plenty of that. If she could only figure out where she was going.

If only she could reach her handbag, which Greg had thrown on the floor near his feet. The gravity of the situation was starting to dawn on her. The bile in her stomach rose so fast, she had no time to stop it, and she vomited all over Greg's lap.

'You fucking bitch,' he snarled as he frantically tried to wipe his trousers. As he bounced up and down in the back seat, Grace saw her chance to make a grab for her handbag, but Eddie still had a firm grip on her arm and he dragged her back, pinning her to the seat with his body.

'If you move again, I will fucking cut you,' he shouted at her. 'Don't fucking try me, you cunt.' Grace realised they weren't stoned at all. They were on something else. They were all fucking lunatics. Her heart started to thud loudly in her ears as she realised she was done for.

Chapter 90

The car had finally come to a stop outside an almost derelict block of flats in Birkenhead. Grace was frogmarched up the four flights of stairs by the two men, while Eve cackled and chain-smoked away in the background.

When they finally came to a stop outside one of the few flats that were still used as a residence, Eve pulled out a key and opened the door. The whole place was rotten – decaying. Even in the darkness it was plain that the net curtains hanging in the windows had seen far better days, yellowed and ragged from years of nicotine abuse.

'Get her in, lads,' Eve croaked. 'Before someone sees.'

Eddie and Greg bundled Grace inside the dingy flat. The stench from inside made her retch and she almost vomited again. She was glad she'd only had a packet of crisps for lunch and had little left in her stomach to throw up.

'In here. It's all ready,' Eve said, grinning as she indicated a door off to the left, and Grace was led into a filthy bedroom which contained one double bed. The sheets were stained brown and yellow with God knows what. An old grubby sheet covered the window as a makeshift curtain. But the worst of it was the crude shackles and ropes which had been fastened to the bed.

Grace thought she must have already died in that car outside, because this was most certainly hell. Her instincts took over and she started to pull at her arms to free herself, but Eddie and Greg were physically stronger than her and she barely made any progress. They laughed at her efforts. She started to scream and shout and Greg took something from his pocket and stuffed it inside her open mouth. It tasted of tobacco and old food and Grace tried to spit it out, but her mouth was already dry and the fabric clung stubbornly to her tongue and palate.

She continued to lash out with her arms and legs as Eddie and Greg tied her wrists and ankles to the four bedposts.

Eddie worked methodically, barely even looking at her, but Greg leered at her, his eyes lingering on every exposed bit of skin as he licked his lips in anticipation.

As he was pulling one of the ties on her wrists to make sure it was as tight as it could possibly get, he whispered in her ear. 'I'm going to have some real fun with you later.'

The stench of his breath alone made Grace's eyes water, but the thought of him touching her made her gag and retch. Soon she was spluttering, choking on the foul piece of material that had been stuffed in her mouth.

'I told you to fucking leave her alone till we get the money,' Eddie snapped as he slapped Greg around the head. He pulled the makeshift gag from Grace's mouth and she gasped for breath. Even the rotten air of Eve's flat felt good in that moment.

'If you scream again, this goes back in,' Eddie barked at her and she nodded her compliance.

'Why have you brought me here?' she asked him, sensing now was the only time she might get a chance to ask.

'Money. We want all of it.'

'I can get you money. Let me go and I'll get it now. You can come with me.'

Eddie shook his head and laughed. 'Do you think we're stupid?'

'Of course not. But how else are you going to get it?'

'Tomorrow, when you've spent the night here, and realised we're not to be fucked with, you will phone your accountant. We know you've got one; we've seen you with him. And he will leave the money in a safe place for us. Once we have it, and we're all far away from Liverpool, we'll let someone know where you are. Once Greg has had his fun, obviously.' Eddie smirked at her and Greg started to laugh.

Grace knew she was a dead woman as soon as they got any money from her. They would be stupider than they looked to keep her alive, because if by some miracle she got out of this shithole, she would hunt the three of them to the ends of the earth and make them pay in ways they could never even imagine.

'How can I be sure you'll let me go?' she asked.

Eddie sat down on the bed beside her and shrugged. 'You can't. But if you don't get us the money, then I will leave you here, tied to this bed, with Greg. At least with me and Eve here, he'll behave himself a little. But if we were to go, who knows what he'd do to a good-looking woman like you. You wouldn't survive more than a few days. I guarantee you that.' He grinned and Greg chuckled in the background. 'He's a bit of a nutter, is Greg. Hates women too. His mummy never loved him, you see. Did she, Greg?'

'You look just like her,' Greg said as he stared at Grace so longingly he was almost drooling.

'But if you get us the money, I've promised Greg we can go

abroad to somewhere where the women are much cheaper, and he'll settle for just an hour or two in your company. It's up to you, Grace,' Eddie said as he stood up.

'I won't give you a fucking penny,' she spat. Her anger was all she had left. If she refused to pay them, they'd have to rethink their plan.

'Fine by me,' Eddie said. 'Me and Eve would just be happy to see you suffer, wouldn't we, Eve?'

Eve nodded furiously. 'Fucking evil bitch,' she spat.

'Why?' Grace asked. Surely it was all about the money?

'Why?' Eddie shrieked, his temper flaring so quickly, he reminded Grace of his father. 'Because you killed my dad, you fucking murdering bitch.'

Grace winced at his words. Her ex-husband's demise was a memory she tried her best to bury in the deepest recesses of her brain. So that was what it was really about for Eddie. But Eve? What was her deal? Surely she couldn't hold that much of a grudge for being thrown out of The Blue Rooms? Before Grace could ask the question, Eve stepped closer to her, with a look of such pure hatred on her face, for a split second it made Grace recoil. But she was Grace Sumner and these three cretins weren't going to get a penny out of her.

'And what the fuck am I supposed to have done to you?'

Eve glared at her, her eyes narrowed into thin slits and her lips set in a grimace. Grace heard Eddie chuckle softly in the background and from the corner of her eye noticed Greg shifting from one foot to the other as a smile stretched across his face.

'What have you done to me?' Eve shrieked. 'You stupid cow. Do you really want to know?'

'Tell her, Eve,' Eddie goaded her.

Grace's heart started to hammer against her chest as Eve

leaned her face close to hers. The pungent cigarette smoke made her eyes water and she blinked as Eve started to grin maniacally, lips peeled back over her gums, showing her yellow dentures.

'I'm Eve Conlon,' she spat. 'You murdered my son. You fucking whore.'

Chapter 91

Eve Conlon scowled at the woman in front of her who had once been her son's wife. She wasn't so fucking stuck-up now, was she? All her money and designer gear meant nothing now that she was in Eve's world. Once they'd milked her for every penny they could get, that Greg lad was going to have his fun with her, and then bury her body where it would never be found.

Eve hadn't seen her son for years before he was taken from her so cruelly. They'd taken him off her when he was a kid and he'd been sent to some care home. It had probably been for the best – she wasn't cut out for looking after snot-nosed little kids. And his dad didn't want to know him. Tommy fucking McNulty – big hard man who'd threatened to kill Eve if she ever revealed Nathan's true parentage. She'd made sure she screwed that bastard for every penny she could over the years though – she wasn't stupid, and she knew her silence was worth a lot to someone like Tommy.

When Nathan had grown up a bit and had finally become someone interesting, she'd got in touch with him, but the cheeky little sod told her to fuck off. She'd reminded him that she'd given birth to him. Had given up her figure and her life for that ungrateful little bastard, but he'd told her he wanted nothing to do with her. She was dead to him, he'd said. He threatened to put a bullet in her head if she ever came near him again, and she sensed that, at that moment at least, he'd meant it. He was just like his father in that respect. But she knew that one day he would come round. He'd have seen sense eventually and welcomed his old mum back with open arms.

When she'd heard he'd been murdered she'd been devastated. There was no way she'd ever get a chance to worm her way back into his affections after all. No chance he could look after her now that she was getting on a bit. She knew his ex-wife had done it. It was all over the papers. But they'd said it was self-defence after he'd almost killed her. Eve had known her boy had a bit of a temper on him and had accepted that these things happen.

But that was until a few weeks ago, when Eddie Redman had walked into her life. He was a mate of Angie Anderson's lad. Eve had lived next door to Angie and her brood, and she'd always liked the woman. Her kids were another story, but Angie was a generous woman who always had a spare ciggie or a can of cider for a neighbour in need.

Eve had been gobsmacked when Eddie had turned up at her flat one Sunday afternoon. She'd been craving a drink and, with only a few pence left to her name, had been contemplating going out and pinching herself some cider from the local offy. Then he'd told her who he was and she could have kissed him. He had the same cheeky grin as his dad and she'd been over the moon that he'd found out about her from Angie and had looked her up. Eve had tried to keep some tabs on Nathan over the years, and she knew all about his other kid, Jake, but she'd had no idea about Eddie. Now here he was, and with a plan to make them both a shitload of money. And when he'd told her what really happened to her Nathan, and how that bitch had tried to burn him alive, well, she'd wanted to kill the little whore herself.

Eddie was a smart lad – just like her Nathan. He had the perfect plan. And tomorrow Grace Sumner would pay for killing Eve's boy – in every possible way.

Chapter 92

Grace blinked as she stared at Eve's grinning face and tried to process the information she'd just been given. Surely she'd misheard? There was no way it could be true.

'What did you say?' she asked

'You heard me,' Eve sneered. 'Nathan Conlon was my boy and you killed him. You scheming little bitch. Now, we're going to make you pay. One way or another.'

Grace shook her head. 'No. You can't be . . . He told me—'

Before Grace could finish her sentence, Eve came closer and slapped her across the face with the back of her hand. Running her tongue across the inside of her cheek, Grace tasted blood. Well, if the old crank was telling the truth, the apple certainly hadn't fallen very far from the tree. But why had Nathan told her Eve was dead? Had he even known the truth?

Eddie started to laugh, snapping Grace from her thoughts.

'Couldn't believe my luck when I found my dear old nan alive and well and living it up in Birkenhead.' He put an arm around Eve's shoulders and she patted his chest adoringly.

Eve nodded. 'He's a good lad, this one. Not like that stuck-up little brat of yours. Letting you and those hired thugs kick me out of his precious little club. When he was the only reason I'd even set foot in the place. I'd been in there every sodding week, waiting for the right time to tell him who I was and then you showed up and fucking ruined everything, you spiteful bitch,' she snarled.

Grace had to shake her head to stop herself from laughing out loud. If it wasn't so bloody terrifying it would have been comical. So, it was all about revenge. The two avenging angels. Nathan's mother, the woman who'd abandoned him as a child and set him on the road to becoming a psychopath. And Eddie – the son whom Nathan wanted absolutely nothing to do with. Whose mother he'd threatened to kill if the truth about Eddie's paternity ever got out. Nathan hated the pair of them so much, he'd denied their very existence, and here they were seeking revenge for his death.

'We'll leave you to think over your options for the night,' Eddie said as the three of them started to leave the room.

'What if I need the toilet?' Grace asked.

'You'll just have to piss yourself,' Eddie replied and the three of them burst into laughter. Grace watched as the door closed and the last sliver of light disappeared. It took her eyes a few minutes to adjust to the darkness, but when they did, she scanned the room for a weapon, or anything that might help her escape.

She saw none and the thought that she might die in this awful hellhole filled her with terror.

Chapter 93

Grace strained to hear what was being said in the other room, but any voices had been drowned out by the blaring of the television. The theme tune of *Coronation Street* confirmed she'd been lying in this filthy cesspit for at least three hours. Her wrists and ankles burned where the rope began to cut into them from all her twisting and wrenching to try and loosen them, but to no avail.

The indignity of it all. Tied, spread-eagled, to a bed. She was desperate to use the toilet now and wondered how long it would be until she had to release her full bladder. God, who would have thought she'd go out like this? Alone, in a dark and dingy flat in Birkenhead that smelled of weed, stale beer and rotten food. She wondered how long it would be before someone would miss her. Jake had discharged himself from hospital and was recovering at home with Siobhan. He would notice when she didn't phone him tomorrow, but would probably assume she was busy packing. Belle was with Michael for the whole weekend, so that was two more days before he'd bring her back and find Grace missing. Libby was probably on her flight to Barcelona by now. She'd gone to join Maria and meet her family. Grace had the weekend off from the club to sort the packing for her move. Who else would even notice she'd gone?

Her earlier terror and fear seemed to have been replaced by an acute sadness. Grace had never felt so alone in all her life. She thought about Marcus. Ben. Nathan. And Michael. Michael, whom, she realised, she loved more than any of them, but had never even had the chance to tell him. He'd arranged to have Belle every other weekend when she moved back to Harewood. But now it looked like he'd have to look after her permanently. It gave her some comfort to know that Michael would be a doting father to Belle, and her daughter would be loved and cherished. But would Belle even remember her? Grace choked back the tears as she realised that she probably wouldn't. Her little girl would grow up without a mother. No one would ever love her as much as Grace did, and Belle would never know it.

Grace was still thinking about her daughter when the door creaked open and the unmistakeable stench of Greg filled the room – sweat mixed with tobacco and stale cider. He walked silently towards her and sat on the bed.

'You're not going to scream, are you? Don't make me put that gag on you again.' He ran his fingertips up her bare leg.

Grace flinched and tried to move away from him but her restraints prevented her from doing so.

Greg laughed. 'Eddie and Eve are asleep. So, me and you can have some fun now, can't we?'

'Fuck off, you dirty little weasel. You're fucking disgusting. You make my skin crawl.'

He laughed again. 'Aw, that's not very nice, is it, Grace? Especially as I like you so much.' He licked his lips as he leered at her. 'I'll show you a good time, don't worry.' He grinned at her, showing his rotten teeth, and she thought she might vomit all over him for a second time that day. He ran his hand further up her leg until it was sliding up under the fabric of her dress and along her inner thigh.

She closed her eyes and tried to pretend she was somewhere else but it didn't work. Maybe there was some way she could use this to her advantage instead? Persuade Greg to untie her? Yes. She'd manipulated much smarter and tougher men than this pathetic piece of shit.

She was thinking about her next move when the loudest bang she'd ever heard and the shattering of glass exploded through her ears. Then what sounded like a small army platoon came running into the flat. Before Greg could move an inch, the door to the bedroom burst open with such force that it came off one of its hinges.

The noise was deafening. Shouts. Screaming. Swearing. Banging. Suddenly, Greg was being lifted into the air as though he was made of feathers. She watched his body as it was launched through the now open doorway.

Then she saw Michael standing beside the bed and her heart almost burst out of her chest with relief. He had come for her.

'Michael,' she whispered, her voice hoarse from lack of fluids.

'Get her out of here. Now!' he barked to whoever was standing on the other side of the room.

'Will do, son.' Grace recognised Patrick's voice as he rushed to her side and Michael disappeared through the doorway.

'You're all right, love. We've got you now,' Patrick soothed as he cut through her restraints. Then he lifted her from the bed with the strength of a man twenty years his junior, and despite hobbling without his stick, he carried her out of the flat. Grace buried her head in his shoulder and clung onto his neck, fearing that if she opened her eyes it would all turn out to be a dream and she would be back in that awful room with Greg trying to rape her.

Chapter 94

Jake was waiting on the doorstep when Patrick pulled his car into her driveway. As soon as the engine stopped, Jake hobbled as fast as he could on his crutches to the passenger door, opened it wide, and pulled Grace into a hug as soon as she stepped out.

'Mum,' he said, tears pricking his eyes. 'Thank God you're okay.' Releasing her from his embrace, he looked her over, as though appraising the damage. She hated the scrutiny and hoped he didn't see how terrified she'd felt – still felt. She leaned against him to avoid his gaze. It was so good to be near him.

'I wanted to come with them,' he said apologetically. 'But they said I'd have slowed them down, and they were probably right.'

'I'm glad you were here instead, Jake.' She would have hated for him to see her like that. 'To wait for me, and to look after Belle. Where is she?' she asked, suddenly anxious to see her daughter. Desperate to hold her soft baby body in her arms. Smell her beautiful baby-powder-scented skin.

'She's fast asleep upstairs. She's fine. Libby and Siobhan are here too. Let's get you inside,' he said as he guided her towards the front door.

* * *

Freshly showered and having sat with Belle in her arms for as long as she could before her daughter started to squirm, Grace prepared to make her way back downstairs to her kitchen where they all waited anxiously for her return and for her to tell them that she was okay. Waiting for her to explain how she'd ended up in Eve Conlon's dingy little flat in Birkenhead. She wanted to curl up in her king-size bed instead and ignore them all. But that would just make them worry more. Besides, there was no way she was going to sleep. She wondered whether she'd ever sleep again. She hadn't felt like this since she was married to Nathan. The nights she'd lie awake waiting for his return, her heart hammering in her chest, blood thundering around her body, wondering what mood he'd be in, and what fresh torment he'd have in store for her.

After straightening her T-shirt in the mirror, she smoothed her hands over her hair. Time to put her game face on and remind the world who she was. She was Grace Sumner. And no one, least of all a couple of crackheads and an old whore, would knock her crown.

'How are you feeling, sweetheart?' Patrick asked as Grace walked into the kitchen. Siobhan placed a mug of hot, sweet tea into her hands as she sat down.

'Okay, considering,' she replied shakily. 'If you hadn't got there when you did . . .'

'Shh, don't worry about that now, love.' Patrick said softly as he put an arm around her shoulder.

A knock at the front door made Grace jump.

'I'll go,' Patrick said.

A minute later he walked back into the kitchen with Sean.

'Michael has stayed behind. He wanted to make sure everything was taken care of.' Sean said pointedly and Patrick and Jake nodded.

Grace noticed the skin on Sean's knuckles was red and bleeding. 'I'm sorry I've had to drag you out of retirement again.' She attempted a laugh.

Sean pulled her into a hug and kissed the top of her head. 'Don't be so ridiculous. You're family, Grace.'

Grace felt the tears welling up again so she tried to change the subject. 'So how did you find me? How did you even know I was missing?'

'It was Libby who alerted everyone,' Sean said.

Libby beamed with pride. 'My flight was cancelled because of the bloody fog,' she explained. 'So rather than go home I thought I'd come here to spend the evening with you. I knew you'd be feeling lonely with Belle at Michael's and since Marcus – well, you know. And I wanted to spend some time with you before you left.'

Patrick coughed as if to indicate she should get to the point.

'Anyway, when you weren't here and I couldn't get hold of you, I phoned Michael. And when Jake didn't know where you were, and Michael couldn't reach you, we started to panic.'

Patrick took over the commentary then. 'Michael got everyone together in less than an hour. Everyone wanted to help, Grace. Even Nathan's old mate John Brennan. Michael had everyone looking for you. The twins are on their way back from London as we speak. It was a stroke of luck that one of the barmaids at the club was late for her shift and saw you getting into Eddie's car. She assumed you were going willingly and she'd remembered him from coming into the club a few weeks ago.'

'But how did you find Eve's flat?'

'Eddie's so-called mates told us he'd been hanging around with Eve. Michael got in touch with his police contact, who gave us Eve's address. And the rest is history.'

Grace shook her head. 'I'm just glad you were able to find me so quickly.'

They all nodded. Then the room was silent and Grace could feel all their eyes on her. Worrying about her. Wondering if she was going to break. She couldn't stand it. She loved them all but she couldn't stand their concern. Not right now.

She forced a yawn. 'I'm really tired. Do you mind if I call it a night?'

'Course not,' they chorused.

'We'll stay,' Jake, pointing to himself and Siobhan.

'Me too,' Patrick and Libby said at the same time.

'I can stay as well if you need me to?' Sean added.

Grace shook her head. 'No! None of you need to stay. I'm a big girl, I can look after myself. Besides, you said Michael had taken care of them. I assume Eddie, Greg and Eve won't be seeing the light of another day?'

'But Grace—' they started.

'No. I love you all and I appreciate the offer. But I really want to be on my own.'

'I'm not leaving you, Mum.'

'You and Siobhan both need your rest, Jake. Please go home.'

'You should really get home and take your tablets, Jake,' Siobhan said as she linked her arm through his and smiled at Grace.

They all argued with her for a further five minutes before she convinced them to leave her house, and only after she promised to keep her phone with her and sleep with a Glock under her pillow. Grace agreed, although she had no intention of using the gun Sean had left with her. She hated guns. She would put it in the safe, out of Belle's reach, as soon as they left.

* * *

As she checked all of the windows and doors for the second time, Grace started to regret sending everyone home. What was she trying to prove? That she was a big girl who could look after herself? Now, in her loneliness, she wondered if that even mattered any more. Wasn't it more important to have people around when you needed them? And as sorry as she was feeling for herself, she knew in her heart that any of them would have been happy to keep her company. Sometimes her pride was her own worst enemy.

She was heading for bed, her foot already on the bottom stair, when she heard the doorbell ring. Her heart leaped into her throat and she admonished herself. *Burglars and robbers don't ring the doorbell, Grace!*

Looking through the spyhole, she saw Michael standing on the doorstep, hopping impatiently from one foot to the other. She wondered whether he was making a flying visit, although she desperately hoped he was going to stay. Maybe she would ask him to?

As she opened the door, he stepped uninvited into the hallway. His hair was damp and she caught the smell of shampoo and soap as he came closer to her.

'I'm sorry I'm so late, but I had to make sure there were no loose ends,' he said, as though it was a given that he'd be there. As though Grace should have been expecting him.

'That's okay,' she said. 'I wasn't expecting you.'

'Really?' He frowned at her. 'After what happened today, you didn't think I'd be here to make sure you're okay?' He shook his head in annoyance. 'Anyway. Where is everyone. My dad? Sean? Jake? Have they left you and Belle here on your own?'

'I made them go,' she said. 'I wanted to be on my own.'

'Well, I'm staying,' he said as he walked past her and headed towards the kitchen. 'Any chance of a drink?'

Grace followed him into the kitchen and poured him a glass of brandy. She didn't bother with one for herself – she didn't think her stomach could take it.

Michael downed his drink in one and slammed his glass onto the breakfast bar.

Grace watched him intently, trying to figure him out. He was so angry. Why was he there? Because of Belle? Out of guilt? Or a sense of duty?

No doubt sensing her watching him, he crossed the kitchen to where she was standing. 'Are you okay?' he asked, his face softening as he took hold of her hand and ran the pad of his thumb softly across the red skin on her wrist. 'Did they hurt you?'

She shook her head. 'No. Not really. I'm fine. Thanks to you, I hear.'

He smiled, his brown eyes twinkling. 'No problem. Just returning the favour.'

'Yes, of course,' she said. Pulling her hand from his, she looked away from his gaze. So, it was nothing more than that.

'Hey,' he said as he took her hand again. 'I'm just kidding. I'd douse myself in petrol and walk through a burning building for you, Grace. Don't you know that by now?'

Shaking her head, Grace bit her lip to stifle the tears that were threatening, fearing that if she started to cry she might never stop.

'I thought I'd lost you,' he said so quietly she almost didn't hear. Then he pulled her to him and she buried her face in his chest, enjoying the familiar smell of him. When he wrapped his arms around her she responded in kind, clinging on to him as though he was a lifebelt in a storm.

'I love you, Grace Sumner,' he said in her ear.

Then she started to cry.

Epilogue

Clad in only her underwear, Grace studied her reflection in the full-length mirror of her large wardrobe and sighed. Seeing Michael walk into the bedroom behind her, she smiled at his reflection. Slipping his arms around her, he nuzzled her neck. The coolness of his hands felt good against her hot skin. She leaned into him, enjoying the feel of his muscular chest against her bare back.

'Hello, gorgeous. How are you feeling?'

'Fed up,' she groaned. 'I have absolutely nothing to wear.'

'You are beautiful,' he said against her neck. 'Anything you wear will look beautiful. Where's Belle?'

'Your dad and Sue took her to buy a new party dress and then they're taking her to their house to show her the giant wooden Wendy house they've had built. I swear it's as big as my aunt Helen's old terrace in Anfield, Michael. They spoil her rotten, you know?'

'I know. But that's what grandparents are for. Don't we spoil Isla just as much?'

'Hmm, I suppose,' she said, thinking of their beautiful eight-month-old granddaughter, who had looked so much like her aunty Belle when she was born.

'We don't have to go, you know.'

'What? And miss our own party? I don't think that will go down very well.'

'Well, you do have the perfect excuse,' he said as he rubbed her seemingly ever-increasing bump. 'I'll tell them you're tired. Then we can spend the night in bed instead.' He winked at her reflection.

She placed her hands on his, her fingertips brushing over his platinum wedding band, the one that matched hers. 'We can't. They'll be so disappointed.'

'I'll make it worth your while,' he whispered in her ear as his hands moved lower. 'Besides, don't they say sex helps to induce labour? It might help move this stubborn little fella? I'm only thinking about you really.'

'Oh, there's nothing in it for you then? You're so selfless.' She laughed.

'I certainly am.'

The truth was, he was selfless when it came to her and their children. They were always his priority. All of them. Her, Jake, Paul, Connor, Belle and this new little boy who was refusing to move from the comfort of his mother's womb.

Michael slipped his fingers under the band of her underwear.

'Hey,' she said, laughing as she slapped his hand away. 'It's your wandering hands that got us into this predicament in the bloody first place.'

'Well, I don't recall any complaints at the time. Or any time since for that matter. I'm going to jump in the shower before we go.' Then with a final kiss on her neck he walked over to his side of the wardrobe and started to get undressed.

Grace lay on the bed and watched him as he removed his shirt and trousers. She loved his body – all muscle and tattoos. She felt safe wrapped in his giant arms. Looking at him still gave her butterflies. He was the type of husband she'd always dreamed about having, but had come to believe never existed.

He was her partner in every sense of the word. He came home every single night, never smelling of drink or another woman. He always answered his phone. He listened when she spoke, and even when she didn't. He always had time for her. He read bedtime stories to Belle. Cradled her while she slept. Soothed away her nightmares. Held her when she was sick. And he made Grace feel like the most important woman in the whole world. She had never felt more loved, or cherished.

She thought about everyone waiting for them to celebrate their first wedding anniversary. His family. Now hers too. Marrying him had given her the family she'd always dreamed of having. Pat and his fiancée, Sue, were doting grandparents. Sean and Sophia were like the brother and sister she'd never had. Then there were her three beautiful nieces, although Steph was more like a younger sister too. Michael's two boys and Jake had become like brothers. Siobhan was like a daughter to her now that she and Jake were married, and baby Isla was a delight, although it had taken Grace a while to get used to being called Nana. Then there was Belle, not quite three years old, who had them all wrapped around her little finger. Sometimes Grace could hardly believe she was surrounded by so much love and happiness.

'Penny for your thoughts,' Michael said as he lay on the bed beside her.

'I was just thinking how lucky I am to have you,' she said, smiling at him.

Propping himself up on one elbow, he brushed her hair behind her ear. His dark brown eyes appeared almost black. 'I think you'll find, I'm the lucky one,' he said.

Then he kissed her.

Coffee and peppermint.

Always.

THE END

Acknowledgements

I would like to thank the wonderful team at One More Chapter for believing in me and bringing this book to life, most especially my squad – Charlotte Ledger, Bethan Morgan and Charlotte Brabbin, who are the most amazing group of women to work with. I'd also love to thank my wonderful editor, Emily Ruston, for her expert insight and advice, which has helped to shape Grace's story into something I had only dreamed of it becoming.

I'd like to give a mention to my good friend and mentor, Mary Torjussen, who has continued to support and champion me all the way, and I will always be indebted to her for her advice and encouragement.

A huge thank-you to my family for their constant love and support, especially my mum and dad, and husband, Eric.

And finally, but most especially, to my three incredible boys – who continue to inspire and amaze me every single day.